HAVOC RED

Surviving the Alaska-Siberia Route, 1943

C. Margo Mowbray

C. Margo Mowbray

ISBN: 0692380663
ISBN 13: 9780692380666
Library of Congress Control Number: 2015901312
Clarity Communications, Polson, MT

HAVOC RED

Dedicated to the Seventh Ferrying Group,
and all ALSIB Route pilots, military and civilian,
who searched and rescued.

There's a land where the mountains are nameless,
And the rivers all run God knows where;
There are lives that are erring and aimless,
And deaths that just hang by a hair.

– Robert Service, *The Spell of the Yukon*

Contents

Introduction

The idea for this story didn't just occur to me one quiet day. It hit me like the prop blast of a twin-row Wright Cyclone. A friend and I had just landed at Watson Lake, Yukon Territory in a Cessna 185. It was a quiet July evening, the slate-gray lake was still, and rain freshened the tarmac as we tied the plane down. I asked about the huge wooden hangar, and he explained its role in the Northwest Staging Route during World War II.

The Army Air Forces ferried Lend-Lease aircraft from Great Falls, Montana to Fairbanks, Alaska, stopping at Watson, one of the hurriedly-built facilities along the route.

"Thousands of warplanes came through here on their way to Russia," he told me, "from P-39s to a B-24." As I walked toward the cavernous building, molting paint but still arching gracefully beneath the Yukon sky, the imagined thunder of those warbirds ran a chill through me. I could almost hear the harmonic rumble of multiple radial engines, and see the array of landing lights as they lifted into a sky that would be black for the next sixteen hours. If their dead reckoning was accurate they would dodge nameless mountains or those with ominous names like Canada's Sawtooths.

But there were no guarantees.

For about what a New York penthouse costs now, the United States bought Alaska from Russia in 1867. The purchase added a territory of more than a half-million square miles, with a coastline six times that of Florida's. Opponents called it Seward's Folly, but by World War II, it was clear why Billy Mitchell called Alaska "the most important strategic place in the world." If a global wheel were drawn with points at New York, Long Beach, Tokyo, Moscow, Berlin and London, the hub would verge on Fairbanks.

The pilots in my story took off from Great Falls, a few miles from where the coldest temperature was ever recorded in the continental United States – seventy below zero – what Jack London would call "one hundred degrees of frost." From Great Falls the young pilots flew north past the sixty-fourth parallel, a mere one hundred and eight nautical miles south of the Arctic Circle. At that latitude, most of Finland lies south of you. Suspended by thin aluminum wings full of aviation gasoline, pilots flew airplanes loaded with bombs, machine guns and ammunition over ice as old as rocks, and mountains thrust a mile-and-a-half high by a restless earth. Extreme cold changes the behavior of mechanical devices, not to mention human tissue. It reduces an antenna's range, and can cause it to snap off at airspeed. To the pilots, it probably seemed as if the cold had frozen the very radio waves. From our moment in time it's hard to imagine flying over a third of the North American continent with only a wavering magnetic compass and a few gyro instruments for guidance. There were hours of nothing but mountains flanking frozen lakes, black spruce and muskeg to cushion your crash if the wings iced up, or your engine seized when its oil gelled in the extreme cold.

Early in my research, I was reminded of the ephemeral nature of these stories. The authors of some of the works I tracked down had recently slipped forever into eternal silence. Even the youngest of the youngsters who fibbed about their age to enlist after the Japanese bombing of Pearl Harbor were in their mid-eighties. This narrative is staged among the Army Air Forces brave Seventh Ferrying Group and their enormous contribution to the victors of World War II. I hope readers find a larger story, beginning with the motives that powered our nation into war.

When I learned that Boeing Aircraft Company had produced three hundred and eighty A-20 Havocs for Douglas, I imagined my grandmother's hand in constructing the aircraft in this story. She set aside her beloved millinery and claimed to be ten years younger than she was in order to get hired at Boeing's Seattle plant. She'd pack a lunch each day, ride the bus to the airplane factory and take her place wiring B-17s. Hats were going out anyway, and I'm sure she figured with her dexterity, she was of more use with a soldering gun, precisely following the big bombers' wiring schematics. Under rooftops camouflaged with faux suburban scenery, Americans produced enough B-17s that if placed wingtip-to-wingtip, would make an aluminum swath stretching the distance from New York City to Richmond, Virginia.

Understanding the milieu of World War II Europe, I was overwhelmed with a sense of privilege. As a free American citizen, there were no restrictions on where my imagination or motivation might lead me. I thought nothing of driving or flying anywhere I wished for research. There were no checkpoints or suspicious, armed sentries. European women didn't have that freedom. Many suffered harassment, assault, exploitation, ruination of their families, and in the case of the Jews, unconscionable wickedness. Here I risk enormous understatement: Post-World War II baby-boomers have much to be thankful for.

Writing flows in an alternating current of uncertainty and inspiration. A dark story powers through obstacles, forcing the writer to bring it to light. When my research uncovered an exploitive side of war harnessing itself to the good, that story prevailed.

This is a work of historical fiction. I ask for tolerance from those who may remember specifics, since I have taken liberties with names and episodes. My focus was on the mission's challenges, its urgency, and the dangers these pilots faced. There was no need to embellish their discomfort, anxiety and naïveté. I refer to the women pilots who flew delivery missions. There is nothing fictional about their courage and contribution. (I felt it was worthy of inclusion, although they began flights somewhat after my setting. The First Special Service Force indeed began training at Montana's Fort Harrison, but not until July, 1942. It was depicted in the 1966 book and 1968 movie "Devil's Brigade.")

There may be a linear mile of good books on World War II. This is not a war story. It's about a couple of boys who came of age when their country was in desperate need of young men motivated by patriotic zeal. Beginning with the excellent coverage of the Alaska-Siberia route to Russia in Blake W. Smith's *Warplanes to Alaska* and *Wings Over the Wilderness*, and the Seventh Ferrying Group's archives and oral histories, I found facts from which to assemble the skeleton of this story. For the blood in its veins, I created Frank Dugan, who seems to have good reasons to make bad decisions, trying to overcome his regrettable past. The spirit of a twenty-something pilot itching to live up to his father's heroism is embodied by Lieutenant Daniel Stanhope, maturing in the wake of family tragedy and driven to construct his own respectable future.

Bullied into a moment of wrongdoing, Dugan's spite takes him on a calamitous path into the shadowy side of war, dumping him in the Yukon wilds during a record-breaking winter.

It will be a tortuous way back to personal peace and reconciliation.

———◆———

It is fact that Franklin Roosevelt and Harry Hopkins – desperate to keep Joseph Stalin loyal to the Allied side – delivered over ten billion dollars' worth of war materiel to the Soviets including a great deal that was immune from search. Between June 1941 and September 1945, promises were made that would stretch American defense resources nearly to the breaking point. There have been allegations of serious breaches in national security including the Manhattan Project. What follows is fiction, but some would say the only fabrications are a few of the players' names.

Other than the actual historical persons in the story, any resemblance to other persons, living or dead, is purely coincidental. Creative license was used with all due respect.

PART I

Prologue

Birch Hill Cemetery, Fairbanks, Alaska – April 1945

The muddy taxi climbed the scar of road, spinning here and there in the gravel. The driver was gabbling something about Roosevelt's sudden death from a brain hemorrhage, but Laura Stanhope only listened half-heartedly. Her mission consumed the rest of her.

The car stopped on a mostly bald hillside overlooking Fairbanks.

"Do you mind waiting here for me, sir?" She pulled on her black gloves. "I won't be long."

She slumped out, teetering against a gust at what felt like the North Pole. She battened her calf-length camel coat closed and made her way up the terraced slope, her dressy heels punching through half-frozen ground. Snowdrifts were bedded in places like dirty lambs. Like the rest of Fairbanks, Birch Hill Cemetery seemed to have been hurriedly scraped from the hillside to handle the hubbub stirred up by the war. There weren't many graves but the place looked old. Leftover blanched grass nearly hid the chalky stone rectangles and squat hand-made markers, none of which pointed directly at the leaden sky. She stepped around several empty graves that gaped open in silent anticipation. They'd been dug before winter's deep freeze, a practicality in the far North.

Having come from the tidy California town of Fresno, she was not accustomed to the frontier atmosphere of Fairbanks, nor the sideways wind that drove ice crystals into her face. She could smell the cold. The sky drooped in gray streaks that slanted behind the low hills surrounding the city, if you could call it that. Between scattered buildings she could see a bend in the Chena River. It was sluggish in the places where it moved at all. She wondered why the war had dropped its military personnel here in the permafrost near the Arctic Circle. She asked herself yet again, Why did my only surviving son have to die so far from home? Why did God take my husband and our younger son, too?

She hoped this journey would tamp down the drifts of doubt and anger. She would see for herself where Daniel's body lay, even if it was in this lonely territory so foreign to her. She hated the way war reached its deadly grasp far beyond the battlefield. Why did it have to consume boys like hers? Clara, the waitress at Leonard's Café, seemed to be the only person who understood Laura's pain.

In December 1941, enraged by the Pearl Harbor attack, Daniel had announced to his mother that he was joining the Army Air Forces. He was so young and innocent – his wisdom teeth hadn't even grown in yet. Then, on a black day in March 1943, two military men had stopped their shiny car in front of her home. She noticed the white star on the car door and sat down, waiting for the knock, her heart pounding. Of course she knew what it meant. They always notified next-of-kin at once.

Back in 1918 they'd brought her a devastating telegram about her injured husband.

Now, another war, another visitation – this time about her son. A personal call meant the worst. She'd wanted to stop the mantel clock, ticking away her last seconds before impact with calamity. After a half dozen knocks, she stood, fighting the urge to run out the back. She approached her front door slowly. It was the only shield between her and a new tragedy.

At first she could not focus on the faces of the two dress-uniformed men. Flatly, she asked them to step in, leaving the door ajar as if to allow the bad news to go back out and not get sealed within her home.

Her thoughts had raced ahead. Her son would be coming home in a box. She would be handed a properly-folded American flag in exchange for his bright future. But they said "missing, in a non-combat-related incident." She collapsed in a chair. They were vague. Lieutenant Daniel Stanhope was "WUK" they explained tersely. "Whereabouts unknown." Someplace she'd never heard of. The Yukon Territory. That was as specific as they got, standing there. They were sorry, they said, putting on their peaked caps. They slipped out the front door, shutting it gently behind them. For these past two years her mind had roiled with circling hope, loss, blame, and wild guesses that awakened her in the night.

Then, just a month ago – it seemed like a century had passed – a tall, dark-haired man had appeared at her door and shocked her with his news. Laura noticed his deformed fingers and his odd way of walking when she asked him into her kitchen.

"I knew Daniel. I was with him on his last flight," the courteous young man had said. Among his disturbing explanation he told her she would find Daniel here.

So here she was, three thousand miles from home to see for herself where her brave pilot boy lay.

The Veterans' section was sparse. A small, weather-worn American flag was planted in one grave, quivering leeward. Naked trees rattled as another flurry deepened the chill. She was too numb to mourn the fact that the grave she was looking for lay beyond the Veterans' section. Laura wondered if anyone had said any reverent words over Daniel's grave. She knew her son had not received the traditional military rifle volleys that he deserved. Who would have known what a fine boy they were lowering into the cold ground?

She nearly stumbled on a small cement headstone, and read:

Unknown male
Died March 5, 1943
Downed aircraft
ALSIB Route

She didn't react to the term "Unknown male." It was as she expected. Her senses had long ago become saturated with pain. Like standing in the rain, a person could only get so wet. A person could only feel so much pain, then the rest poured over, creating an impenetrable shroud.

While Stalin's armies were bashing into Hitler's bunker in Berlin, and Winston Churchill agonized that most of Europe would be awarded to a thug as power-crazed as Hitler, Laura stood over a silent rectangle of earth.

The bloody moil of a world war was reaching a crescendo as she walked peacefully back to the cab, idling in its cloud of exhaust.

CHAPTER 1

Becoming Dugan

Where tyrants' hold is tightened,
Where strong devour the weak,
Where innocents are frightened
The righteous fear to speak.
– TIMOTHY TINGFANG LEW

Montana State Prison, Deer Lodge – Autumn 1940

The seven a.m. rising bell jarred Dugan awake. In the outer chamber, a guard shouldered the grated door closed, its iron-on-iron squeal and slamclatter echoing between the moleskin-colored walls. Dugan resented being wrenched from his dream's soft buttery light, the warmth of friendly faces, and the smell of fresh-baked bread, to endure another day between cement walls as thick as a man's broadside.

He sat up and during the morning's body-count, took up his stub of pencil and wrote in his deliberate printing.

Fresh bread. What I'd give for a loaf of warm bread. And plenty of butter. That's what I'm looking forward to when I get out. Warm bread and butter.

His pencil, the only writing tool he was allowed, was so short it could not possibly be turned into a lethal device. Prison guards had taken away his long pencil when they discovered another inmate had turned one into a weapon. The guy had purloined a nail, sanded off the head against a rough place on his cell wall and affixed the little spike in place of the pencil lead. He'd made a hobby of quietly sharpening the point against his cell wall until it was confiscated.

Dugan could get all the paper he asked for. He didn't care that it was tissue-thin typewriter copy paper. So far, inmates hadn't managed to inflict paper cuts with the flimsy stuff. But he was not allowed extra toilet paper because guards had discovered a rope woven from toilet paper during a cell search. Dugan had felt the momentary fraternal cooperation as he and the others pooled their supplies for that project.

He pinched the stub and continued writing.

> *ARSE. That's what they call me here, I <u>hate</u> the nickname. My name is Frank Dugan. They love to torment me, but I will keep quiet and my fists down. It is the only way I can win. It's worse than my given name Proinsias Maloney – Is there a worse name?*

He underlined the word "hate" so hard he cut right through the paper.

Dugan's mother had been to a revival meeting the night Dugan was conceived. In the rapture of lovemaking, her favorite saint winged into her mind and she vowed to name her next baby after him, boy or girl. When the baby boy came along, instead of "Francis," she got the notion to honor their Irish lineage. She found a dusty book with that ancient name in it. No one, not even her husband could change her thinking.

> *Since my dad give me my last name, my mother got to brand me with my first name. It means Saint Francis. In Butte, the other kids tried to call me princess – – Princess Baloney!! They learned to duck. I decided to use my middle name Dugan. It's my mother's unmarried name. For a trip to the courthouse and a dollar I became Frank Dugan.*

He slipped his paper and pencil back under the mattress as his door was released, sounding the familiar series of clanks. Dugan folded his arms and lined up six feet from the man in front of him, as was the rule. Staying inside the yellow line painted on the floor, he walked passively with the others toward the dining hall for another chipped bowl half full of mush with a sprinkle of sugar.

———◆———

Even after his dense tousle of dark hair had been shaved, Dugan stood six feet tall. He had to dip his head to clear the opening to his six- by eight-foot cell. A thin mattress of rough ticking lay atop a narrow woven metal bed frame. The bed, cold-water-only sink and toilet were all bolted solidly to the wall. The Hudson-green Palmolive soap helped mask the stink left by the previous captive. The door, vertical iron bars sloppy-painted black, locked with a heavy-gauge mechanism. It grumbled open and shut on a rail. Only the cell house guard could unlock it, invisible in his cage at the distant end of the cellblock.

These walls are solid. I feel safe in here. It's the up-down bars of my cell door that's trying to split my soul into little strips that wouldn't do anybody no good on the Outside. But I am not going to let it. I must think of ways to keep my soul from turning to shreds.

The bells of Immaculate Conception Catholic Church rang out a few blocks away, making him think of Butte again. They always made him think of home. At first, it pained him to think of Butte, the bells, the past. But he'd taught himself to use the sound to conjure pleasant memories. Now the bells comforted him, like a benevolent warmth, ringing tones of redemption in the air. He recalled St. Mary's, and the over-his-head stained glass windows where miners were pictured hobnobbing with the saints. After his father's death, Dugan saw Pop up there in heaven with them. He was a good man. Dugan remembered him saying, "Don't let the words of God fall to the ground." Now the lead lines between the blue and blood-colored panes held Pop from falling. Dugan remembered after-church suppers, making silly faces at his siblings when no one was looking and distracting the elders while his younger brother stuffed extra dinner rolls under his shirt.

Winter blanketed Butte's raw hills with plenty of snow for sledding. While autos skidded and tangled at the bottom, the kids would skip school and race downhill on coal shovels and garbage can lids. A favorite run began at the top of State Street and went nearly to the edge of town. A slag heap ramped the careening sleds to a lurching stop, scattering children over the mullock of arsenic grit. When the ponds froze, they'd put together pairs of hand-me-down ice skates with knotted laces. Sometimes they could find extra socks to keep their feet from freezing for awhile. It helped the old skates fit tighter, but their ankles still caved in.

Shopkeepers hired Dugan to wash windows and shovel snow off their sidewalks. Once Mrs. Duffy gave him a knitted cap and mittens she'd made just for him. "I wish I was twenty years younger, you good-lookin' boy," she'd said with a wink, turning her broad backside to him and going back into her house.

He'd helped Mr. Agostini, sweeping the bakery floor or scrubbing his pots and cake pans and polishing his glass case full of baked goods. On icy winter mornings, warm baking aromas spread out the front and alley door, cheering up drab, cold Butte. Every other week, Mr. Agostini gave the boy fresh bread along with a couple of dimes. It was hard not to devour the warm, fragrant loaf, but he'd felt proud to bring it home whole to his ma.

Dugan saved his dimes and took his younger brother Patrick to a movie once in a while. The Marx Brothers' *Animal Crackers* was their favorite. They watched it over and over. With his curly hair and round eyes, Patrick would mimic Harpo. Dugan used his mother's grease pencil to smear on a black mustache and eyebrows. He would twiddle a fat stick cigar and mock the uppity people they knew. The boys laughed until they rolled on the floor.

Pop had played an old button accordion and sometimes sang to his family. Pop never showed that temper that folks associate with the Irish. Maybe temper skipped a generation, Dugan figured. His grandfather was known for his temper, and it might have been his undoing. The senior Mr. Maloney had been on his way home from Duluth, but never showed up in Butte. The story went that he got in a bad fight and was rolled off the train in the dark of night, someplace in North Dakota. Pop always said temper turned a person crazy.

"Don't eat the bread of wickedness nor drink the wine of violence," he'd recite, "Proverbs." He had tried to coach his boys to do something brave instead of sticking their chins out and swinging doubled-up fists. But the day Dugan and Patrick came home, bloodied from their encounter with the cross-town rowdies, Pop understood why Dugan had fought to defend the boy. The troublemakers had called them "dirty micks" and pushed Patrick to the ground face-first and tried to hold him there. Pop showed his pride in his eldest son.

"They won't do it again, son," he said. "Boys, you'll learn that bigotry is the seed of ignorance; hatred its bloom." As Ma tended Patrick's bloody chin, she just clucked, "Protestant ruffians."

He would never forget how Ma looked when the men brought news that Pop had been killed in the mine explosion. Or the morning she gathered them together when his baby sister died.

We were all sitting around the wobbly kitchen table. Her face looked like it was changing shape. Ma was pretty, but not then. She said: We lost the baby. At first, I wondered why everyone just sat there. I thought we'd all better scatter to look for it. My older sister Margaret laid her hand over my arm and whispered: baby's lost up to heaven. Dead and gone. I would of looked stupid bolting out the house to look for it.

It's cold and it's not even winter yet. Another winter com-ing on in here. My 3rd inside the old stone walls of Montana State Prison. Once you're inside you forget which way is which. Directions don't matter because you're not going anywhere anyway.

Once I got in these walls I never saw another tree. Leaves fall, snow comes, snow goes, they turn green again. Leaf trees tell time. I miss the trees. Pines just stand tall and don't change. They make no demands. You can count on the pines. If Pop was a tree, he would of been a pine. Tall – strong – peaceful.

Dugan never could write nice Palmer Method script. It was easier for him to print. He continued.

The one good thing about MSP – There's plenty of time to think and write. I'd sure love a piece of Mr. Agostini's bread right now. There is nothing like it here. And I could sell Mrs. Duffy's hat and mittens for a good price in here. Enough cigs for six months. Then I could trade the cigs for something I need. Another blanket. I can get back to sleep after the 3 a.m. lights-on body count and the shouting when there's a recount, but the cold slicing right through me keeps me awake.

After his last year of high school, there wasn't much better to do. He had no college money – just part-time jobs and cocky little Jack McCoy, Sean Massey and their gang of troublemakers who sometimes pulled Dugan in to menace the neighborhood. At first it was harmless stuff . . . putting mice in old ladies' mailboxes, letting air out of the tires when some rich guy parked his car near their street. Probably a mine owner. Maybe even a Protestant. They were to blame for killing Pop. They were too stin-gy to keep their exhaust fans running right, and the mine dust and gas exploded. Dugan always thought pranks against them kind of evened up a score. He even showed Patrick how to bleed the air out of their tires. Massey, the punk they called "Mash," came up with a way to put a penny in a gum ball machine and empty it out. He could put a single nickel in a soda machine, and jam it so they could help themselves to all the bottles.

Dugan had tried to keep Patrick away from the older boys. He'd scowl and tell his little brother to "get lost" in an angry voice, but sometimes the kid would sneak around behind them. Dugan never told his brother about the bad stuff they did, always goaded by Jack. The boys called him "Joker," but he was the kind who tore the wings off flies for fun. Once Jack threw a rock at a bird, knocking it out of the tree. He gave the live bird to a cat so he could watch its tortured death. Dugan realized too late that Patrick had watched the cruelty. He never forgot the pain on the kid's face.

Once Jack caught a stray dog, doused its tail with kerosene, and lit it on fire. The dog sprinted away, yelping. Dugan had been helpless to do anything. It wasn't just the smell of burning dog that sickened him. He began to hate Jack, deep in his heart.

When Pop was killed, Ma cashed in his two-hundred-dollar union death benefit.

"Handy that the funeral parlor was put right across the street from the Miner's Union Hall," she'd said at the time.

She and Pop had already borrowed forty-five dollars against the benefit to bury the baby, so with what was left, she paid for Pa's "arrangements" – the undertaker's catch-all term. After a bit of hand-wringing, she chose a commonplace casket to save a little money. She managed to keep the house going for a while – a ramshackle company house on Mineral Street. Dugan's oldest sister found domestic work in Anaconda and moved out. Single men boarders drifted in and out. His mother did the housekeeping, cooking chores and took in extra laundry with help from Margaret, Dugan's remaining sister. The three children still living at home had few clothes, but there was always a hot breakfast, dinner and a box lunch. Then Ma got sick, lingered awhile, and died. No one ever asked questions. There was some bustle right after she passed. Parish women darted in to drop off hot dishes and cakes in shifty ways, but no one stayed to comfort the children.

After Ma died of that hushed-up sickness it turned different. I hated the pity in the neighbors' eyes when they looked at me and Patrick and Margaret. They acted like they knew something we didn't. How could they know anything? They didn't live there like we did. Folks shunned us after that. Like we already committed some sort of crime. Like we were dirty in an invisible way.

Then, not even a month went by and the Company turns us three kids out of the house. I'm glad Ma wasn't there that awful day. I went against Pa's wishes and lost my temper. Funny − − you just get your temper back again. I wisht I could lose it so it never came back.

Ma had begged her sons not to work in the mines. One of her church friends vouched for Dugan and he got a job bussing tables and washing dishes for Mr. and Mrs. Vucinich at the Placer Street Diner. He moved into Mrs. Trbovich's boarding house. Margaret and Patrick went to live with an aunt in Anaconda. Before she left, Margaret insisted on blessing Dugan's new room with holy water to purify any evils lingering from the previous tenant.

"I know it's a *nice* place," she said as she sprinkled water from a vial. "But you never know who lived here before." Giving the bed an extra dose, she whispered loudly, "could of been a *harlot*, or, or a *pimp*."

Dugan was filling into his gangliness and his dark hair had a slight wave which stood it up in an Errol Flynn way. He'd inherited his father's good looks and smooth voice.

Dugan worked hard at the diner. He was always there to cover for the others when the place filled up, and soon Mr. Vucinich had him take on more duties. Dugan appreciated the extra hours. The customers liked him, too. He could make a joke and they would laugh along with him. His broad smile revealed a grille of good teeth, even though the quartering pair fit in sideways. Crescent-shaped grooves lined up beside his grin, which the girls thought was cute. The Placer Street Diner started serving a lot more high school girls who'd linger all afternoon over their nickel sodas. When the meal trade increased, Mr. Vucinich raised Dugan's pay fifty cents a week. Mrs. Vucinich usually stuffed a brown paper bag with kitchen leftovers and set it beside Dugan's coat for him to take. When he got to Trbovich's, he would share the food with any other boarders who were home.

Working at the diner was pleasant but it didn't cover the pain of losing his Pop and Ma, no matter how busy the place got. The hardest thing he had to do was serve the mine managers when they came in for lunch. He hated them for ruining his family, his life. His blood boiled when he watched them eye the menu like they expected something special. But he forced a smile and served them dutifully, out of respect for the Vucinichs. He couldn't look them in the eye, though. God, he missed his Pop.

Dugan wanted to do right by Mr. and Mrs. Vucinich, but the job lacked excitement. All his life he'd heard men talk about The Great War. He decided serving in the Army was what he needed to do. It would be a good way to make something of himself. The dignity of a uniform and important duty would make his Ma and Pop proud when they looked down on him from above.

One summer evening he finished at the diner, threw his apron in the bin, and stepped outdoors in time to see dusky light lingering on the west face of the Boulder Mountains, like the sun didn't want to to drop below the horizon just yet. Magenta folded into dark sage grays and long shadows deepened to indigo. It seemed a fitting display for the sunset of this part of his life. He wondered about the places he'd see in the military.

The boisterous gang approached, jostling around him.

"Hey, it's Sarge!" one chided. "Been practicing your salute?" Another knocked Dugan's knit cap off his head. He bent down to get it and someone else placed a foot on it. His anger was about to explode, but he managed to keep from making fists.

"The girls will be all over you, in your u-nee-form," one of them said sarcastically.

"Unless you're all over them first," another bellowed, to bawdy guffaws.

Jack glared up at him belligerently from beneath his cocked hooligan cap, motioning to the others. They surrounded Dugan. Why not drink a little beer with them? He was leaving soon and it would be their way to celebrate his decision. They hustled him off into the twilight and Dugan gave in to the foolery of Jack's gang that regrettable night.

CHAPTER 2

Visit

Those who are good suffer for it as well as those who are bad . . .
— WILLIAM FAULKNER, *LIGHT IN AUGUST*

The uniform he wore now was hideous, reeking of disinfectant, especially when they threw a laundered one his direction after group showers.

> *God! this is a boring life. If you can even call it LIFE.*
>
> *Most men here celebrate evil. The worse your crime, the higher your rank. Except the monsters who done crimes against kids. They have to watch their backs all the time.*
>
> *Most guys think my conviction is something to honor. Every day I wake up sick with regret. Some of these men have no conshence. Bad is good and good is bad.*
>
> *Some of the convicts say horrible things about the guards and the judges who sentenced them. They had their weapons stripped from them, but they still try to hurt with words – the only weapon they have left. They are the ones who get slammed below in solitary. But you can still hear them curse.*

He missed Patrick but the idea of the boy seeing him locked up disgusted Dugan. Margaret visited only once. He'd watched her stiffen as the prison matron ordered her to remove her coat and shoes for a body search. She'd stood in her stocking feet, enduring the indignity as inmates shoved each other for a glimpse of his attractive visitor and made lewd gestures. The dill-pickle-faced matron sniffed Margaret's shoes, then groped her roughly from her armpits down to her knees and eyed her pretty legs jealously.

It was obvious that it pained Margaret to see her brother through the bars in the small visitors' chamber. The matron hovered behind her. Margaret leaned forward to speak to Dugan and he tried to scoot closer to the opening but his chair was bolted to the floor.

Patrick was getting middling grades and eating like a horse, she told him.

"How 'bout the gang?"

"Mash's pa tars hoist cables for the Company, and got Mash work as a mucker at the Alice," she explained. "You remember my friend, Lillian?" He nodded. She lowered her voice. "There was trouble between Joker and her. He threatened to choke her dead if anyone found out the baby would of been his."

She told him she had to sell their father's accordion. Dugan felt a wave of loss. He'd liked playing it when no one was around. He always thought he might make some real music with it some day. He recalled its decorated casing, pearly buttons and its woody breath when it came to life in his arms. It was the only thing of value their father had owned. How could some junk dealer value it the way Dugan did? But it was gone, turned into nothing more lasting than a few canned goods for Margaret and Patrick's pantry.

The matron cut Margaret off with a rude order that visiting time was over. His sister reached between the bars and squeezed Dugan's hands, tears brimming in her troubled eyes.

Everyone inside here thinks they do not belong. But I am really an ice block in hell here. I am surrounded by guys like Joker and Mash. It's like it was at its worst in Butte. I don't fit. Everyone in here is a misfit in society, but what are you when you are a misfit among misfits? What is left?

Prison completely undid a young man. It had long ago stripped him of his sense of humor, his energy, his ideas, his dignity. The only pleasures he had left were a few hours of darkened solitude and his fading fantasies.

They call this place a "correctional facility" but it don't correct anything. If a man is rotten, he only gets more rotten within these walls. If a man is good but unlucky enough to get locked inside, he has to fight to keep his goodness.

Ma taught us kids to pray for forgiveness. There's even a chaplain in here for confession. I think some of these convicts just ask for forgiveness before they sin – – kind of like buying grace insurance.

I would count the stones in the outside wall, except I think that's bad luck. I already know more than I want about this place. Back in '93 big Frank Conley got rich while his chained-up convict-slaves hauled and set these sandstone blocks that would pen them in. I guess a working day passes the time better than not.

All the guards are armed. I hope to God I never see any of them have to shoot an unarmed man in the back.

He rested his aching fingers a moment, then repositioned the stub and continued writing.

Sometimes I feel like someone is standing on my chest. The air in here gets too thick and foul. It's like breathing muddy water.

Does prison do this to everybody or am I going crazy?

CHAPTER 3

Between Two Wars

Power will be the arbiter.
– JACK LONDON, *THE IRON HEEL*

Fresno, California – November 1940

The cluster of local men gathered as they always did about ten o'clock on weekday mornings at Leonard's, the storefront café on Fresno's Main Street. Clara had the coffee ready. As the men scooted their chrome and vinyl chairs, she approached with the big glass pot in one hand, a half dozen ceramic mugs splaying from the other. As they took their places at the formica table, she noticed their mood was dark.

"I don't care if the Germans *are* overrunning Europe," Hal began. "It ain't our war!"

"But Roosevelt's drafting men between twenty-one and thirty," Walter reminded him. "First peacetime draft in U.S. history."

The last war was still fresh in everyone's mind. Each of them knew untidy veterans with visible injuries who shambled around town with vacant eyes. Others vanished into hermithood, overwhelmed by mustard gas and shell shock. Everyone knew someone who'd been killed in Europe. Each year since, on November 11 they pinned red paper poppies on their collars to commemorate Flanders Field, and at eleven o'clock in the morning, stopped what they were doing for two minutes of reverent silence.

"This big new German offensive is gonna threaten our country. We can't just put our heads in the sand with all them countries fallin' like dominoes," Walter continued. "Churchill says Britain is stripped to the bone. London is under blackout orders cuz o' the bombings." Jabbing his chest with his thumb, he added, "*I* sure don't wanna huddle in a bomb shelter ever' night."

Clara returned, pretending to check on a nearby table. "Another foreign war is unthinkable!" she blurted. "My son Donnie is in the Merchant Marines and my youngest boy will graduate from high school in the spring. I'm darned if I'm gonna see him go off to war!"

"Looking back at the last war, I wonder if we got a little snookered by the Brits," Roy said, raising an accusing finger. "You know, maybe they were 'crying wolf' to get our help."

"Charlie Lindbergh says we should stay outta this one," Hal insisted, "and he's been to Paris and such."

"Yeah, but he's a Nazi sympathizer," Walter argued. "Him and his rich friends like Henry Ford. They preach Isolationism, but all they really care about is the money they could lose if the market goes bad. I think they'd be smart to start tooling up to build armored rigs."

"I sure don't want to see the last war disaster repeated," Roy said.

Clara rested the coffee pot on the table and put her hands on her hips. "This country needs a break from war. Look what it did to ol' Dan Stanhope!" The others nodded. Everyone missed Dan. He used to be one of the regulars at Leonard's where they could gossip, leave their spoons in their mugs and put their elbows on the table. Clara would watch them lean their heads in when one started telling a risqué joke. Dan had seemed comfortable being among the men who ignored his injury.

"Ol' Dan changed after he got shipped home from Europe," Hal said. "At first he seemed fine, but then he got pretty touchy, and thought ever'body was starin' at him."

"I don't like that our military has slipped to such a low priority," Walter muttered. "Didja know our soldiers are usin' wooden rifles for their drills? I read that the Air Forces only have a few hundred aircraft, some of 'em just fabric biplanes left over from World War I! Why are we ignoring that crazy Hitler? He ain't gonna stop with Poland and France."

The others just shook their heads.

———————

The café's festive holiday decorations should have cheered Clara, but something was pressing down on her mood. Even though the coffee bunch never tipped much, she liked waiting on the fellows. But lately their conversation had frightened her. Then there was the president's fireside chat last night. She'd heard the gravity in Roosevelt's voice. It was like he was forcing each heavy thought through the radio. He'd said, "You wouldn't deny your neighbor the use of your garden hose if his house was on fire." Then he referred to America as the "Arsenal of Democracy." Clara thought of Donnie. Would it affect him? His letters hadn't mentioned anything but routine duty in the Atlantic.

Everyone had heard the broadcast, and the fellows began discussing it before she poured their coffee.

"Now that President Roosevelt's won his third term, he's pretty cock-sure he's got our backing," Hal observed. "He wants to send planes, equipment and food to the Brits. I wonder when he's gonna start sending our boys."

Clara turned toward the group. "And I voted for him because I *trusted* him!"

"You can't disagree with FDR's point about lending and leasing equipment to Britain," Ernie said.

"And it's not sending our kids into war," Hal said, looking up at Clara.

"I don't know much history, but what war was ever stopped by lending garden hoses to a neighbor?" she asked.

CHAPTER 4

Franklin's Plan

London – January 1941

Harry Hopkins chomped another antacid as he was whisked into the special car at London Airport. He felt enormously important, being the United States president's closest confidant, but was anxious about meeting the British prime minister.

"We are being eyed constantly through German bombsights," the driver said, handing Hopkins a gas mask and a helmet. "So far, they are only terrorizing us at night, but keep these handy at all times, sir." Hopkins lit another cigarette.

It was several miles to the underground War Rooms where he would meet Mr. Churchill. It was mid-morning, but it was a ghostly city without people. They passed dreary winter gardens and rows of naked fruit trees.

"The Red Cross has set up bomb-resistant work rooms around the city," the driver remarked. "Volunteer women sew bandages. They are the only women permitted in the city. The rest were evacuated to the countryside along with all the children."

As they neared their destination, uniformed men and women hurried about. Hopkins saw pocked buildings. Heaps of charred rubble still smoldered. They passed the Parliament building, crossed the Thames, parked, and a clerk ushered Hopkins into Churchill's underground command center. Thick steel plates were bolted to the ceiling beams, color-coded phone lines strung along the walls, and clerks in drab military wools clattered at typewriters. A faint bouquet of the prime minister's cigar drifted in the close basement air. In spite of the whitewashed walls, Hopkins could see that Churchill and his staff lived a badger's lifestyle.

They passed a very small room with a single bed, nightstand with an ashtray and a cluttered bookshelf.

"Mr. Churchill's private nap room," the clerk said, deftly closing the door and nudging Hopkins farther down the narrow hall. They entered a larger room. The prime minister was extending a typed page at a secretary, pointing to a particular place on it with his other hand, a cigar pinched between his fingers.

"My dear woman, ending a sentence with a preposition is something *up* with which I will *not put*. Please revise that paragraph and *then* I'll sign it." She dashed out and he swiveled toward Hopkins with a wink and a devilish smile. How could anyone keep his sense of humor in this gloom, Hopkins wondered. The man's energy lifted him from his fatigue as they exchanged proper greetings. The prime minister was wearing a dark suit and flawless white shirt that set off his large forehead and wide-set eyes. He pushed the ashtray toward Hopkins, and placing his hands wide apart on the desk, leaned toward the American. His face took on a fierceness and his chest seemed to swell. Hopkins could see why the press characterized him as a bulldog.

"Do you believe the audacity of that bloodthirsty little guttersnipe?" Mr. Churchill began, surprising Hopkins with his bluntness. "If Hitler were to invade *hell*, I'd make a compact with the *devil himself!*" He swiveled in his chair and retrieved a large map. "Our metropolis here, the greatest target in the world, is a kind of tremendous, fat, valuable cow tied up to attract the Aryan beast of prey."

Hopkins should have felt sorry for the man, with his nation teetering in such a tenuous position, but the prime minister radiated such verve that pity was far from his mind.

"We cannot move London," Mr. Churchill stated simply. With his cigar still wedged between his fingers, he outlined his markings and continued. "The Nazi juggernaut must be stopped. The life expectancy for our British officers in France is an appalling *three months!*" His face soured. He leaned toward Hopkins again. "American help is imperative if the final curtain is to come down on this horrendous act Hitler calls the 'thousand-year Reich.' "

Hopkins conveyed Roosevelt's promise to lend aid.

Shuddering with disgust, Churchill added, "an alliance with Russia is inevitable, even though Stalin's industrialized savagery is abominable. Nor do I trust him. He is a burglar who tries to break and enter. If he fails, he invites you to *dine* with him that evening."

Hopkins was pleased that the prime minister had brought up Russia first.

"Yes, a careful alliance was our plan as well, Mr. Churchill."

The prime minister settled back, his air reflecting a new strength. Hopkins had no doubt that this man could deploy Britain's mighty defenses from these small chambers.

"Mr. Hopkins, did you know that Shostakovich lost family, friends and colleagues in the Great Terror of 'thirty-six? He was moved to capture the pathos in his music. Russian audiences openly wept at his tragic Fifth Symphony."

An aide brought a tray with glasses and a decanter of Johnnie Walker scotch. The two of them sipped drinks and smoked as they discussed details. Hopkins commented on the provisional command center.

"This is no time for ease and comfort," Mr. Churchill replied, waving his cigar stub. "It is time to dare and endure." Catching the fried-cabbage fragrance escaping the small kitchen, he added, "Something reminds me. I believe it's time for our luncheon."

Hopkins returned from London, fortified with Mr. Churchill's convictions. He was so sure of Franklin's plan to lend and lease war equipment that he was surprised when members of the president's own Democratic Party argued bitterly against it. He watched in disgust as hostile debate lasted weeks. Standing just a few feet apart on the Senate floor, men verbally attacked one another.

"Mr. Roosevelt is trying to flim-flam the American public!" Montana Senator Burton K. Wheeler declared, his face flushed. In an apoplectic staccato he added, "The president's request is shocking. This is the most dictatorial and asinine piece of legislation ever in Congress in the eighteen years I have been here!"

Appalled at the attack on his friend, Hopkins was relieved when the chairman pounded his gavel. "You are out of order!" he declared.

Congress finally passed the Lend-Lease Act in March. It was obvious that the American public approved of Franklin's "Arsenal of Democracy" with their buying binge on Wall Street. Hopkins had seen where Brits had planted cabbages in their coal bins to survive, but clever American investors were now enjoying caviar days and a surge in stock prices. Each time Hopkins saw a "Now Hiring" sign, he glowed with admiration for his president and friend. Good business was good politics – even if it was fueled by war.

CHAPTER 5

A New Enemy to Hate

Hitler's not going to teach my children!
— Canadian Advertisement to buy war savings stamps

Montana State Prison, Deer Lodge – Spring 1941

Butte's daily newspaper appeared in the prison library a day late after the mailroom reviewed and censored it first. Dugan and some of the others pounced on it. He craved any kind of news. After discovering the toilet paper escape rope, the guards were extra vigilant that no one take any of the newspaper back to their cells. Dugan managed to tear out a liberty bond advertisement and sneak it in with his loose sheets of paper. He liked to look at the image of the young soldier, rifle at his side and fighter aircraft streaking past in the background.

Between the newspaper's black blockouts he read that war was spreading. Rommel's Panzers had whined north through Libya toward the Mediterranean, stopped only by some Australians. "Hurrah for those Aussies!" Dugan blurted.

It alarmed the shift lieutenant, who ordered him to pipe down.

The others peered over Dugan's shoulder, asking him to read the story to them.

"Squealing blind through sandstorms," he began, keeping his voice low, "the German tank column could have closed the Axis grip on Alexandria, Cairo and the Suez Canal but for a handful of gristly, Australian commandos, blasting the invaders from inside scattered foxholes."

The news gave the inmates a new enemy to hate, a fresh target, instead of hating the prison, the guards, and each other. The diversion of war was medicine for their ailing souls.

"Chrissakes!" hissed one man, pointing at the tattered paper. "It says here the Brits are even drafting women!"

———

In the paper dated June twenty-third, Dugan read the shocking news that Germany had violated its non-aggression pact with Russia and had attacked in an all-out assault. The Red Army's tanks and aircraft had outnumbered the rest of the world's armies combined. But the paper reported that "within the first eight hours, the Luftwaffe turned nearly two thousand of the Soviet's first-line aircraft into smoking heaps of scrap." It quoted Hitler's vain claim: "Barbarossa is a German success. Before three months have passed, we shall witness the collapse of Russia, the likes of which has never been seen in history!" A photo of Churchill showed that beneath his black top hat his face was pinched with worry. The caption quoted his outraged response: "We must do everything we can to keep Germany from ruling the skies!"

Passions heated up in the prison, along with the men's malignant feelings of impotence and helplessness. Dugan imagined a legion of jack-booted men in gray uniforms backed by the German flag with its black swastika. To him, the symbol, set at its malevolent angle, looked like a saw blade poised to cut down everything in its path.

Waking up on his twenty-first birthday, Dugan felt a rush of shackled impatience. He would have dashed to the nearest draft board – if only he were on the Outside.

CHAPTER 6

In the Den of the Bear

Moscow – July 1941

Hopkins lit another cigarette from the glowing end of the one he held between his nicotine-stained fingers. He felt drafts even with his full-length wool coat buttoned to his throat. God, Moscow was a long way from his cozy rooms near the president. He'd endured the long trip and was just about to meet the Soviet premier face-to-face in this austere room. His meeting in London had exhausted him, but when Franklin asked him to travel to Moscow as his special envoy, how could he decline?

Hopkins peeled another antacid from his little foil roll. Damn this ulcer. I don't dare let on it's kicking up again. He wiped a fleck of calcium carbonate from his lips as he heard a tattoo of bootsteps approaching in the outer hall. Several impeccably uniformed men appeared, flanking a much shorter man, not much over five feet tall. Hopkins suppressed his surprise at Joseph Stalin's appearance. The man did not resemble his official image – the one Stalin approved after executing several of his hapless portrait painters. His mustache was streaked with gray. His face was pock-marked.

The stocky commander nearly crushed Hopkins with a hug. His intense dark eyes showed no warmth. When he stepped back, Hopkins noticed his oddly shortened left arm before he expertly positioned himself so it was inconspicuous again. He sat facing the door on the high-backed bulletproof sofa he'd designed for himself.

Stalin was forceful, but even though he spoke through an inter-preter, Hopkins could tell he was not articulate like Mr. Churchill. He spoke in a monotone, with frequent animated outbursts which made his interpreter wince covertly. In spite of his bluster, Hopkins thought he had the flinchy demeanor of stalked prey. He seemed unable to look the American directly in the eye. Instead he directed his eyes at a shoulder or lapel. Two of his bodyguards remained in the room for the entire meeting. They sat rigid and officious but their eyes showed the rancor of abused, caged animals.

The German double-cross had obviously shaken his host to the core. Stalin – whose assumed name meant "man of steel" – boasted that he'd executed his Air Force commander over the Barbarossa disaster, adding, "another of my generals saved me the trouble by committing suicide." At this repellant news, Hopkins shifted uncomfortably but tried to appear supportive. Mr. Stalin did not reveal that he feared his own people as much as the invaders, and had ordered masses of com-rades executed. He was so mistrustful that he'd had all rugs and carpets removed, so he could hear footsteps when someone approached. He'd had all the drapery shortened so he could see the feet of anyone hiding behind it. Outside of his tight orb of armed henchmen, the starving cursed him and relished the chance to stab him dead. They mumbled grace over breadless meals of thin broth and couldn't ease their chil-dren's hunger with dogma. They prayed for German victory. Stalin ed-ited that fact in threatening remarks to Hopkins.

"Maybe tomorrow I decide mighty Red Army shall fight *with* Axis. What would Mr. Roosevelt say then?"

Hopkins knew it was imperative to stanch Stalin's inclination to switch loyalty. He assured Mr. Stalin that the United States was geared up to send huge quantities of food, planes, tanks, trucks and ammuni-tion. Hearing that, the man's teeth showed slightly beneath a twitch of his mustache. He called for vodka, and settled back on his sofa. He insisted on delving into more detail of the commitment and contin-ued the dialogue. His conversation ranged widely, but the brute never revealed that his own son Yakov had been captured fighting the enemy and that Stalin refused Germany's offer to release him in a prisoner trade. Having three sons of his own, Hopkins would not have understood a father letting his son die in a stalag.

He included a bowdlerized lecture on Russia's brand of socialism. Hopkins found himself agreeing more and more as time wore on. Exhausted, he risked a discreet glance at his watch and realized they'd been meeting for six hours.

Stalin stood abruptly and moved toward Hopkins who wobbled up from his chair. The Soviet premier placed both hands on his visitor's bony shoulders and leaned in. His breath was hot vodka and digesting onions.

"Hitler's propaganda minister, Joseph Goebbels, said Americans and Brits would never find common ground with *Bolshevists*." He sneered at the misnomer. "Mr. Hopkins, I am counting on *you* to make a fool of him."

On his long trip back to Washington, Hopkins smiled to himself thinking of how well this meeting went. Once he reported the real Russian situation to Franklin, the "Big Three" would certainly prove Goebbels wrong.

CHAPTER 7

Natural Causes

Clear the decks for action
The time for speech is past
Let's do the job we have to do
And get it over fast.
— ABE LYMAN, *LET'S PUT THE AXE TO THE AXIS*

Fresno, California – December 1941

"**I** can't believe Roosevelt's just sitting on his hands!" Daniel Junior exclaimed to his mother. "It's been a month since the German U-boat sank the Reuben James! We're just standing on the sidelines, watching Britain and Russia fall to the Germans while Japan is raping China!" He could see the term he used shocked her. He felt very adult after he'd said it. It annoyed him that his mother had stopped looking at the papers. "Mother, did you know Germany is torpedoing unarmed civilian ocean liners?"

He'd been watching the construction of a temporary Army base just beyond Fresno's outskirts. It thrilled him to see the olive drab vehicles with white stars on their sides coming and going, their canvas tops concealing stockpiles of exciting military equipment and weapons. Daniel had hiked over and strolled between the neat new barracks and buildings. Each plane that flew over quickened his pulse.

Ever since the day thirteen-year-old Daniel Junior looked up from his position in the sunny outfield and watched a Jenny fly overhead, he knew he wanted to fly. The biplane's OX-5 V-8 engine sputtered and went silent, leaving only the hum of the wind through its rigging. Daniel and some of his teammates abandoned the ball game and ran to the field where the biplane had skidded to a dusty stop. Daniel never forgot how the pilot looked, climbing out of the open cockpit, lifting his goggles with invincible flair. The man saw the boys' mitts, smiled at them, and called, "who's winning?" It was a question Daniel's father never had the chance to ask.

Even before Daniel graduated from Fresno's Edison Tech High School, he had told his mother that he wanted to attend a college where he could take ground school and flight instruction. He passed near the top of his class and finished with a college degree, pilot license and a fiancée. He'd dated Beverly some in high school, and when he was away at college, their letters to one another had become passionate and he'd proposed. They were planning to get married after he was established in his Army career. Beverly kept up on war news and supported Daniel's ambitions. She'd often told him she loved the idea of being an officer's wife – especially a pilot.

The blaze of war blew up in Europe and turned coffee shop opinions toward entering the conflagration. As the president fussed over opinion polls, War Department brass paced back and forth, champing to get past his equivocating and start dropping bombs.

Then Japan's attack on Pearl Harbor upended America. Radios were tuned in for Roosevelt's "day of infamy" speech. The reality of another world war burst through the shield of American neutrality, intruding into American homes, farms, factories and passions. News echoed from radios, and newspapers got snatched up and passed around like never before.

The *USS Arizona* was still burning in her Pearl Harbor berth when Hitler declared war on the United States. The alignment of international battle buddies was about to shift. Roosevelt began referring to Stalin as "Uncle Joe, our gallant Soviet ally."

———

"It's about time!" Daniel shouted when he saw the block-type headline "US Declares War on Germany!" He continued reading to himself for a moment, then became even more animated. Laura looked into her son's eyes, which projected new fervor.

"I'm joining the Army Air Force!" he declared, slapping the paper on the table. "I'll be damned if anyone's gonna stop me."

Laura stared at her son, just a boy with barely enough facial hair to shave. She wished she'd never loved her boys so much. Daniel's fierceness would be easier to accept. Love was a dangerous slope. The more you invested, the higher the precipice from which you fell when you lost them.

———◆———

Laura would never forget that horrible day in November, 1918 when the Western Union man approached her home, a yellow envelope in his hand. Her heart racing, she stood and opened the door immediately upon hearing his knock. She knew he probably brought some tragic manifestation of God's will, and she would be powerless to do anything but endure it.

Her husband had enlisted, rather than wait to be drafted. She hated that Dan had chosen to put himself in so much danger. Laura, whose schoolgirl face was framed with an attractive wreath of soft, sand-colored curls, enjoyed teaching elementary school. She and Dan had been looking forward to starting a family. She wanted to stay home with babies, once they came along. He'd just been promoted to supervisor at the Fresno canning plant. His decision interrupted their orderly lives and plans.

Without delay he was trained for combat, a rough-hewn human gaffe with nothing more than a steel hat for protection. The Army handed him a rifle and a pistol, and sent him to the trenches in an unpronounceable European city to throw grenades that would shatter the lives of other young men with plans.

The telegram simply stated that Sergeant Daniel Stanhope was injured while carrying out his honorable duty, and was recuperating in hospital. What it didn't say was that he'd left an arm and much of his scalp and face in the mud near Ypres, Belgium. Laura learned that herself when she first saw him in the flesh – what was left of it. He walked unsteadily toward her, his empty uniform sleeve pinned to his side. His face had changed. Pink putty-like patches of skin on his forehead and down the side of his face showed recent burns trying to heal, flake by flake. A mortar shell had exploded near him. When burning debris lodged beneath the rim of his Brodie helmet, he was too stunned to yank it off with his good arm and drop and roll. His Army doctor had told him he nearly lost his eye and that he was a very lucky man. Sergeant Stanhope had silently and bitterly disagreed.

Everyone in town recognized the man with one arm. Wide-eyed children stared, but most folks tried to ignore his scarred face. Dan was well-liked and people presumed all kinds of heroics, repeating ever-enlarged details of his battle wound. The man was becoming a legend. He hadn't had to pay for a cup of coffee since he came home. Friends and even strangers bought his meals when they saw him at Leonard's.

One Memorial Day, he rode in the parade marshal's cabriolet, ahead of the color guard, the band and all the flag-wavers marching down Fresno's Main Street. The crowds waved and saluted him.

Laura could sense that Daniel Junior's pride in his father was mixed with childish angst, as if a storm cloud followed him everywhere. The boy would cry out for her at night, short of breath. He told her of nightmares in which he was running up an endless staircase. Sometimes he struggled with a heavy burden. Sometimes a large creature was chasing him.

In spite of the hero's welcome, Dan Senior didn't last very long after coming home from "the war to end all wars." It wasn't just his arm and the skin on his head that he'd lost. Laura had to cut his meat, and button and unbutton his clothes for him. The injury had stripped him of his dignity. He stopped going to Leonard's for coffee with the fellows.

When he and Laura lost their younger son the summer the boy turned six, Dan Senior's eyes narrowed to disapproving slits beneath his graying, unruly eyebrows and he quit laughing. He seemed to give up. Laura realized he'd used up all his fight half a world away, trying to survive the ear-splitting purgatory between machine-gunnings from the sky and the earthy hell of gangrenous trench foot. He stopped breathing before Daniel Junior turned twelve. He was only forty-two. His obituary said that he died of "natural causes," but any soldier knew there was nothing natural about being the target of German flammerwerfer, mortars, stick grenades or the Fokker scourge.

———————

"We'll get those Huns this time," Daniel cried, slamming his fist into his other palm. All this talk made Laura's heart sink like a ton of stone. There was no stopping the boy. News of the war thrilled him. She imagined the Bible picture of stern-faced Abraham, poised with the sword over Isaac's neck, preparing to kill his only son. To her, Abraham's sword stood for this outrageous war. Unless God intervened, she could lose her only surviving son.

Beverly sent him off with kisses, and high hopes. Laura wrung her hands and dropped, powerless, into a chair. She sat silently as he left for the nearest recruiter. Her son couldn't understand that you can't backfill the loss of a loved one, no matter what you do.

———————

But to Daniel, the conflict had come along at the ideal time. It would be his way to settle a score, even if his dead father would not be around for the payoff.

CHAPTER 8

Merchant Marine

The chatter at Leonard's centered around who had joined up – someone had noticed another home displaying the gold-edged pennant with its big blue star. Talk of the war echoed around the tables all day long. Leonard taped war bond and recruiting posters on the walls. Clara tolerated the posters as a matter of duty to her boss. She dreaded the possibility of her younger son being plucked from home like ripe fruit, but like most young men he imagined only the heroics of war. In the occasional letter from Donnie, the Merchant Marine still sounded safer than the infantry.

A new Abe Lyman song, *Wrap Your Dreams in the Red White and Blue* had been added to the jukebox. Ernie selected it and sat down with the men for coffee. Clara had already heard it so many times, she knew all the lyrics – that song and his silly *We're in the Army Now*.

After his friends gathered, Roy brought up a story he'd seen in the newspaper, nearly buried among other small articles. "Didja see that now we're sending aid to the Reds?" The men hadn't seen it. "If we outfit the Russians, they can whip the Nazis for us."

"That must be the idea. Seems like a good plan to me," Hal said.

Walter had read in the morning paper about "America First," Senator Burton K. Wheeler's anti-war group. "That stubborn son of a gun tried to stage a rally in Seattle, and the audience heckled and threw eggs at them."

"He got what was comin' to him," Ernie said. "That jackass Wheeler leaked information about the Army's victory plan to the newspapers."

"That's right. Didja see today's editorial?" Walter continued. "Says Wheeler is just watching American history pass him by, that he has little to look forward to but . . . let's see if I can remember the exact words . . . 'insignificance and obscurity.' "

As the men tossed coins on the table for Clara, Walter put a nickel in the jukebox and they all left to the brassy sounds of another Abe Lyman hit, *Let's Put The Axe To The Axis*.

———————

When the men gathered the next day, Leonard greeted them from the top of a step stool beneath the wall clock. "Gotta get used to Roosevelt's 'war time' starting today, fellas," he reminded them, turning the hands an hour ahead. The men murmured agreement and adjusted their wristwatches. Grim-faced, Clara shuffled out from the coffee station.

"G'mornin' Clara, how's it goin'?" one of the men asked.

"Didn't you hear?" she bellowed. "Donnie's ship went down in the North Atlantic!" The men glanced at one another awkwardly. Hal took her hand and held it. She plopped in a chair and sobbed into her other hand. They all shared their condolences as she tried to compose herself and Leonard – just as surprised as the others – put his hand on her arm and kindly led her to the back. He sent her home with two days' pay.

"What a tragedy," one of the men said, slowly shaking his head.

Leonard returned with the coffee pot. Between sobs, Clara had told him that her son was on a convoy of thirty-four ships when they were attacked, sinking twenty-one of them.

The men sat silently, looking at their hands. No one spoke.

Finally, Hal cleared his throat and spoke up, a quaver in his voice. "This may not be 'our war' but American wives and mothers like Clara have already sacrificed their husbands and sons."

CHAPTER 9

Motivation

In the shadow of his hand hath he hid me,
and made me a polished shaft;
in his quiver hath he hid me.
– ISAIAH 49:2

Montana State Prison, Deer Lodge – December 1941

The emotional shock wave of the Pearl Harbor attack penetrated the thick walls of the prison. Guards disappeared to enlist, and new ones replaced them. When inmates exploited their inexperience, Dugan was afraid prison officers would cut the only privilege they had – the newspaper. Soon the new guards toughened up, the atmosphere returned to its pathetic balance of keeper and caged. The men resumed their places within the yellow lines painted on the floors and Dugan worried less about losing his connection to the Outside.

The prison began allowing personal mail – heavily censored at first. Between smudge-blacked words, the prisoners read of cohorts joining up. Young American men were receiving military orders to report for duty. And the inmates envied them. They breathed each others' caged air, filling their lungs with distilled zeal.

Margaret wrote that Mash quit his mine job and joined the Army, just one step ahead of the law. Joker had bragged about joining up, but wrecked his chance when he blew his hands off in an explosion. He'd stolen blasting caps and dynamite from a mine supply shed. Margaret didn't know of anyone who felt sorry – especially her friend Lillian who said he got what he deserved.

The Brits cheered that America had joined the war, and were pictured in the papers lifting their chipped, pint-sized canning jars in toasts with whatever they could find to drink. Germany's declaration of war on the United States amplified Dugan's craving for retaliation. His restless thoughts cycled through hatred, anger and revenge. New energy seeped in and constructive thoughts began to form.

It is bigger than Montana State Prison. It is bigger than Montana.

It has lined up and straightened my mind and body. I am a killing arrow pointing out of these bars aimed right at the enemy. I need to get out and fight.

I want to kill Germans. They are rotten.

———•———

"Can you believe this? All men eighteen to sixty-four hafta register fer the draft now," an inmate whispered, trying not to attract the guard's attention. That kind of news was supposed to be censored for fear it would agitate the prisoners. Thanks to a mailroom oversight, the government notice had slipped through on the society page next to an article about Louise Martin's bridge club.

"Christ! If they're askin' old men to go in, they must be desperate!" Dugan scratched his head.

The prison lay at an elevation of forty-five hundred feet, a dozen miles from the Continental Divide. Whether it was ninety degrees in blazing sun, or blizzarding at twenty below zero, all inmates were sent into the recreation yard every day. They were to move about beneath rifle-toting guards who paced back and forth on the top of the wall. The men began to holler back and forth during these outings beneath the Bastille-like towers.

"Stubs baby, you can't get drafted, cuz they don't take no one with the clap!" one yawped.

"Bad newth for you goonth who can't read!" another lisped through his missing front teeth. "You ain't gotta chanth to get in the Army."

"Hey Chief! Could you scalp a Jerry who's wearin' one of them helmets?"

"Beanpole, give it up! You don't weigh enough soakin' wet to get in. Ya gotta be at least a hunnerd 'n five pounds or the Army don't want ya!"

"Hey Arse! I hear *you* wanna fly *airoplanes*! But yer so tall ya better hope they can find ya one o' them open cockpit biplanes!"

"They line ever'body up fer physicals. The doc sticks his finger in yer mouth to check yer teeth, then he waggles it up yer ass. He goes to the next guy and does the same, right on down the line!" another yelled to loud "na-a-h's" and huge guffaws.

"Silence in the yard!" a guard ordered.

Dugan recalled a line from Zechariah and thought of the prison as the "Stone with Seven Eyes." But there was one corner of the yard where only one guard could see them. This was one place the eye blinked. The inmates drifted in and out of that corner so as not to arouse suspicion. They began making a plan in intermittent collaboration. Dugan saw where inmates had hunched there and scratched its red bricks with their names, MSP numbers and hometowns. Some had added hopeful dates of their release, many years in the future. Dugan was tempted to scratch a swastika with an arrow piercing it, but instead turned his attention toward their plan.

It was very chancy, drafting a petition intended for Governor Sam Ford. Discovery would trigger punishment for conspiracy. The only way they could be heard was for one man to file an interview request with the deputy warden. They nominated a scribe who would make the request. Dugan slipped him sheets of paper and lent him his pencil stub. Over the next few days they gathered in the corner, the scribe memorizing the prisoners' message. When he finished writing it all down, he smuggled the document back to the corner, where Dugan and two hundred and ninety of his fellow inmates squeezed their signatures into blank spaces, writing carefully against the coarse brick wall, so they wouldn't punch through the paper:

> Dec. 19, 1941
> We feel that we who have erred and who have suffered imprisonment as the result of so erring would make excellent fighting men for the following reasons:
> 1 - We are well schooled in matters of discipline
> 2 - We have probably a greater love of freedom and its underlying principles than those who have never been deprived of their freedom, and
> 3 - Deprivation and hardships are not strangers to us.
> Therefore we petition you to seriously consider the advisability of issuing pardons to all of us, who, in your estimation, would be valuable additions to the armed forces of the United States, contingent upon the immediate joining of the armed forces by any man receiving such a pardon.
> We are eligible for enlistment except for our felony. We are willing and anxious to serve our country.

They also wrote to Warden Dudley Jones. The scribe again took up Dugan's writing stub and on the one remaining sheet, he wrote:

> We are not trying to get an easy way out. If we have a debt to society to discharge, we could better discharge it by offering our lives to our country than by serving out our terms of imprisonment.

It sounded real legal-like. The fellows did a good job. I didn't know all the bigger words like 'deprivation' but I know a lot of it happens in here when big guys bully the smaller guys. Some things shouldn't even make it to confessional. Anyway, I had nothing to lose by signing it.

The inmates' rumblings took on hopeful undertones. The smell of male perspiration became pervasive as Dugan and some of the others began doing pushups on the cramped floors of their cells. Grainy war images penetrated Dugan's dreams. He could almost hear the sharp cadence of German troops goose-stepping, their right arms aping the heil Hitlers of the men around them. He could imagine himself sitting in the cockpit of a fighter or pulling a grenade pin and heaving it. Maybe he'd fire the canon from atop a tank, or swivel an ack-ack gun into a sky filled with Messerschmitts. His writing was filling with words that revealed his appetite for war.

CHAPTER 10

All Eyes On Alaska

He who holds Alaska holds the world.
– BILLY MITCHELL TO CONGRESS, 1935

The White House – Early 1942

Hopkins had summoned the president's closest advisors to the Oval Office. Even with the light coming from behind Franklin sitting there at the huge desk, Hopkins could see new lines of worry on his gray face. He wondered if the others noticed the anxiety in his friend's demeanor. Admiral Stark wouldn't sit, and just paced back and forth in the intimate space, irritating Hopkins.

Everyone had war jitters. As eager as Americans were for revenge after the devastation of Pearl Harbor's fleet, a counter-attack was impossible. In a hand-wringing attempt to do something, the president had asked Hopkins, as chair of his Advisory Committee, to call this emergency meeting.

Roosevelt led off by announcing his intention to round up all Japanese-Americans. "We've estimated a hundred and ten thousand of them," he began. "They will be interned in camps throughout the western states." In the hushed room, leather creaked as the men leaned forward in their chairs to tap ashes into bronze ashtrays.

Secretary of War Henry Stimson finally broke the silence.

"I don't like the way the Japs are flexing their muscles. They're all fired up by the wreckage they caused at Pearl Harbor. I predict they're sharpening their Samurai swords to attack the mainland with no warning."

"You could be right, Henry," the president said. "Our aircraft industry is shaken, especially those on the west coast. The Douglas plant is still managing to roll out one of our valuable C-47 Skytrains each day, in spite of the distractions of blackout conditions." His face was even more grave as he continued. "Our civilian spotters have just reported Japanese subs near our western shores." The men shifted and looked at one another. Ice tinkled as someone set a glass down. Hopkins shook out another cigarette. He started to light it from the smoldering butt in his other hand, but instead accepted a light as the man next to him extended his gold Ronson then snapped it shut.

"The Boeing plant is vulnerable to shelling from those subs," Stimson added. "One attack could interrupt our essential B-17 assembly line!"

The president nodded at his secretary of state, Cordell Hull. At the cue, Hull began to speak.

"We've anticipated that, sir. The plant manager has requested our Army Engineers Passive Defense Division to camouflage their twenty-six acres of roofs," he explained in his leisurely Tennessee patois. "It's beginning to look like a little residential spread of tidy homes, streets and fences." With a hint of a smile he went into details. "They even put up little street signs. 'Synthetic Street' and 'Burlap Boulevard.' "

"That's nothing but a risk," Chief of the Army Air Forces Hap Arnold snorted. Aiming his frown at Hull he added, "Those names risk exposing the tactic to the enemy."

"With all due respect, sir," Hull replied, "those miniature street signs would be impossible to read from a diving Zero at two hundred miles an hour." Arnold shook his head, his gray eyebrows converging into a fierce "V" clearly not amused.

"We are providing protection from both without and within," Hull continued. "We placed anti-aircraft guns in the mock buildings, and armed security guards are now patrolling the plant and rooftop to catch saboteurs."

"Now you're talking," Arnold said, dropping both thick fists down on his chair's arms as if he were cracking walnuts.

While the others droned about camouflaged rooftops, Hopkins wished they would move on to the problems of delivering equipment he'd promised to Russia. He'd been getting frantic calls from the Kremlin for more fighters, medium and heavy bombers. He needed the floor and as Roosevelt's top deputy, was ready to assert himself. He raised a bony finger.

"Yes, Harry?" the president responded. Each head turned toward him.

He edged his narrow hips forward from the lap of the large armchair and cleared his throat with the phlegmy sound of a career smoker. "I trust this new threat from Japan doesn't derail our intention to fulfill our *president's* promises to our staunch Russian ally against Germany."

Arnold immediately reacted. Hopkins had expected it.

"At this time, we've only got forty B-17s and one B-24 for our Pacific group. I heartily oppose equipping the Soviets at the expense of our own Air Force!"

"It would be unwise to give away airplanes for sentimental or goodwill reasons," Stimson ventured.

"Well put, Henry," Arnold said with another fist-fall.

Chief of Staff George Marshall agreed. "I'm uncomfortable giving anything to the Russians without strings attached."

Hopkins stole a quick glance at the president. These men couldn't possibly know the volume of aircraft the president had already promised the Russians. Already, American-built aircraft, trucks, tanks, weapons, ammunition, fuel, food and supplies were steaming out of east coast ports bound for depots at Archangel and Murmansk. Loaded Liberty ships cast off, their highest plimsoll lines dipping nearly below the waterline. But Doenitz's wolfpack lurked beneath the North Atlantic shipping lanes with orders to fire at will with deadly results that made big news.

"We've beefed up our convoys' defense with armed Navy escorts," Stark stopped pacing to report, "but those dastard German U-boats are even firing on us from the surface! Our dazzle-camouflaged escorts can't fool them completely." He had made a calculation and shared his grim discovery. "The enemy is marking up *seven kills* for every Liberty ship we launch. Our intel found that the Germans are launching seventeen new U-boats *every month*."

Dispensing with the decorum expected in the Oval Office, the admiral approached the desk, put both hands on it, leaned toward the president, and added, "I don't need to tell you that German torpedoes are sending tons of equipment to the bottom. We've lost five hundred and eighty-four aircraft to U-boats." There was a collective gasp in the room.

The president lowered his gaze, silently shaking his head back and forth slowly. "I asked for the straight facts, and you've provided them." His eyes pierced through his pince-nez at the man. "Anything else, Admiral?"

"Sir, their bombers have exploited the Atlantic air gap – the swath where it's too distant for us or the Brits to provide top cover. We've stretched our fighters to the limit."

"I understand."

"But more importantly, Mr. President, we've lost thousands of our Merchant Mariners. One out of twenty-four sailors . . . a statistic I – and I'm sure you – find unacceptable." He straightened up and resumed his annoying pacing.

Hopkins didn't need the reminder. Ships that made it through the murderous gauntlet were at risk of freezing in port. The icebreakers could do very little at that latitude. And the Luftwaffe had already proved that the rail lines from the ports were in range by bombing them. Stalin and his Stavka – his military confidants who'd survived his latest purge – had made their demands very clear. Stalin valued fighters and bombers more than men. The Russians brushed off Hopkins's explanation that the southern route cost a lot of time and labor. Departing Miami for South America's east coast, then crossing to Africa, through the Persian Gulf through Iran required either dismantling the aircraft first or the risk of very long flights. Flying them seemed logical, but the Wrights and Pratt and Whitneys didn't do well on a partial diet of sand and had to be torn down anyway, he'd tried to explain. But it didn't appease the sharp voices on the other end of his phone connection.

The president's voice boomed through Hopkins' thoughts. "My biggest fear is that Russia can't vanquish our mutual foe; that they capitulate and come to terms with Germany on a separate peace." He held up both hands holding the portentous silence. "We simply *must* provide Russia what they need." Marshall and Stimson looked at Arnold, who sat, stoic, outranked by his commander-in-chief.

"The stubborn problem is how to get our aircraft safely to the front," Roosevelt began again. "How ironic that our fastest, airborne tools of war are stranded half a world from where they need to be!" The men shifted uncomfortably, but Hopkins leaned forward, hoping to keep the momentum of the conversation going.

"Gentlemen," the president continued, taking the cigarette holder from between his teeth, "we need to put our American ingenuity *fully onto this problem now!*" He punctuated each word by pounding it out on his desk.

The men spread maps across desks. They pulled out rulers and string, and peering through the tobacco smoke, laid them different ways over the maps. All eyes turned toward Alaska, the land Billy Mitchell – once court-martialed for insubordination – had called "the most strategic place in the world."

"Our planes could be flown intact from the factories and staged somewhere in the northwest," the secretary of war said. "From there, they could fly over western Canada into Alaska." He stretched his string over the narrow sea between North America and Siberia. "Do you realize it's just a hop of fifty-three miles over the Bering Strait to the Russian mainland?"

"It's the most direct route to the Soviets," Roosevelt concurred.

"From Fairbanks," he continued, straightening up after making a final measurement, "it's three thousand, five hundred miles to Moscow. It's less than two thousand miles from the Montana border to Fairbanks. Add another thousand miles for our aircraft coming out of California, or seventeen hundred miles for those coming from the Bell factory in New York."

"And it's entirely through friendly skies. Our Canadian friends will no doubt agree," Hull speculated.

"No more U-boat torpedoes," the admiral observed. "No more aircraft disassembly. No more risks of damage during hoisting on and off the ships. This plan frees up ships and manpower to do more productive tasks!"

"Flying at over two hundred miles an hour, this plan will cut delivery travel time by days!" the president emphasized.

Hopkins settled back in his chair again, crossing his legs. Now we're making progress, he thought.

"But Alaska Territory has few roads and only a handful of places you could remotely call an 'airport'," Interior Secretary Harold Ickes protested. "Some call it 'Seward's Icebox' for a reason. Most of the landing strips are just crabgrass clearings on the tundra or river gravel bars that disappear at high water! What isn't permafrost is swamp. We've estimated three million lakes!"

The secretary's reaction concerned Hopkins. The others, poring over their two-dimensional maps, only had a drawing room idea of the proposed route. Alaska seemed to be just an empty land of glaciers, volcanoes, fur-fringed Eskimos, pointy-eared dog teams, trappers, sourdough gold miners and little else. And then, the Siberian crossing had to be reckoned with.

Ickes interrupted, his face darkening. "They'll need fuel and repair facilities. They'll need barracks . . . latrines . . . mess halls for the pilots and support staff. Septic systems! That means supply roads into each. I've seen the so-called airports in Canada that your proposed route would include." He looked at the president and each of the others. "None are hard-surfaced, or more than two thousand feet long! Only experienced bush pilots can land safely on them. I just received news that one of our light bombers landed at Edmonton's *paved municipal airport*, and it punched through the asphalt and sank to its hubs!" Hopkins chomped another antacid. It seemed impossible, but the other routes were frustrating his efforts, and were indeed deadly.

The men looked to Roosevelt for his reaction. He just stared at Ickes, unmoved from the plan. "Naturally, it will be a huge challenge to create a network of landing fields for the lend-lease aircraft flying through," the president acknowledged, his head tipping from side to side like a metronome. Hopkins recognized that quirk of his. He did it when he wanted to get his way. In a child, you'd call it petulant.

———————

The Russian half of the route spanned more than three thousand miles, and the Soviets balked at the plan. They were too busy killing Germans to carve airbases out of their vast hinterlands.

Hopkins needed their cooperation. More desks needed pounding, from the White House all the way to the frenzied lend-lease expediter in Newark – an Army captain trying to carry out safe shipments through lethal waters. He was exhausted from writing letters home to the families of the lost mariners.

Hopkins endured more meetings and made more promises. Avarice taints the pure custard of the socialist ideal as well, he discovered. Once he convinced Stalin's satraps that it could mean a lucrative fringe benefit – a widened pipeline for black market items that millions of Russians craved – they nodded their approval in greedy anticipation.

He was beginning to feel indispensable to this lend-lease project. Good connections mean job security, no matter which side of freedom your boss works.

Now Hopkins had even more to smile about.

CHAPTER 11

Cat-skinning to Russia

Winding in and winding out
Fills my heart with serious doubt
As to whether the dude that built this route
Was going to hell, or coming out.
– SLOGAN PRINTED ON ALASKA HIGHWAY STATIONERY

A hundred species of game wandered through Alaska's virgin spruce forests. Alaskans counted animals by herds. Their backcountry was home to four kinds of bears. Gold fever had hit in 1897, and one hundred thousand hopefuls had trudged into the Yukon and Alaska territories. Nourished by bannock and rhubarb, they jammed picks into ore-rich tunnels; panned, sluiced and dredged tons of waterway gravels feeding the Klondike and Yukon rivers. Well-tramped pathways twisted around little mining settlements. But over a half-million square miles of unaxed Alaska slumbered in wolf-howling wilderness until early 1942. Tracks from elk, moose, caribou and grizzly bears were overrun by the clodhoppers of surveyors, staking out a supply route that roughly connected several backcountry Canadian landing fields. Between Dawson Creek, British Columbia and Fairbanks, Alaska, thousands of military personnel and civilian laborers punched D-8 Caterpillar crawler-tractors around the muskeg, pioneering a trail that would become the Alaska-Canada highway, or Alcan. American and Canadian men, bundled against bullying weather, slept in wind-blown tents as they frantically carved the road through the boreal forest. Warm weather brought

52

swarms of black flies that could kill a horse. The adrenaline pulsing through the nation, awakened by the Japanese attack on Pearl Harbor, motivated the men to complete one thousand, five hundred miles of road in less than a year. A dozen wide, hard-surfaced airports appeared between rivers and trees, on an arc from Great Falls, Montana toward Nome, Alaska. The new airway was christened the "Alaska-Siberia Route" – ALSIB in military jargon.

At the same time, Russians scraped out airports along a flyway from the frozen coast of the Bering Strait to Krasnoyarsk. The Russian approach to the project was brutal. The Soviet government tapped its Gulag labor camps and forced thousands of men to work punishing fourteen-hour shifts in the cold forests, wresting roads and runways from the stubborn taiga with hand tools. In rare moments when they had energy for conversation, they furtively exchanged bits of personal history.

"Someone overheard my jest about our government. Next thing I know, I'm thrown onto the cold concrete floor of a stinking prison."

"Third time I showed up late for work they hauled me in. Gave me three years."

"I was locked up for swiping a head of cabbage for my family."

"Me? They called me 'kulak' after collectivization. I got ten years for gathering potatoes from the fields I'd owned before they confiscated all our farms." Casting a glance at their surly crew boss, he added quietly, "they dared not cut off my hands. What good is a slave with no hands? Some of us will freeze to death out here. But it's said that *no one* escapes Stalin's choking, crumbling mines." He raised his pickaxe and shuffled back to work.

The target of their hatred would soon appear on the cover of Time Magazine. Joseph Stalin was the editors' choice for 1942's "Man of the Year."

Meanwhile in Washington, Roosevelt wielded the awkward alliance to keep the Soviet bear engaged with the Nazi eagle. "A common enemy has bonded us," Roosevelt said privately to Hopkins. "We are allied now even though our social and economic ideals are repellent to one another. Harry, I demand discretion in the press about this agreement with the Soviets. I'm uncomfortable how Americans would receive news that we have become allied."

By now, the White House was at odds with its own War Department. Roosevelt was unsinkably optimistic that he would be able to count Stalin as a friend in peacetime; the War Department had no such confidence. They were pulling at each other like two dogs over a sweaty soccer sock. This was not the story the President wanted the public to know.

Not only did Hopkins bury the details, he masterminded a game in which each of his players were kept ignorant of anything but their own moves. Details were "like an iceberg, slipping from public view," one journalist would later write.

As an inmate in a Montana prison did pushups on his cell floor, he had no idea the way in which these new allies' mutual growing distrust was going to consume him.

CHAPTER 12

Heady Freedom

For brethren, ye have been called unto liberty;
only use not liberty for an occasion to the flesh,
but by love, serve one another.
– PAUL'S LETTER TO THE GALATIANS 5:13

Montana State Prison, Deer Lodge – Early 1942

The petition had an effect. Dugan and most of the men were elated, imagining the kind of duty they might get. For others, the joy was muted with anxiety. Like captive boars, they'd become habituated to the austere routine of prison. For years they had not made their own decisions. They had settled into the wretched community of prison life, and had developed defenses from the men surrounding them, both within and outside the bars. Freedom frightened a few of them. But not Dugan. He was ready for the next change, whatever it might be.

Anything would be better than prison life, where you get punished from two directions. Society punishes you by locking you away from it; convicts punish you within these walls. One little boner and they jam your arm in the chow line, making it look like you dropped your tray. You don't get a second meal. In fact, you have to clean it up then sit silently while everyone else eats in front of you.

I see myself in the tight-fitting cockpit of a fighter, the control stick in my hand, my thumb ready to press the trigger of a machine gun.

Now Dugan had a reason to rise in the morning. Inmates were leaving, one at a time. He would hear their names called. He'd heard that they were being bussed to Army processing centers. Would he be next?

As Montana prisoners were freed, the first wave of Axis POWs were arriving on U.S. soil, from overcrowded camps in Europe. Dugan read the news in a magazine. "For some of these poor bastards, their life is about to get *better*," he said. "They can thank the Geneva Convention. It's the law for humane treatment of prisoners. Enemy soldiers have to be removed from the combat zone. These guys come off the battlefield all dirty and hungry and are marched up gangplanks into Liberty Ships. U-boats lay off the torpedoes, knowin' the ships are full o' their own," he paraphrased.

Another man grabbed the magazine. "Says here one POW bragged that he gained weight in prison camp even after the labor he done!"

"Jesus, man! I'm gonna sign up with the Germans and get myself caught, so *I* can go on a ocean cruise," one joked.

"They're guarded by the Civilian Control Administration, it says. Gotta be better'n the goons we got here guardin' us!"

"Didja know there's a camp at Fort Missoula?" one added. "Just think! Some of us are goin' right past them when we get outta here." He stuck his thumbs in his ears and wiggled his fingers.

Dugan was in his cell when he learned he was not eligible to enlist in any branch of the military. His crime was too serious for release into a non-supervised position. Anger coursed through him. His head felt hot, and the walls pressed the breath out of him. He wanted to slam his fists into something. He kicked at the wall. When the pain was unbearable, he collapsed onto his mattress.

He counted the hours in prison as others were released and trained to fight. He'd nearly given up hope. The papers kept reporting that manpower was desperately needed. He'd even have taken a job in the mines, in spite of his ma's warnings. War changed everything. He knew she'd have understood.

In April he learned that he would be released to work on a crew, building up air base facilities in Great Falls. He was relieved that he was not being turned over to the Anaconda Copper Mining smelter west of Butte. A lot of Butte people worked there. Except for Margaret and Patrick, he wanted nothing to do with his past. He was turning north to a city near the Canadian border, and hoped never to return. A lightness came over him. He felt like dancing. His euphoria faded when he realized he wouldn't be flying a fighter or firing any kind of a gun at the enemy.

I should be happy just to get out of this prison purgatory but I want to tell people I was in the war. Not just a sideshow nail pounder or grease monkey thousands of miles from combat action. I will keep straight and narrow. Maybe they will lose so many soldiers, they'll need me to fight.

CHAPTER 13

Welcome to Great Falls

Our city has become a sea of khaki.
– GREAT FALLS, MONTANA RESIDENT

While the inmates had waited for a reply from the warden, the Army Air Forces Ferrying Command was building up its headquarters at the Great Falls airport less than two hundred miles away, near the border the U.S. shares with Canada. Great Falls was a logical place to stage lend-lease flights over the new ALSIB Route. It lay on a Great Circle route from the states to Siberia. Its clear weather was ideal for visual flying and the high plains were a good proving ground for cold weather preparations. Also, it was five hundred air miles inland – far from the threat of Japanese bombing.

Still, the War Department issued precautionary orders to its residents.

"Here are your blackout instructions," uniformed Girl Scouts told Great Falls folks on door-to-door campaigns. Camp Fire girls conducted grease drives since the fat left over from cooking could be used to make explosives. Housewives got in the patriotic spirit and imagined protecting their husbands and sons while scraping waste grease from their pots and pans. Grade schoolers liked the "Slap the Jap" posters for scrap metal collection. They trained their eyes over ditches and crannies for tin foil gum and cigarette wrappers and scrap metal that would be turned into proud battleships. They bragged to each other how much they had donated, not like big-city kids who sold their pathetic scrap for pennies.

"Let's sign up as Victory Belles!" one young woman exclaimed to her friend, stopping in front of an Army poster of a smiling girl dancing with a handsome young man in uniform. "It'll be fun to dance with the new soldiers!"

"And join all those khaki-wacky girls?" her friend asked. "You gotta be kidding!"

"It's all above board, come on. Let's!"

"I will, if you will," her friend conceded.

The two young women joined nearly a thousand other local girls who'd signed up in a rush to respond to the Army's request.

Great Falls had been selected in haste, and Army staff rolled in before there was sufficient housing. The city opened their Civic Center as a place to bunk and feed the first hundreds of men arriving to outfit the Seventh Ferrying Group. Cots were lined up in a neat grid, with just enough space between for a fellow to sit and lace his boots. Racks for hanging uniforms provided a little privacy between the rows.

———

A guard brought a canvas duffel bag to Dugan's cell and shouted Dugan's name at the cell house guard. The door rolled open, he set the bag down and told the prisoner to report to the administration office. Then he disappeared and the cell door was left agape.

Dugan stared out at the empty cell house gallery. The usual noises of his fellow inmates, barred in their own cells, faded. Instead, he heard rushing, as if a current of water flowed past – an invisible river that was about to sweep him away. In an unthinking reflex, he stepped against his back wall. He took a deep breath as if he were about to dive, before digging into the bundle. He pulled out a new chambray shirt, Levi's jeans, a new flannel-lined denim jacket and new underwear. His hands shaking, he threw on the new shirt and fumbled with the buttons on the jeans. He picked up the bag and reached under his mattress for the collection of thin papers he'd stashed there. He pulled out a couple of blank sheets, folded them into his bag, and left those he'd written on. They were part of a dead past he no longer wanted. Slipping his pencil stub in his breast pocket, Dugan put on the stiff denim coat and walked out of his cell for the last time. He resisted a whim to skip out of the monstrous cellblock, and paced deliberately across the yard into the administration building.

The man behind the barred window gave Dugan a bus ticket, a ten-dollar bill, drew a line through his name on a list, and told him to go to the main gate below Tower Seven. Dugan thanked him, even though the man had already turned away. He walked past the chaplain's open door. The seat behind the little desk was empty, or he'd have said goodbye to the kind man. Dugan stepped out of the building and approached the guard standing at the main gate, and noticed he was unarmed.

"Good morning, Mr. Dugan," the guard said.

Dugan extended his arms, palms together, expecting to be handcuffed.

Their eyes met and the guard smiled and patted his shoulder.

Dugan smiled back. "Just an old habit, Mr. Ramsey," he mumbled, dropping his hands. Their breath made little puffs in the chilly air. Dugan had never really looked at a prison guard as a person before.

Ramsay walked him beneath the ramparts, unlocked the first of the two iron gates set within the arched portal. They stepped in the small chamber and Mr. Ramsey unlocked the outer gate. As he jingled through his keys and elaborately secured it behind them, Dugan stood in the sunshine, surveying the twenty-two-foot-high gray sandstone wall. They were the stones that had penned him inside for the last three years, and now their freedom-facing sides reflected sunlight as if celebrating. Dugan raised his arms high and placed both hands on the stones. The morning sun had taken the chill off them. He stood there for a moment, eyes closed, and allowed his forehead to touch the wall while a rush of gratitude filled him. His long, barren wait was over.

"We have time to walk to the Brakeman Café and you can wait for the bus there," Ramsey said patiently, gesturing toward the center of town. They walked alongside the wall, which paralleled Deer Lodge's Main Street.

Dugan smelled bacon each time someone opened the café door. His mouth watered and he fingered the bill in his breast pocket. But it would be uncomfortable to enter the place full of locals – they'd know where he'd come from. He was relieved when they spotted the bus, sun glinting off its split windshield. The guard looked at him again, gave him a friendly shove, and said, "get a Jap for me, son." He vanished, leaving Dugan there alone, a free citizen waiting for a bus. The man's courtesy and respect brought tears to his eyes.

Never had the idea of a bus ride thrilled him so. He felt like a child waiting to be carried away to Pleasure Island. The bus wheezed to a stop, the door swung open and he stepped on board. He smiled at the driver and handed him the ticket. Several riders moved aside to open a seat for him. The strangers' friendliness and the heady tonic of freedom overwhelmed him. He chose a seat near the front, bent down to shove his bag under the seat, and wiped his face with his sleeve so no one would notice his tears. The bus pulled out, its engine howling for the next gear.

"I'm Edward, from Billings, and I'm on business," his seat mate said, extending his hand. It was awkward trying to shake his hand while sitting so close, but the gesture pleased Dugan. Dugan stood back up to wriggle out of his new coat. He assumed the man could recognize the clues – a single man boarding in the prison town, wearing new work clothes, an institutional haircut, and his Irish, sun-starved complexion.

"Heading out west?" the man asked.

"To Great Falls, sir," Dugan replied.

"So am I," he said, "to Gore Field. I'm a civilian under contract to the Army. I've been assigned to oversee some electrical work."

"I believe I'll be doing construction at my new job there," Dugan said. He appreciated the man's kindness, but didn't want to give any more information. He didn't know what else to do, so he reached beneath his seat and pulled a sheet of blank paper from his bag.

"Are you a writer?" the man asked.

"Not much of one, I'm afraid. I write . . . to my younger brother." He started fingering his breast pocket for his pencil, but decided not to bring the silly stub out.

"Here. Looks like you need one of these." Edward offered a beautiful fountain pen. "It's an extra."

"Oh, thank you but I . . . I wouldn't take that from you, sir. I thought I had a pencil, but I must've . . ."

"I see. Here, I've got extra pencils, too. An engineer always carries extras." He chuckled.

"Thank you, sir." Dugan admired the new pencil like a precision instrument. "I will use this. Yes I will."

"Thomas Edison used only pencils, even though he was such an innovator. And, really, a fountain pen can leak in high altitudes. A pencil eliminates that risk."

Sensing the conversation was heading in a safer direction, Dugan asked, "why does high altitude make a pen leak, sir?"

"Atmospheric pressure. As you go higher in elevation, the air is less dense, and a sealed container will become internally pressurized; and drat! Your pen oozes permanent ink on your brand new shirt!"

Dugan knew his shirt with its storage-folds could give him away. He was getting overly warm again. He felt more like an escaped convict, rather than a man legitimately released by the Governor of the State of Montana. He'd been given a second chance, but that didn't erase his crime or the past three years he'd moldered inside the prison.

At Garrison Junction the bus stopped to pick up a passenger before turning north toward Helena.

"Care for today's paper?" Edward asked, offering his *Billings Gazette*.

"Sure!" It would delay more conversation. No doubt his seat mate had his hunches. Handling the fresh paper delighted Dugan, its clean pages still smelling of printer's ink.

"Keep it," Edward told him. "Just pass it on when you're done."

"Thank you, sir." Dugan savored it slowly and completely, then carefully rolled it into his bag.

Before entering Helena, the bus stopped at Fort William Henry Harrison. The sign over the entrance reminded Dugan that Mash had been sent to this place. Margaret had written of it. Edward explained that the Army was preparing an elite group of soldiers for parachute and snow operations at this fort. "It's called the First Special Service Force," he said. Funny that a do-nothing kid from Butte would be selected to defend his country on a pair of skis. But Mash was one tough kid, and would do anything to prove it. Maybe he'd finally make something of himself, Dugan decided.

"You and I will be working with the Air Transport Command in Great Falls," Edward said as the bus motored onto Highway 191. "It's the staging area for the new Northwest route to Alaska."

Dugan nodded. He wanted to act like he knew all this, but decided not to bluff. He trusted this man from Billings. He seemed so sincere. Dugan hoped to encourage more talk of the job.

"I see."

"After new airplanes are delivered there, the Seventh Ferrying Group pilots fly them to Fairbanks. From there, the Russians fly them on to their battle front."

"These are the 'lend-lease' planes that I read about in the paper?" Dugan asked, pleased that he could make the reference. "I was only aware of the aircraft going to Britain."

"Yes. This Russian alliance is new. Just added to the original lend-lease operation. And the Women Airforce Service Pilots will be delivering some of the aircraft to Great Falls. So if someone asks if you want to meet a 'wasp,' jump at the chance! They aren't the stinging kind." Edward grinned. "Maybe you'll find a honey!"

Dugan gave him a bashful smile and squirmed in his seat, but was grateful for the information.

He spotted the Anaconda Company's smokestack in Black Eagle well before they reached Great Falls. A five-hundred-foot shrine to soot-faced copper smeltermen, he thought. It reminded him of the huge stack above Anaconda, the pinnacle of the company town skyline. Like a maypole, as long as it spun with paychecks, everyone danced. He thought of Margaret and Patrick. He would start writing to his brother, now that he had something positive to say.

A long bridge carried them over the Missouri River. Dugan watched gossamer wisps rise off the slow waterway. He was on the move too, free of the stagnant backwater of prison. And, like the river, he was the sum of all that had flowed into his past. Pretty soon, he'd be separating from the refuge of the bus and his thoughtful friend. Dugan realized he couldn't just drift downstream in his new freedom. He'd need to steer carefully into the changed current of his new life.

The bus geared down in the mid-day city traffic. It wended around a couple of corners, and stopped in front of the classic-columned Civic Center. Several uniformed men brushed past Dugan with their big duffels and unloaded. The bus turned back west, crossed the Missouri again and dropped into low gear to climb a hill just west of town. From the top of the west bench, Dugan got his first glimpse of Gore Field. After pulling through the entrance gate, the driver shut the bus down. The remaining few riders got out and joined the people clutching luggage and pointing. There were Red Cross men and women and men in coveralls. The chaplain was easy to spot, his collar visible above his overcoat. Evidently, even tough, clean-cut military men needed a dose of God once in a while.

Dugan spotted nurses in their dark blue capes and imagined their snug-fitting white dresses beneath. Other than the old prison matron, they were the first women he'd seen for so long, it was hard to resist staring at them. He queued up with Edward and the others at the

Personnel office, avoiding eye contact with strangers to head off new conversation.

He was assigned a place in a civilian dormitory and told where to get his base pass and identification card. "The twenty-four-hour cafeteria is open for civilians," the clerk told him. "Sometimes their special is T-bone steak or a fried half-chicken. May as well enjoy it. You'd never know the rest of the country is under rations!" Pointing past a large building, he added, "You'll pass right by the post exchange – the 'PX' – on your way."

Edward wished Dugan the best of luck, gave him a friendly wave and walked in a different direction.

Dugan entered the PX and leisurely strolled the narrow aisles between stacks of new clothing, insignia displays, a case of Orpheus wristwatches and electric "Roto-Shavers." He loved the smell of new textiles, but it was nearly overpowered by a recent application of floor wax. He fingered his ten-dollar bill, feeling powerful among this array of military greens, browns and grays. It was a garden of colors to him after the drabs of prison garb. He ran his hands over the new towels as if they were fine angora. He smiled as he tried on a woolen knit hat, remembering Mrs. Duffy. He also bought a writing tablet, jersey work gloves, two towels and a Schick razor. Reluctantly he purchased a bar of prison-smell Palmolive soap. There were no other choices.

His dorm smelled of fresh varnish. A tall clothes cabinet stood between his bed and the next. A large olive drab foot locker rested at the foot of his bed with a hasp for a padlock. It squawked open on virgin hinges. He organized his few things, sat on the bed and stretched out. No more lying at a diagonal like he had on the prison mattress. He stroked the new wool blanket. He took up the new pillow and held it to his face, flooded with recollections of the room and bunk beds he'd shared with his brother and their pillow fights. Dugan knew he was only a hundred miles from the Canadian border. For three years, he'd heard inmates whispering of it – the imaginary line between captivity and freedom. How odd they'd release him to a place with no high fences strung with barbed wire; and a civilian's ID card in his pocket.

But holding the pillow with its fresh linen smell, any idea of escape faded. He never thought of running again.

CHAPTER 14

The Only Weapon

At first, Dugan was given a nailing apron but few tools. He was paired with an experienced laborer who gave instructions on the jobs he was expected to do. There would be framing, roofing, siding, painting; and windows and doors to install on the new buildings. The work was strange to him, but once he saw how it was done, it made sense.

Dugan thought of all the things he wanted to write to Patrick. Barely two years old when Patrick was born, he'd pronounced his baby brother's name "Patswee." The younger child became "Patsy." When Dugan began his first letter to him, the nickname seemed childish.

> ~~Patsy,~~ Patrick,
> It feels good to work again and get away from the stink of MSP and I don't mean only the smell.
> We eat in a mess hall, and sleep and relax in a dorm for civilians. I don't have to duck under the door anymore, but it's a hard habit to break. It probably looks funny to everyone else.
> I actually report for work, and by 8 aclock, I am ready to.
> Some people must know my record but nobody asked me.
> Sometimes I feel pretty useless in this big war. I know that even women are building airplanes and making ammo. I hear they fly airplanes from the factory. And here on base, planes with machine guns and bombs are showing up but my only weapon is a caulking gun.

Dugan was lonely, but he didn't venture getting friendly with the people around him. He was courteous, keeping conversation to the tasks at hand. It helped that everyone was intent on the project. His past seemed to be of little importance up here.

"That Dugan feller's a hard worker, no doubt about it," he overheard his supervisor saying. "He don't waste no time jawin', just does what's he's told."

It's beautiful here. The Rockie Mountins are all around and I'm outdoors a lot, so I see them in all shades of sunlight. I can see colors I had forgotten. Almost too powerful to take in so I close my eyes sometimes. The picture is still there, even though my eyes are closed.
Your brother Dugan

"They built this air base here cuz the weatherman promised three hunnerd days o' clear flying weather," a laborer said to him as they sat cross-legged against a wall and began eating from their box lunches. "But they didn't say nuthin' about the three hunnerd and sixty-five days o' wind." He cursed as his sandwich blew from his lap and cartwheeled downwind, becoming bits of flotsam whirling away. Dugan offered half of his.

The wind bullied its way between buildings, like it was angry at the interruption of its urgent path across the prairie. Gusts tested the fitness of windowpanes. Everyone else complained as cans, dropped rags and tumbleweed rattled and bounced across the tarmac. Dugan found it lively. At night it soughed through the compound. It reminded him he was free of four tall sandstone walls. Rain sometimes pattered the new shingles just a few feet over his head, a sound he'd forgotten in his ground-floor cell that sulked beneath an identical tier of cells. Now he, too, owned the sky, its stars, its clouds and all its moods.

"You need wind for the wings to fly," the man told him, interrupting his thoughts. "But it helps if it's blowin' more or less down one o' the runways. That's why they built four of 'em. I guess they figured eight headings oughtta be enough for *ferry* pilots." He thanked Dugan for the sandwich. After a pause, he added, "I saw the wind lift a B-17 right off the ground, and that ain't no joke."

Each day at Gore tapped Dugan's mind in useful ways. Roosevelt's east coast voice bugled encouragement over their radios.

"The defense of the Union of Soviet Socialist Republics is vital to the defense of the United States," he declared. Dugan knew the president was speaking of Gore and their work launching ALSIB. They were building up the place where his "Arsenal of Democracy" would be delivered. Dugan was at the front door of ALSIB, feeding Russia's insatiable back door, safe from U-boats and air attacks. It brought out a spirit of cooperation – this time fueled by patriotic pride instead of desperation to escape.

Galleys of news and rousing display advertisements whipped up American patriotism. President Roosevelt implored people to conserve rubber and gasoline, driving slower and only when necessary. The public was asked to limit train travel so the seats could be devoted to military men on orders to report for duty. Nestle chocolate was "fighting food." Floor wax and furniture polish ads nagged housewives to do their duty to preserve their furnishings and appliances. Crates of shiny propellers and cosmolined engines poured urgently from factories that had been building refrigerators.

Dugan saw Edward once in a while, and they talked about the news and what they'd each been working on. Edward was the one who told him that their incoming mail was being censored. "Typical military protocol," he'd said, brushing it off. "They're looking for Nazi infiltrators."

CHAPTER 15

A Pleasing Roar at Gore Field

Summer days were long on light for framing, tar-papering, roofing, siding, painting and caulking. Dugan's supervisors left him alone to work. A Post Engineer would stroll by from time to time with plans tucked under his arm. Rolling them out in a crackling scuffle with the wind, the engineer would nod approvingly at Dugan's work, roll the plans back up and walk away.

One day Edward told him his work was complete and that he would be returning to Billings. Dugan was very sorry to see him and his pencils and fountain pens leave.

> Patrick,
>
> There won't never be a war bond poster with a man holding a putty knife, but I like my job. They show me what to do, and leave me to it. Someone comes by to check only once in a while. It feels good to be trusted with tools like saws and hammers. They tease me when they see me shine them.
>
> It's like a race against an invisible enemy around here. There is a hurry-up to everything we do. Airplanes show up, and there is only one hangar so they get worked on outdoors. I hope the meckanics are more careful than we are out here with tools – slap dashing the framing up and slapping roofing on, and pounding it down as fast as we can get our other hand

out of the way. God forbid when it gets cold and one of these potbelly stove chimneys catches fire. The whole row of shacks could go up in minutes.

———•———

Bell P-39 Airacobras from New York arrived almost every day, as well as Douglas A-20 Havoc attack bombers and C-47 Skytrains from California; a few AT-6 Texans, and North American B-25 Mitchells from Kansas City.

Dugan loved the profile of the C-47s. Resting on their haunches, they nosed longingly into the sky. They became graceful birds after tucking their wheels on climb-out. The tricycle-gear Havoc parked level, its large nose gear gangling from its narrow fuselage. Straight on though, it was a war machine, its plexiglass nose bristled with machine-gun barrels. A pilot and bombardier could indeed wreak havoc. The sporty Airacobras had an impatient look, like they hankered to get into the air and strafe something. Dugan loved that he was surrounded with gutsy machines of war. It amazed him how their wings could lift them so high and fast. He never missed watching a takeoff.

He was also alert for a glimpse of the WASPs Edward had told him about. He imagined shapely women with pretty painted lips who'd remove their flying helmets, letting their unpinned hair toss in the wind. Their khaki flight suits and parachutes wouldn't conceal their femininity. The pilots seemed aloof, and the women's quarters were separate. They did not spend much time before they got flown out of Gore for their next ferry flight, but he kept hoping to meet one – a tall, slender one.

———•———

Dugan was hanging a door on an outbuilding, struggling to keep from pinching his finger again, when he heard a twin-engined Havoc start up. Four more started their engines, adding to the robust roar, and he set his tools down to watch. They lined up, their twin-row Wright R-2600s at high RPM for their takeoff roll. They lifted off and headed north out of Great Falls for their one-way trip to Russia. The sight took his breath away. He watched until they faded to specks in the August sky, scattered with brilliant towering cumulus.

Dugan had no way of knowing that these were the first of nearly eight thousand aircraft that would depart Great Falls for Russia over ALSIB – so many that if lined up wingtip to wingtip, they would stretch seventy-three miles.

Not all of them would make it.

You're on top of the world here at Gore. Not like the choking air of Butte, where you feel like you are closer to the bottom. I can see almost to Canada. When I breathe in the clean air of these high plains I feel rich. The fellows belly-ache about stuff – – their superiors, the long hours, the wind, not enuff women but I have not felt this happy since I don't know when. I agree about not enuff women.

Bad news, tho. A squadron of attack bombers took off out of here and we herd later that weather got bad and when they turned around to come back, one hit the hills and crashed and burnt up.

Your brother Dugan

"I was given a target of four hundred and forty-five aircraft to deliver by now," Dugan heard a major tell a captain. "But we've only managed to get thirty P-40s and two dozen A-20s outta here so far. The bottleneck we need to solve is aircraft preparation. We need more personnel on it!"

"Yes sir," the captain replied. "I will scour the place for anybody who can spin a wrench, sir."

"It would help if they know a tech manual is good for more than a doorstop."

"Yes sir."

The tamaracks turned, stippling the slopes with gold. The snow line lowered on the mountainsides, and men talked of hunting. Fall brought even more frenzy to the place. It was freezing at night and Dugan had to feed coal or wood to the stoves in the barracks, administration buildings, shops and hangar. The burst of construction had slowed down, and he was sent to work under Mel's supervision. Affable Mel, the bill of his cap bent up in a permanent salute over his large forehead, had a chronic gray grease smudge on his chin. He showed Dugan how to load cargo, using the Load Adjuster, a slide-rule-like device to calculate safe load limits.

> *Patrick,*
>
> *Now they got me working some on the planes. I am learning meckanics. Mel my work partner sent me to the tool master to get a left-handed screwdriver. Well, that made him laff until I got the joke. Next he asked for a Whitworth cressent wrench. I fell for that one, too. But when he told me to run and fetch six feet of fillopian tubing, I stopped and thought it out, and saved being laffed at. If you don't know what that means, I will explain someday. Don't ask our sister. It will imbarrass her.*
>
> *I got him good tho. I bought a wooden snake at the dime store and set it where he'd see it up close when he took out a radio panel. The next I know, he's clear across the hangar yelling for us to kill the son of a bich.*
>
> *When we're done with them, our planes fly all the way to the western edge of Alaska. Russians fly them all the way to a place I can't spell where they get into the war against the Germans.*

Dugan relished the work that placed him inside the airplanes. The Russia-bound aircraft smelled like brand new rubber and paint mixed with a hint of high-octane aviation gas and cosmoline. Some were fully armed. Seeing the bombs and machine guns made Dugan proud. The well-used cargo and crew transport planes smelled like spent oil and burnt-macaroni electrical wiring mixed with av gas. His footsteps echoed within their fuselages, until they were stuffed with cargo. When no one was around, he'd slide into the cockpit for a look at the sleeping gauges. The seats sagged where bottoms had pressed parachutes for hours on end, and the control wheels were unblacked where pilots' hands had worried them through turbulence or darkness split by lightning. In the close space, a hint of anxiety mixed with all the other smells.

Dugan was curious what was in the sealed shipments. There were crates of mortars, ammunition, truck and auto parts, tools, military uniform material, skis and medical supplies. Sometimes there was time to pry the tops open and admire the new weapons a moment before tapping the crates closed with his claw hammer. He and Mel got a shock when the top accidentally popped off a crate of thousands of pairs of false teeth.

It seemed a lot of stuff was getting shipped that had nothing to do with fighting a war. An undercurrent of traffic had begun, and the Russians jealously shepherded it along the route. The duty-free pipeline was beginning to bulge but Dugan knew better than to stick his nose into that business. He'd learned discretion in prison where some of the guards were in on contraband trafficking. If you were stupid enough to make a careless comment, the next day someone would have replaced your lightbulb with one filled with kerosene, a Molotov cocktail that blew up when it switched on. Dugan understood that silent cooperation was wisest on the Outside, too.

There were boxes of fancy women's clothing and packages of lingerie. He saw cardboard folders of new silk stockings. That puzzled him, because he'd seen newspaper ads asking American women to turn in their silk stockings so the military could make them into gun powder bags. Since they couldn't buy them anymore, he'd heard that women were painting thin black lines up the backs of their legs to fake the seams.

There were boxes of cosmetics and cans of foods Dugan had never heard of.

"This sure ain't Spam," Mel exclaimed, rubbing his chin. "Look at the picture on these cans!" They'd peeked into a crate of smoked oysters.

"I'd have to be starving before I'd eat something that ugly," Dugan said as he heaved the crate into the belly of the plane.

Mel levered his hammer over a crate marked "Medicines." The lid skitched off and his eyes opened wide like it was full of girlie magazines. "I thought the Ruskies had plenty of vodka, but take a look at *this*!" It was packed with bottles of Kentucky bourbon.

"If they lose the war, at least they'll be able to medicate their sorrows away," Dugan said, laughing.

Mel pulled a bottle out and squeezed a bottle of carbolic acid in its place.

Dugan acted like he didn't notice.

Once they were rushing to load a flight for an impatient pilot who'd been delayed by weather. As Dugan hurriedly handed a box off to Mel, they dropped it, and the pungency of strong perfume saturated the air. They couldn't get rid of the smell, and for days the other men teased and called them the "foo-foo twosome."

There were cases of technical data. Things like maintenance schedules, wiring schematics and drawings of American equipment they were using in battle seemed legitimate, but some of the material began to arouse suspicion from Dugan's higher-ups. An American major came striding into the hangar where Dugan and Mel were sliding cartons around preparing to load another C-47 bound for Russia.

"Why do they need the plans for a tire factory?" the major asked no one in particular as he pried open a carton. He rifled through large sheets with heavy blue marking on them. Mel and Dugan stepped closer to the crate. They could smell fresh Ozalid photostat chemicals. "And what is all this stuff about the chemical make up of synthetic rubber? Can't they figure that out on their own? And how about all these maps of our railroads?"

A Russian officer suddenly came around a corner and fixed a patronizing smile on him. "Your very own Mr. Roosevelt is sending this to us with his compliments," he said. "If you have any doubt, telephone Mr. Hopkins." He stood imperiously as the major gestured to Mel to seal up the crate. As the major turned on his heel and strode back out, he declared, "this base is about as secure as Coney Island!"

Just like the cold overtaking the fading warmth of autumn, Dugan felt the distrust creeping into the storerooms and hangars. Russian officers hovered closely as the men readied the aircraft for their flights to Fairbanks.

Time was always short. The pressure lit the fuse on tempers, especially for the mechanics when stuffy Russian officers paced back and forth in their shop areas.

"They get their orders from Colonel Mitrov," Mel said quietly as one of them strutted nearby.

"Mitrov?" Dugan asked.

"Can't miss him. His boots squeak and he wears enough cologne that if he lights up a smoke, he could go up in flames." The men snickered.

"They're supposed to authorize the final winterizing and sign off each plane before it heads to Fairbanks," Mel explained, "but with their awful English, they just point out stuff they claim are defects, and we gotta remove the cowling, and re-adjust whatever they think is wrong," he added, with a sideways glance at the Russian.

"These pompous bastards make me nervous," another mechanic groused, pulling his arms from deep inside an engine. "What do they know about the valve adjustment on a Wright twenty-six hundred?"

Hearing his tone, the Russian stepped behind him and peered over the mechanic's shoulder silently with his hands clasped professorially behind his back. The mechanic ignored him. "Every time I have to re-do something, I risk messing it up." He sounded angry enough to heave a wrench through a window, but instead threw his grease rag down, making a pathetic *fwip* sound.

"I'd be careful about what I say," Mel warned the man.

"Why? These gorillas don't know what I'm saying."

"Don't be so sure. Elaine in the steno pool – you know, the brunette bombshell with the cute ass – she told me one of 'em was gettin' too friendly with her, pawin' at her, acting like he didn't understand that she was telling him to take a hike. She heard him later, speaking perfectly good English to Major Crane."

Dugan and Mel obediently loaded the Russia-bound planes. There was a lot of "diplomatic mail" and fake leather briefcases with "Executive Immunity" stenciled on them. No one ever checked their contents. "Upper brass is sure free-spending with their favors to the Reds," Mel said one day. "I guess the patriotic thing to do is keep 'em happy so they keep killin' Germans. If your enemy is my enemy, that must make us friends." That was the unofficial slogan around the place.

"Have you noticed that they've started securing their luggage in locked rooms around here?" Mel asked Dugan one day. "Shipping labels have gone missing; they could be placing legitimate labels on contraband. Once it's sealed, no one would suspect it." As intriguing as it sounded, Dugan ignored this, too. He'd learned a long time ago not to go looking for trouble. It always seemed to find him.

Suspicion made its way up the brass ladder. As the attitude of the Russians became ever more chary, messages hissed up and down Gore's chain of command. The intelligence department created the code-cracking Venona operation expecting to discover Nazi radio signals. What they heard instead were signals to and from the Soviet Embassy in Washington, D.C. to the NKVD, the forerunner of the KGB.

"You catchin' what I'm catchin'?" Mel asked Dugan. He rubbed his chin, depositing the day's smudge. They were safely out of earshot of any officers. "Uncle Sam's finally gettin' curious about some of this stuff gettin' free rides straight to Uncle Joe's desk."

"We better just do our jobs, and not talk to anyone we don't really know," Dugan said.

While the men speculated, the Russians got chillier. A policy statement went up in each work area:

The United States should continue to furnish lend-lease supplies to Russia to the full extent of our capacity, provided – and provided only – that Russia cooperates with us and takes us into her confidence.

But the suspicious shipments continued.

PART II

CHAPTER 16

Lieutenant Stanhope's Orders

When Daniel finished advanced flight training and officers' school in October of 1942, he excitedly dialed Beverly to tell her that he now wore the Lieutenant "butter bars" and soon he'd be flying fighters. And he'd been nick-named "Hopie." They lingered on the phone until his coins ran out. He bummed more coins and called his mother to tell her, hoping she'd be proud. But he could tell she did not share his joy like Beverly did. He had to let his mother haul that cross on her own, he decided. He promised to write, hoping his letters would reassure her.

Laura had pinned a calendar on her kitchen wall. She'd thrown away the one the American Legion sent her, with patriotic pictures. With enormous guilt, she'd ignored their request to send a donation and instead spent her dollar at the five-and-dime on a calendar with inspirational verses on each page. It had out-of-focus pictures of Jesus, lilies and lambs. Each day that went by with no bad news, she marked with an "X" in green Crayola. She knew Beverly always glanced at it each time she stopped by. Laura didn't tell her that she kept a red and a black crayon in a drawer in case she received another Army telegram or visit.

Daniel ripped open the official envelope with his orders, only to learn he'd been assigned ferry duty. "Damn the Army!" he burst out loud. *"Ferry duty?"* They must not think I'm a very good pilot, he thought.

"Ferry duties have become a top priority," the letter stated. The military was still squeamish about publicity, so Daniel had no way to know how many thousands of fighters and attack bombers Harry Hopkins had promised Joe Stalin, leaving it up to others to make good on the deliveries. Hundreds of rookie pilots like Daniel were getting the same letter. He was assigned to Gore Field at Great Falls, Montana, a place he'd never heard of.

———————

Peering out the C-47's small passenger window for his first glimpse of Gore, he was shattered. What could ferry duty way out here have to do with the big conflicts making headlines? He thought of Beverly. What would he write her? How could he make her proud of *this* assignment?

As the plane descended for its approach, Daniel spotted two crashed P-39s lying, contorted, a few miles from the airport. A third one, covered with oil, burned just off the end of the runway. Men were clustered around it, trying to squelch the flames. Some of the dry grass beneath the wreck had caught fire and a body lay flat on the ground near the plane.

His transport landed and taxied to a stop. Daniel and the other new pilots hefted their duffels and hopped out, shielding their eyes from the low autumn sunlight. A new flag snapped from a pole in front of a white clapboard building. Ground crews scurried around some parked airplanes. Guys were painting huge bright red stars on the American-made planes. The stars stood out in stark contrast to their drab green sides. The foreign insignia puzzled him. A captain ushered them across the new pavement toward a small building. The husk of a burst baseball skipped across in front of them, headed for a pile of tumbleweed lodged against a building.

They entered the briefing room, stirring dust motes in the light slanting in. Once his eyes adjusted, Hopie saw a large map on the front wall that had been tiled together from smaller maps. The men milled nervously in the warm room, their travel-weary bodies filling it with the smell of yesterday's uniforms. Daniel noticed warning posters along the side wall. Silhouettes of German and Japanese aircraft appeared side by side with Allied models that looked similar. The headlines read, "Which one would you shoot?" He felt a surge of envy for the fighter pilots.

A colonel with a neatly trimmed mustache entered and pivoted to the front of the room. He saluted, then eyed each of them as they stood at attention, his hands on the hips of his impeccably creased trousers.

"As you were," he said. "I'm Colonel Horner. Welcome to Gore Field.

"I know, you-all think you're in a backwater, being called for ferry duty stateside when you thought you'd be sent into combat right after A-T. Well, we won't let you-all get bored. You haven't heard much about this operation yet because we aren't sure how the public would appreciate that we're in bed with the Russians. It's complicated, but you-all can understand that your skills are *needed* and needed *now*."

His voice was honey-buttered southern – Georgia or maybe the Carolinas – but honed by years of speaking military jargon.

"Our job is to get thousands of new *airoplanes* to Fairbanks, a flight of two thousand miles over some pretty rugged terrain. There are *no* nav aids, *no* decent forecasts, *no* paved roads, *no* railroad tracks and *very few* nice, wide airports in case you get lost or have engine trouble.

"You-all thought you could always depend on your magnetic compass. Maybe so, here in the lower forty-eight, but up there, solar winds and magnetic disturbances in the ground will confuse it. Study your charts. *Memorize* them. Topographical knowledge is as critical as knowing how to fly. There isn't even a *search* detachment with enough personnel or equipment to come after you if you go down. I've had to send a *dog team* to pick up downed pilots. Don't let anyone rag you out of taking decent survival gear. Put your matches in something waterproof. If you need matches, you're going to be glad they're *dry*. Split them up and stash them in different places, *on your person*, just in case."

Taking a small mirror from his breast pocket, he flashed reflections of the overhead light bulbs onto the men's faces and continued speaking. "This ten-cent signal *mirrah* could keep you from becoming a *land*-mark. Always have one in an accessible place on *ev-er-y* flight. It's a good idea to carry a pair of snow goggles so you won't go snow-blind if you end up *out*side your aircraft for a time.

"You'll sleep in tents, eat field rations, and freeze your asses in pit latrines. You might freeze to death in your own sweat. You'll dump your bird at Fairbanks, and turn right around and fly back here in an unheated C-47, and do it all over again until you drop from exhaustion. So, you see why we tapped you-all. Each man here was selected for his demonstrated a*bil*ity." The room was silent except for the droning wind.

"You-all are as green as halter-broke mustang colts, so here are your P-39 manuals." He gathered the books into his arms and began passing them deliberately, pausing a moment to look each pilot in the eye. The colonel's eyes were gun-metal blue beneath authoritative brows. Daniel saw no trace of emotion on his pencil-mustached face.

"I advise that you read this here little book day and night, and *dream* about flying these things, so at least you get some make-believe flight time. You cain't log it, but it may be the only experience you-all get before strapping into one and taking off for real. Any questions? Good. Now report to Major Ross for your specific orders. Dismissed!"

Before he turned sharply away, his eyes showed a fleeting look of pity for the condemned.

The men silently filed out.

"That guy sure knows how to serve up a shit sandwich," one mumbled.

"How so?" Daniel asked.

"Didja notice how he started with a compliment to butter us up, then laid on the talk about bad conditions and no rescue, then ended with our 'demonstrated ability?' That's a shit sandwich."

Daniel looked inside his manual to begin studying the twelve-hundred horsepower Bell P-39 Airacobra, a single-seat tricycle-gear fighter. He had no time to sulk because his orders were to fly in the morning. At first light, he'd be taking off in a plane he'd never even sat in, for the two-thousand-mile flight to Fairbanks over empty territory with sketchy paper maps. Sparse markings showed peaks and rivers. Some had native place names and others, like Devil's Gorge, Deadman's Slough and Hell's Gate sounded like cleaned-up curses of trappers and miners.

For this first flight, he would be placed in a group of three other Airacobras, including a lead pilot who'd flown the route several times.

He found his barracks, threw his gear on his bunk and headed to the mess hall, hoping a meal would settle his nerves. He filled a tray and sat so he could watch the activity through the divided window-panes. In the last light of the evening plenty was going on. Towed planes were nosing back and forth, and men wielding fuel hoses rose on ladders, pumped gas into planes and descended beneath his line of sight.

"There were no P-39s on the field where I trained," a voice said, bringing Hopie's attention back inside. The pilot sat across from Daniel, his brown eyes intense. "When I got here, they just gave me a tech manual, and let me sit in the cockpit and read it over. Not even a blindfold test. I was told I could practice on the way to Fairbanks. No one in my group waited around, so I had to fire it up and just take off – kinda reminded me of my first solo, only that was in a forty-horsepower Cub with a cruise speed of seventy-five miles an hour!" He spoke right into you, Daniel thought.

"I guess it's pure on-the-job training," he said.

"I'm Caspari. Tony Caspari."

"Daniel Stanhope." They shook hands. "But you can call me Hopie." It was the first time he'd introduced himself like that, and he felt self-conscious. He paused a moment, then recalled the deadly evidence he'd already seen of this seat-of-the-pants-training. "What's the deal with the wrecks around here? I saw three P-39s rolled up in a ball out there, and one looked pretty bad."

"That one crashed off the end of the runway this afternoon. A fatality, I heard. It was coming in from Bell's factory in Niagara." He paused. Looking down at his clasped hands, he added, "it was a WASP. I don't know why that should make any difference, but . . ." His voice trailed off and both men sat silently for a moment.

"The other two happened yesterday after take-off. They may have taken too much time idling on the ground. The Allisons are finicky about engine temperature. They overheat easily. Once in a while, the engine quits."

Horner hadn't mentioned that little fact. Hopie silently vowed to burn it into his memory.

"My training was in an AT-6," he told his new acquaintance. "I can count on one hand the number of hours I have in anything even resembling the P-39."

Caspari had made several flights already, so Hopie asked him more questions about the Airacobra and the route, recalling some of Colonel Horner's disquieting comments. Others joined them, eager to share their knowledge.

"The 'thirty-nahn is jes fahn till they bolt that goddamn belly taynk on. That thang dirties it up sumpin awful," one drawled as he slid in across the table next to Caspari.

"It raises your stall speed, so you really gotta watch your approach speeds," another chimed in.

"It's got the most vicious spee-in of any airplane ah've ever flown," the Texan added. "It's sweet on the controls, but with no warnin', will turn on ya and bite. Ya gotta hayndle it careful but without fear – just like you'd hayndle a desert rattler!" Hopie stopped chewing and stared at the man.

"A fighter pilot told me that in training, they tested that whopper thirty-seven millimeter nose cannon," one said, holding a fist out and dropping his thumb. "It really packs a punch. Fires two rounds a second. He says you can feel each one. Wicked recoil."

"Well, we'd get busted playing with the armaments," Caspari warned, tapping the Seventh Ferrying Group patch on his jacket.

"Can't we do a little hunting on the way up there, you know, provide cover for the highway crew? Take out a few bears for them! Who'd notice a few rounds missing?"

Caspari waved him off with a smile. "Bears are hibernating anyway."

Another pilot jumped in. "I was feeling pretty cocky, having just finished advanced training. I took off with full tanks in a 'cobra, and tried an Immelmann without getting up very high."

"Bad idea," someone broke in.

Nodding agreement, the speaker continued, extending his hand, rotating it palm-up. "So now I'm totally inverted, right? Ready to roll back to level, right? But she stalls and goes into an inverted spin." He flipped his hand in a half-twist. The others craned forward.

"At least I had the presence of mind to push her nose down to stop the spin. When I recovered, I was prob'ly only a hunnerd feet off the ground."

"Shoulda started higher."

"And not in a fully loaded bird."

"Ya coulda bought the farm."

Hopie appreciated the guy's story. Usually pilots clammed up when they messed up. The chatter paused, and he rose and excused himself to begin studying his new manual.

He didn't rest well his first night at Gore. He drifted in a raft of anxiety and every new sound disturbed his shallow sleep. He woke in the predawn dark, snapped on his light and thumbed through the manual to the section on stalls again. He memorized the speeds and configurations. He dressed in his flying clothes and returned to the mess hall, hoping Caspari would show up and help sort the truth from the ballyhoo.

He didn't recognize any of the men shuffling in and around the food and coffee counters. He ladled hot cereal into a bowl and slid it along the counter, but none of the pans of steaming foods aroused his appetite. He took a couple of plump sausages and sat alone. Stars disappeared where the sky faded into turquoise in the east windows.

"Wanted to beat the morning rush, Hopie?" Caspari's cheery greeting came from behind him as he speared his last bite of sausage. Caspari sat beside Hopie and peppered a large heap of scrambled eggs.

Hopie waited a moment for the two men sitting nearby to rise and leave the table with their empty trays. He brought up the Airacobra again.

"I have no tricycle gear time," he began, trying not to sound edgy.

"Don't sweat it,' Caspari said with a dismissive wave of his table knife. "There's really no difference in technique between the tail wheel and the nose gear. You'll like that the tail is already up. You can see where you're going when you're taxiing, so there's no need to 'ess' back and forth." It was as if his voice was propelled by a sudden insight. "You're in my squad this morning," he added with a big smile.

Hopie helped himself to a second cup of coffee he didn't want, waiting for Caspari to finish his eggs and hash browns. They walked together outside in the blushing pink morning light. Two other pilots, McCann and Hays, gathered for their flight leader's briefing. To stay on course, they were to keep Caspari in sight, since his was the only aircraft with a navigation radio.

Caspari explained that their first stop would be the mandatory landing in Edmonton. "Gives us a chance to refuel and check our aircraft and gear to see if anything's amiss – that is, needs adjustment – before the wilderness section of the route. Keep me on your right wings. We need to be able to see each other." He demonstrated a few hand signals including the gesture for a forced landing. "Not that you're gonna need it," Caspari said confidently to Hopie.

Looking at the sky, Caspari said it looked like good visual flying weather, and they'd get a new forecast in Edmonton.

"Seems the weather forecasts are just a toss o' the dice," Hays commented.

"Yeah, but at least we know if it's snake-eyes," McCann replied as they started toward their planes.

Caspari paused alongside Hopie's plane to answer any more questions the new pilot may have thought of. Hopie walked around his aircraft conducting his pre-flight inspection. He stroked the cold aluminum gently, as if he were getting acquainted with a skittery horse. Under his breath he said, "okay sweetheart, you know the rules better than I do. Get me to Fairbanks safely, you understand?" He came around the tail to the right side and groped for something to hold while stepping up on the wing. He opened the Airacobra's distinctive car-like door and gracelessly dropped into the cocoon-tight cockpit. After rearranging his bulky parachute seat pack several times, he reached for his shoulder harness and buckled it.

"She'll fly at ninety, and she'll land at about ninety, too," Caspari reminded him, pressing the door closed and gesturing at Hopie to latch it. He stepped off the wing and with a twirl of his index finger, signaled the pilot to start his engine. With a big grin and a thumbs-up, he headed to his own plane.

Now it was up to Hopie – his head swirling with facts and vital numbers – to get the bird to their first stop at Edmonton.

CHAPTER 17

Flight

In the sky, a pilot and small crew enter into single combat
with a rush of approaching danger.
– EVERETT LONG AND IVAN NEGANBLYA,
COBRAS OVER THE TUNDRA, TRANSLATED
FROM ORIGINAL RUSSIAN TEXT

Hopie was eager to start the engine and get busy with the demands of flying. He hoped it would kill the butterflies in his stomach. He folded the first of his navigation charts to display their first leg. As he opened the throttle on the big Allison, he nervously watched the temperature gauge, keeping a steady eye on it throughout his climb-out.

"Ferry flight departing Gore, this is Ferry six-two-zero. Turn to a heading of three-one-zero," Caspari radioed, having calculated the right heading to correct for the westerly wind.

Like all flights in the single-engine fighters, this was supposed to be in daylight with visual contact with the ground. Hopie recalled the colonel's order to memorize the terrain, so he began immediately. Landmarks would be reassuring backup to Caspari's radio navigation.

Climbing to ten thousand feet tamed the imposing heights as they flew along the Rocky Mountain Front. The California browns and farm-row greens of his past turned to Montana's wheat-soft golds and faded-denim blues, jibed with slopes of primal white. It was a landscape that made him feel small.

Hopie pulled his thoughts back inside the cockpit. He relaxed his grip on the control yoke letting color back into his knuckles. He unfolded and repositioned his chart as the land slid past below. He watched out the window for the few landmarks noted on the charts. The air was smooth so he acquainted himself better with the aircraft. Closing his eyes, he named each instrument, then reached out blind and touched it, opening his eyes to see if he was right. Navigating was easy. They stayed over the plains, keeping the mountains on their left. Hopie checked his compass heading and scanned out the window for the other three aircraft in his flying group.

He spotted Edmonton laid out in the middle of the prairie. Its approaches were wide open for miles. He liked the looks of the place. The airport was paved and close to town. He'd had the notion that the elevation had risen, but he was now thirteen hundred feet lower than when he departed Great Falls.

He taxied in behind the others and shut down. Caspari helped each pilot with a careful walk-around while the aircraft were fueled. He got a weather forecast and shouted to them to mount back up so they could use what daylight and passable weather remained to get as far as possible. Stratus clouds had appeared to the west, and Caspari feared a weather front.

Northwest of the airport, city structures turned to a neatly squared patchwork of farm fields narrowing to the horizon. Shelter belts shielded houses and outbuildings, telling of the prevailing surface winds. The flat farmlands spread out in a tranquil landscape, far from where the chaotic edges of the continent sparked with impatience. It seemed a land immune from the drama of war. Caspari's voice came through his headset. "Inside those Canadian homes, women are knitting caps and mittens for their troops while they listen to war news on the wireless." How quaint, Hopie thought.

Caspari followed the radio ranges to their next checkpoint at Grande Prairie and they overflew it, right on course. They landed at Fort St.

John for fuel again. They took off and flew over Beaton River, Fort Nelson and Smith River, not much more than villages with big runways carved from the forest. Sometimes Hopie heard no reply to Caspari's position reports, but it was reassuring when a weak voice could be heard through the static. At least someone knew their whereabouts and time crossing that station.

The weather held so they flew on. Canadian homesteads dotted fields cleared from forests. A school, a sawmill and church among several small homes made a town. The leg between Fort Nelson and Watson Lake was more challenging, as Hopie tried to match his mapped landmarks with what he spotted on the ground. Some of the lakes seemed to be in the wrong place. He had a hard time telling which way the drainages ran. He constantly watched for Caspari and the others. Even with decent visibility, it was impossible to pinpoint his location. There were none of the familiar landmarks from his training flights. No paved roads, railroad tracks or power lines pointed the way. No neat towns with streets that ran north-south and east-west. There were just vast spreads of trees with a random mountain rising above the tree line, exposing ancient rock. Even the sun seemed to be hanging in the wrong place in the sky.

They landed for a layover at Watson Lake rather than risk the weather since it would be dark before they made Fairbanks. It was outfitted better than stations like Fort Nelson and Fort St. John where you got your water from a stream.

Caspari told them to relax, and he'd arrange for fuel-ups and morning pre-heats. Hopie heard the diesel generator throbbing from inside a shed as he followed the others into the building spread beneath the log control tower. They tossed their bags down and stood around a little stove in the weather station area. A mechanic came in, rubbing his hands together and backed up to the stove.

"Hey! It's Mac!" he exclaimed. "Haven't seen you for awhile. Not since you got lost and landed in that farmer's field to get directions." He gave the red-headed pilot a friendly shove.

"Hell, I wasn't lost," McCann defended, "I thought I'd just drop in to impress the farmer's daughter."

"We knew what happened. How else could you explain the cow shit on your 'cobra's underside?"

The men laughed.

"I guess to a flatlander from Kansas," the mechanic added, "these mountains all look the same."

Hopie didn't admit that they all looked pretty similar to him, as well. He decided to re-read the navigation section of the airman's information manual, his adopted bible since receiving it at the start of his flight training. He was never without it. With the airman's bible in hand, he felt he would have less need for the holier one. Of course he had his Dalton "Whiz Wheel" navigation computer. It worked fine in theory. But when the wind changed on you, it just dumbly kept its heading while your airplane was carried downwind. You wouldn't know unless you spotted some landmark before getting too far off course.

Caspari entered as Hays was saying, "yeah, but there's that dog-leg, and a ninety-mile radio blank where there's no range signal."

Hopie asked where the showers were.

"Showers?" The mechanic laughed. "Only cold water up here. A couple of meatballs thought they could rig up a water heater. They wrapped raw wire around a chunk of ceramic sewer tile and dropped it in a drum of water. They darn near electrocuted each other!"

Nervous chuckles tittered from the others.

"Let's get some grub," Caspari said. "Don't expect gourmet, but we'll eat better than before the Alaska Highway came through. Everything used to fly in by a Norseman C-64 on skis. Even potatoes were a luxury since they cost ten times what they did in the states!"

The men joined a few others in the cookhouse.

"Ever have Yukon shrimp?" one of them asked Hopie, forking several finger sausages onto his tray. "Fresh outta the can!" They all laughed. "Here we have homesick potatoes and plenty of saltines."

Hopie filled a bowl with chili and took a scoop of the pasty white matter, noticing there was no butter or oleo. He found the salt and pepper, and used it liberally.

"I see you've discovered the imported exotic seasonings they treat us to up here," Caspari said. "How about some Army strawberries for dessert?" They placed dried prunes between more saltines and drank vile coffee that had simmered in the big aluminum percolator all afternoon.

"If you're hungry enough and wash it down with plenty of this blackstrap they call coffee, you can imagine it's a slice of Mom's mince pie."

"My mom is a better cook than that," another remarked.

"How 'bout yer wife?"

"Well, not so good with pies, but give her a chub of bologna and she turns into Betty Crocker. Ever have bologna gravy? It's pink!" They all laughed.

"Hopie, how ya gettin' along with the peashooter and that try-sickle landing gear?" Hays asked.

"So far, so good," he replied. "I don't see a difference in landing. You just hold the yoke back and let it decide when to put its nose wheel down," he said. "I wonder about crosswinds."

"Easy as pie," Caspari replied. "You'll just want to keep the upwind wing down, and keep it going straight, just like your AT-6. Nice thing is, the engine's already behind you so it won't tend to swap ends, like the taildraggers."

"I see. What I am not getting along with is my flight-school issue clothing. I'm going to find an Eskimo and get some advice on what to wear in this country, even if I have to use sign-language."

Caspari disappeared and joined him a few minutes later. "Here are some mittens and a cap."

"Say, thanks!" Hopie said, "I should get my own at the PX here."

"Well, the PX here at Watson is just a few boxes of chewing gum and playing cards all piled in a corner. Keep these till you get your own. I brought spares."

"They should put my mother in charge of cold-weather clothing up here," Hopie told his friend. "You should see how she would dress us for sledding!"

"Your family went sledding? In California?" Caspari asked, his dark eyebrows arching in surprise.

"Sure. Up in the Sierras. My little brother and I before he . . ." His voice trailed off. "So where do we bunk?"

Caspari led them to the line of pyramid tents. They ducked through the flaps, re-sealing them against the cold and selected cots. Hopie set his duffel on an up-ended corn crate and laid out his sleeping bag for the first time.

"I've never had a sleeping bag with a page of instructions stamped inside," he joked.

"Well, pay attention to the rule about keeping it dry – or you could freeze in your own breath," Caspari said.

Hopie started to climb in with his jacket on, but re-read the warning stamped in his bag:

Don't wear all your clothes to bed. Put them under your bag. Cold comes up from below. Use clothes, pack-board or fir boughs beneath the bag.

"Fir boughs?" he asked aloud. He spread his clothes on the sway-backed canvas and replaced the sleeping bag over them.

He knew better than to complain. He wondered about Fairbanks. What would the facilities be like way out there? He took his spare clean shirt from his duffel and laid it over the dingy stuffed ticking that was supposed to serve as a pillow. He shivered, wondering if he had a defective sleeping bag. He was grateful for Caspari's knit cap.

The generator finally clattered to a stop. His ears, assaulted from the long flight, were ringing in the new silence. He heard a deuce-and-a-half, its distant sound carried on the cold night air. Its engine paused in a long sigh, skipped a gear and lugged on. It, too, had made a long journey north. Not above the wilds on wings but through mountain cleavage, gaining each arduous mile on knobby tires.

Waking up with his eyes burning from too little sleep, Hopie was glad the military had abandoned six o'clock reveille on the ALSIB route. The men waited until nearly daylight before rousing from their tents. They gathered, rumpled, at the cookhouse where the coffee smell greeted them along with the steamy warmth of the room. They sat down for a hot breakfast of cream of wheat, white sugar and more prunes, this time soaking in tepid water. Hopie had looked forward to the tart wake-up flavor of coffee. He was disappointed that its taste was far short of its aroma and decided to load his mug with sugar.

"I've discovered there's plenty of water up here, and they're using it to stretch supplies," McCann said, looking into his mug disapprovingly.

"Let's hope they're not using it to stretch the av gas!" Hays growled in agreement.

"Say, Hopie," McCann said, "ya gotta try the moose milk we sometimes get up here." He had a small pitcher and poured a generous amount into Hopie's mug. "It's a real northern delicacy," he added with a straight face. The others eagerly added some to their mugs and watched as Hopie sampled it cautiously. He ruminated a while before announcing his opinion.

"Kinda gamey," he said, "Smells funny, too. I guess I prefer canned milk."

The others burst out laughing as the instigator revealed an opened can of Carnation condensed milk.

"You got me there, you buggers," Hopie admitted.

They gathered up their flight bags and Hays suggested that Hopie take his turn first in the canvas-shrouded pit latrine. The others stood at a discreet distance and exchanged smirks when they heard his burst of "Ke-e-e Ryst!" from within. As the new guy, he'd fallen for the trick of taking the chill off the seat for the next sitter. Hopie couldn't believe a toilet seat could be so cold. He was afraid he'd leave a circle of his hide on it when he stood up. It was enough to constipate him. Maybe the facilities at their next stop would be heated, or at least the ambient temperature would be warmer.

The men regrouped in front of Caspari's plane for a briefing. Glances were exchanged, but no one said anything about Hopie's latrine initiation.

"Keep me in sight at all times," Caspari reminded them. "That crack about the radio blank was no joke. I'll be using dead reckoning to navigate to the next radio range signal, and trying to round you guys up could put all of us off course."

Each pilot walked around his aircraft, scraped ice crystals from their windshields and wings and loaded up. The ground man killed the motors on the portable heaters and rolled them away. With chocks slung over one arm, the man gave each the start-up signal with his three-fingered mitten. They fired up, idling just long enough for their temperature needles to reach the green arc, taxied back into flight order and took off.

Clouds lowered halfway down the mountainsides. The terrain brooded in the colorless shadows. It all looked the same to Hopie. He wanted to study his strip map but didn't want to lose sight of Caspari's plane. There were mountains in all directions. He was sure he was looking down on lands where no man had stepped. There were burned areas left by the summer's forest fires. His feet were very cold. With the engine behind him, there was no heat coming from the firewall. All he had so far was his standard-issue footwear. He'd swap them for something warmer the first time he had a chance.

The Alcan was nothing more than a muddy trail cut through the dense forest. Funny, Hopie thought, that to the men down there, it was their entire world. Their days were spent between the trees, clawing a yard at a time. To pilots like himself, their effort was a mere slit in a huge land. And to any man below spotting a plane flying over, Hopie's entire world of gauges, controls and speed was a momentary glimpse of a blister on the back of a sliver of aluminum.

The highway zig-zagged around muskeg swamps. It was lost in the trees unless you were directly over its chicanes. And now that the dry season was over, the equipment didn't raise telltale clouds of dust. Hopie found it nearly useless for air navigation. If the Japs attacked, they'd sure have trouble strafing a supply convoy snaking along it. That was one advantage, he thought.

It confused him when, about fifty miles out of Watson, they turned nearly south. He checked his magnetic and gyro compasses and looked out his window for reassurance, sighting the others as rugged scenery drifted past only a thousand feet below. He knew that the farther north he flew, the greater the difference between magnetic north and true north. Dashed lines on their charts indicated the variations, but the value surprised Hopie. It was critical to figure in this calculation to stay on course. His training hardly even mentioned the phenomenon. Let's see ... "east is least and west is best," he recited from his ground school. Even though I'm in the west, I see it's an east variation, so I *subtract* the value from my magnetic heading to get my true course. Or do I subtract it from *true* to get *magnetic*? I'll just keep the others in sight and worry about it later, he decided. Checking his chart, he realized if he had it wrong coming out of Whitehorse, within only a hundred miles he'd find himself over Kaskawulsh Glacier, instead of Kluane Lake and the Alcan. His confidence slipped away like the slow but sure needles on his fuel gauges.

They approached Teslin. The long, narrow lake was easy to correspond to his strip map. He relaxed his clenching grip on the yoke again. At its north end, they turned southward, but Hopie had no further doubts about the direction Caspari led them. He pulled out his sack lunch and managed to swallow his "Yukon pie" – peanut butter and jam on field bread – with coffee from a small thermos. He smiled, recalling the fellows' moose milk prank.

They flew through a mountain pass that opened out over the Yukon drainage at Marsh Lake, and followed it to Whitehorse for a fuel stop. Caspari announced their incoming position to the tower and added to his squad, "take a look, boys. This is as close as you'll get to red-light Klutchie Town on this trip!"

They took off again and beneath overcast skies headed west through a wide valley and picked up the twisty Dezadeash River. There were very high mountains ahead. Kluane Lake was another good landmark, since Hopie couldn't get a bearing by the sun. They continued northwest an hour or so. Caspari told them if it was clear, they'd see Canada's highest mountains off to their left, including volcanoes. Caspari called in over Burwash Landing and Snag and before he called in at Northway, he announced that they were in Alaska territory. The Nabesna River was an easy landmark. Caspari called in at Tanacross, where the Alaska highway crosses the Tanana River, another reliable landmark.

Grinding on, Hopie was snapped from his lassitude when his magnetic compass twitched and bobbled to a sixty-degree deflection before it returned and settled to its previous heading. What the hell caused that, he asked himself, tapping the little kerosene-filled globe. He dismissed the aberration, thinking it must have been magnetic dip as they turned westward from their northerly heading. But they'd held a steady course. Had he imagined it? A pilot could always rely on his mag compass, they taught in flight school. Then he recalled Colonel Horner's warning about solar winds and magnetism in his little "welcome to Gore" speech – the guy wasn't bullshitting. He kept a close eye on it and made frequent, tiny adjustments to his gyro compass to keep it from precessing very far.

Hopie thought that Fairbanks should appear just over the next horizon. But another, fainter horizon would appear far ahead. Big Delta Army Airfield was easy to spot, south of the confluence of the Tanana and Delta Rivers. In dwellings scattered below, lights were twinkling on. They drifted backwards like the running lights of southbound ships.

Caspari interrupted his thoughts. "Ferry group with six-two-zero, we're gettin' close. Ladd Tower will prob'ly give us left downwind to runway two-four. We'll land in the same order we took off. Leave some space for wake turbulence. Switch to tower freq and I'll see you on the ground." The airport appeared. Hopie could make out a few rows of buildings in the town of Fairbanks to the west. After flying for hours over wilds that could swallow a downed aircraft, the sight of five thousand feet of concrete and the cluster of neat Army-style buildings made Hopie giddy. He surged with new confidence, even though he'd depended on Caspari's shepherding.

It felt good to hop down off the wing of the new plane two thousand miles from where he'd started. Heat quivered from the engine compartment. He reveled in the smell of hot oil and metal and the ticking of the engine as it cooled. The twilight air was near freezing, but adrenaline was keeping him warm in the twenty-knot breeze.

He patted its side. "Thank you for the flight, baby," he murmured, lingering alongside the bird.

"I know." Caspari said as he approached. "It's like saying good-bye to a friend."

CHAPTER 18

Ladd Field

A door spilled light as a squad of fellows in bulky coveralls emerged from the huge hangar. They fanned out to take responsibility for the planes.

"I bet that runway looked pretty good to you, Hopie," Caspari said. "Here at Ladd, they claim it contains more concrete than all the streets and sidewalks in Alaska Territory." Even a strip of hard gravel would have looked pretty good to Hopie.

A C-47 was parked on the tarmac, its wheels chocked and its doors propped open. Pilots with musettes and duffels slung over a shoulder tottered toward it in a reluctant rush back to Great Falls. In its dim interior light men were settling on its benches. Caspari sent Hays and McCann to the transport and told Hopie he could lay over. They made that exception for first-time pilots. Hopie could fly back on tomorrow's transport. "In fact, I think I'll take a layover. I've lost track of how many days I've worked straight. Maybe nine . . . more like twelve. They aren't gonna bust me for taking one layover in twelve days." Hopie now appreciated the ferry pilots who'd endured weather delays along the route at the slap-to barracks and tents, the unheated latrines and scrounged-up meals washed down with see-through milk from a mechanical cow. He was grateful to stay long enough for a hot meal and overnight here at Ladd and was pleased that his mentor was staying.

"We may not get this luxury again, unless the weather's too poor for flights out," Caspari explained. "Come on. I'll show you around."

"That reminds, me. I gotta stop at a real PX for some long under-wear and stuff."

"Get a needle and white thread and stitch your initials into all your clothes," Caspari advised. "If and when they pick up your laundry, you'll want to get it back."

"Right."

"It's not a problem here at Ladd, but they gather dirty laundry along the route and fly it to Edmonton. Otherwise it's up to you – and you've seen how scarce hot water is."

"What do the mechanics do about shop clothes?"

"They douse 'em in gasoline then wash 'em with 20-Mule Team Borax in a parts-cleaning sink."

They entered the east end of Hangar One. A mechanic wiped his hands on a clean red grease rag and greeted the two pilots.

"This is Ladd's Cold Weather Testing Detachment," Caspari began, once they'd introduced themselves.

"You just missed our commander, Colonel Gaffney," the mechanic told them. "We showed him our successful results to twenty-five below, but that wasn't good enough for him," he added, shaking his head. "We call him the 'screaming eagle of the Yukon,' and his performance didn't disappoint us." Hopie and Caspari exchanged looks. "He was pretty clear that since you pilots face conditions well below that, we need to keep pushing our limits."

"We appreciate that," Caspari said.

An understatement, Hopie thought.

"He says this route's as tough as the Hump from India to China, 'cept it's five times farther. I don't envy you – forcing lightweight metal skin to fly thousands of miles, ramming frigid air into large-displace-ment engines at two hundred miles an hour. Do you realize that aloft at sixty below, you guys are really test pilots?"

"It's an unforgiving environment, for sure," Caspari said. "I've wit-nessed the needles of flight instruments freeze in place, and had con-trol cables shrink out of adjustment . . . " He stopped there. "I've met

Gaffney. He's pretty passionate about the testing and how it will help improve our chances – both the machinery and the men."

"What's this?" Hopie asked the mechanic, handling a long rod-like item with a power cord.

"That's the electric dipstick we developed. It does a fair job keeping the crankcase oil liquid enough so the oil pump won't blow a seal before the engine warms up. We learned this thanks to the Germans who kept dropping out of the sky during their winter attacks on Russia."

"Clever," Caspari said. It was just one of the innovations the Cold Weather fellows had come up with to trick the combination of air, spark and gas into firing within the frigid steel cylinders before the spastic moving parts tore themselves apart.

"This might be the ideal place on the globe for cold weather testing, but we'd be hard pressed to find a worse place for our creature comfort," the man said, turning back to his work. Hopie recalled the big framed canvas nose hangars he'd seen outside, snugged over engines to block the wind so mechanics could perform maintenance without freezing to death.

What's going on in the west side of this indoor football field?" Hopie asked, facing a massive door that split the huge building into two halves.

"That is *Russian* side. Yanks are forbidden to *never* enter Russian side, okeh?" Caspari replied, rolling his r's in a fake Russian accent.

"I thought we were on the same side of this war," Hopie said.

"Some are not so sure about that," Caspari said, arching his eyebrows.

The Russians were steadfast that the handover of aircraft occur at Ladd. Their attitude was ever more opaque, like the partition splitting Ladd's big hangar in two. It was definitely not the spirit of mutual trust that the man in the White House envisioned.

"Let's head to the mess hall," Caspari said. "We'll get better grub here than the kennel rations they serve along the route. You'll see why we call this place the 'country club.' "

All this development at Ladd had started pretty recently, he explained. "Kind of an engineering marvel. Fairbanks used to be just a trading outpost. There were only eighteen military aircraft in all of Alaska. Then the Japs attacked Pearl Harbor and they landed in the Aleutians. Alaska offered plenty of space for defense. All that and this Russian deal changed everything. This place got beefed up in a hurry."

Hopie started to head back to the door, and Caspari instead led him down a short stairway into a passageway of steam pipes and utility conduits.

"Utilidoors," Caspari called them. "Engineered large enough to serve as walkways. They connect each of the buildings."

"Looks like the only thing you can't do underground is fly airplanes," Hopie said, opening his coat in the overwarm passageway.

———————

"This is the Ritz after Watson Lake," Hopie said when they re-emerged in the spotless mess hall.

"Hey! It's Caspari." Someone motioned for them to join his group. A fellow who was telling a story paused.

"Hi fellas. This is Lieutenant Stanhope from Fresno," Caspari interjected. "We call him 'Hopie'."

The men acknowledged the newcomers and the one called "Lasso" went on with his story. Hopie tried to listen through the clatter and bursts of jovial conversation echoing in the busy room.

"They figured ice was a possibility, so they slobbered tar-like de-icer on my 'cobra's prop. So, that natcherly makes the Allison's long driveshaft even shakier." The men nodded in agreement. "About half-way to Grande Prairie, it starts shaking awful. I lost power, and the cockpit filled with steam. I could smell coolant and rolled the window down, thinking it would clear so I could see, but guess what – it just drew more fog inside, and then it turned into a real fire."

"Fire scares me more than any other in-flight emergency," one interrupted.

" . . . so I pulled the emergency door release and had to kick it away. When I jumped, the horizontal stabilizer smacked me in the back. I pulled the ripcord and the shock of the chute opening yanked my boots off!"

Hopie wished he was exaggerating, but knew better.

"Gawd, Lasso, this goes from bad to worse," one said.

"You ain't heard the worst of it. I landed in a bunch o' jackstrawed timber right close to the plane. Course it was burning like hell. Somehow I managed to crawl far enough away that when the oxygen and rest o' the fuel exploded, I was okay. The next morning a 'T-6 dropped a duffel with canteens o' water, good boots, a police whistle and two cans o' beer. Good thing I drank the beer before I read their note that says, 'if you are hurt, stand up and wave your arms!' Now ain't that the Army way? It also told me to get myself *six miles* back to Horseshoe Lake where they could land and pick me up."

"Jesus, man, were you able to walk?"

"Barely, but the good part was that it was so cold, there were no bloodsucking mosquitas!"

No one could top Lasso's story.

"Hey Fresno," one hailed, his voice like a bronc bursting a rodeo gate. "This your first time at Ladd?"

"Yep. Just got here."

"Flew up in a Bell Booby Trap, didja?"

Hopie glanced at Caspari.

"I'm from Salinas, neighbor," the man continued. "Arrived at Gore late August and been makin' this li'l milk run ever since. Retrieved a coupla half-repaired 'cobras and flew 'em back to Great Falls for better coolants. They're prone to losing their altimeters, too."

Hopie extended his hand to shake, but the man waved him off.

"Skip the friendship, Fresno. I don't get chummy with anybody up here." He crossed his arms in front of him.

Caspari broke the awkward moment. "We came up in a flight of four 'cobras. Say," he directed to the group in general, "did any of you fellas notice your compass tumble somewhere between Tanacross and Big Delta?"

"Right-oh," one replied. "Must be a mineral deposit or something. Coulda been a solar disturbance, too, this far north."

Hopie figured Caspari already knew the answer, but was helping a novice save face.

"I was flying one night in a Havoc when the northern lights were active," another added. "It was too confusing trying to watch my compass, so I decided to placard it and just keep an eye on my gyro." What other surprises could this God-forsaken route spring on a pilot, Hopie wondered. He'd read that the Indians called the northern lights "dance of the spirits." No doubt the phenomenon would take up his compass as a dance partner some dark night.

The voices got louder as more men jostled in friendly ways toward the chow line. Hopie noticed the Russians for the first time, all edging toward one side of the large room. There were a dozen or more of them. They wore light brown tunics belted at the waist and trousers with a wide red leg stripe, tucked inside tall leather boots.

Caspari explained that Ladd hosted hundreds of Russians. "Of course they have their own quarters, but share the mess hall with us."

"What are they like?" The foreigners seemed exotic to a kid from a California farm town. "Are they friendly?" He tried not to stare. They looked older. One had an eye patch, another limped along with a cane. "I mean, do you ever talk with them?"

"Most of these guys are fresh from the front," Caspari said. "Even flying through weather over the Bering Strait is powder puff duty. After surviving combat with the Luftwaffe, Ladd is rest camp. Ferry duty in brand new Yankee machines is their reward."

As more arrived, Hopie noticed some had scarred faces. One was missing some fingers. Others had a haunted look in their deep-set eyes.

"They love to fly, just like we do," Caspari added. "Some of 'em have shot down dozens of Germans. They can be standoffish, but don't take it as a brush-off. None of them speak English very well."

"Sure. I hadn't thought of the language problem," Hopie said. "It's hard enough to get through all those tech manuals in your own language. I guess the photos are pretty clear."

"They can fly fine. They just need to get the hang of the peashooters and bombers."

"More seat-of-the-pants training, huh?" Hopie asked.

"There's a lady interpreter around here. Not date bait, but no dog biscuit either," one of the pilots chimed in. "The Russian pilot straps in the seat while one of us gives instruction. She kneels on one wing, and does her best to explain what we just said. Once he fires up, further talk's impossible, so away they go."

"Russia's on the metric system," Caspari added, "so they're also trying to understand our airspeed indicators and placards. All the stall speeds are in miles per hour; inches of manifold pressure and so forth. And our charts, y'know – altitudes and terrain markings – all in feet."

"I guess the only thing that needs no conversion is RPM," Hopie observed.

"That, and the silence when an engine quits. That's a universal signal to pucker yer asshole," Salinas burst out, looking side to side at the others for a laugh. He dug a fork into his mashed potatoes and gravy.

Hopie and Caspari got up and joined the chow line, filling their trays. Hopie spotted a tub of oleo and took a dollop for his hot biscuit, then took a ladleful of canned mixed fruit. There were pans of warm brownies for dessert.

"The Reds are experienced all right, but they're new to the liquid-cooled Allisons," one explained when they sat back down with the group. "I warn them that it's best to get your taxiing and run-up done quickly and get into the air to keep the engine cool."

"Then there's the bruiser who doesn't even take time for a proper mag check."

"Or they go yahooing around the tarmac, and redline 'em before they take off. Last week a pair of them weren't paying attention and both their engines quit and they ended up in fatals."

"But they don't want some Yank kid tellin' *them* how to fly. I was explaining the checklist, and ol' Ivan waved me off, pointed for me to get off the wing and started cranking. I could only hope he latched the door. If that thing flies loose, it hits the tail and you're a goner."

"His name was Ivan, too?" Caspari asked.

"Aren't they all named Ivan-this or Ivan-that?"

"At least they can ride along in the Havoc."

"How? There's no room for anything but the pilot."

"If they pull out the bank of radios, they can lie on the shelf and observe over the pilot's shoulder."

"Yeah, but they still brush us off."

"Maybe you'd better brush up on your sign language, Dunce. You might be making obscene gestures at them and not know it!" They all laughed.

"How about talking to the tower?" Hopie asked. "What about traffic control?" He suddenly realized the danger of flying in and out of Ladd where half the pilots couldn't understand instructions intended to keep aircraft from colliding.

"There's one Russian-speaking controller, but . . . the pilots often make their own rules," Caspari replied tactfully. "You'll see. I let *them* maintain separation. We have no idea what they are going to do, but if they see you, they'll avoid you."

"Sounds like the voice of experience?" Hopie prodded him.

"Yep. I was landing a 'cobra here, all set up on short final, when two of them flew right over me, hauled on full flaps, and slowed smack in front of me. I shoved the throttle forward and tried to climb above their their wing vortex. I was still getting tossed all over the place!"

"Some training flight," Hopie said.

"And I bet you weren't expecting training on how to launder your trousers!" Salinas burst in again, his mouth full of brownie.

"Why don't they let us Yanks fly on into Russia?" Hopie asked, ignoring the crass comment. "Looks like the Reds are hurting for able-bodied pilots."

"If any of those sorry Commies caught wind of how good we got it over here, they'd stow away in one of our returning transports and defect," Salinas declared. Casting a look at the cluster of brown uniforms he shook his head. "And they don't want any Americans anywhere near their country. They're suspicious that we'll see something and shut off their black market."

"And cozying up with the Americans could blow their neutrality pact with the Japanese Empire, now that we're at war with the Japs," Caspari added.

"You called it a 'powder puff' reward, but now they gotta meet their own deadlines, facing bad weather, flying airplanes they've never seen before," Hopie observed. "It's a helluva long way to Moscow, isn't it? I wonder about facilities along the route."

"Right," Caspari agreed. "Once past Nome, they're over the Bering Strait, with its ice fog and storms and forty-five-degree water. If they go down, they know they can't survive. The Russian land crossing's lethal as well. There's still smoke from taiga fires. Their winters are worse than ours. At their 'cold pole' it gets down to ninety below zero! I hear they harness reindeer to come after their downed pilots."

"Even if a pilot survived a forced landing," Salinas barged in again, "nothing but wolves would prob'ly find him . . . because all the bears would have hibernated."

Caspari paused after the morbid comment then nodded at the line of joking Russians filling their trays.

"I suspect there is some liquid courage involved in the form of fermented potatoes."

"Fermented potatoes?" Hopie questioned his friend.

"Vodka."

After eating, Caspari took Hopie to the officers' club. It was as nice as the mess hall. Men were settling in with magazines, pulling up chairs around card tables and the soft shuffle of cards could be heard between bursts of poker lingo. A can was punctured open, sounding a carbonated *pisht*. Most of the talk centered around the weather.

"Wait'll you fly into some pea soup fog," a pilot started in, trying to top the last anecdote about flying through the convective turbulence of forest fires and blinding smoke. "Ice fog forms over the rivers. You don't get any warning, it just fogs up to about pattern altitude. It gets bad over the Chena right off both ends o' Ladd Field." Some of the pilots looked up from magazines. The card players got quiet.

"Flying over the field," he went on, "I could see down through the fog all right, but when I turned onto final, I lost all visibility forward and to the sides. So on short final I just set up my descent at two hundred feet per minute, and let her land herself. I used up the whole damn runway!"

Ground crews began using another valuable trick they learned from the bush pilots. After it snowed, they laid tree boughs along the sides of the runways. Pilots depended on the makeshift markings when river vapors blended sky and earth.

"Beer, Hopie?" Caspari asked, one in each hand.

"Sure."

"Y' know we're not s'posed to horse the Wrights to redline during break-in," a pilot began, his cigarette bobbing with each word. Squinting through a curl of smoke, he continued. "But I was bringin' a Havoc outta Long Beach for Gore and got in some bad weather over the Sierras." He stubbed out the cigarette. "There were thunderstorms all around. I could see a gap ahead of me, and I needed to get through before it closed up. I had no choice but to cob 'em."

At the mention of Long Beach, Hopie thought of California, and its shirt-sleeve weather.

"Boy, could I use a little warm sunshine about now," he said to the group, with an exaggerated shiver. "My feet haven't thawed since Jefferson Barracks!"

"Well kid, ya better get used to what we call 'frozen sunshine' around here," one of the poker players replied. "The sun's shining, but it's still snowing! This is nuthin'. When it actually gets *cold*, you'll want to cover yer mouth with somethin' to keep yer fillings from droppin' out. And find some heavy mittens, or yer fingertips'll freeze off within ten minutes. It's a little harder to manage the controls, but beats losin' fingers!"

Another embellished the warning, "Then, when the wind blows, the snow falls horizontal. You'll see the drifts we'll get after a blow. I've seen 'em twelve feet high!"

"Yer bee-essin' me," Hopie said, and belched, tasting the sour vapor of cheap beer.

"He ain't," another added. "You'll see! Around here, the biggest event of the year is guessing when the Yukon breaks up."

"What do you mean, 'breaks up'?" Hopie asked.

"The river freezes. Sometime in the spring the ice breaks up and starts flowing again. You put five bucks in the lottery with your guess when it'll happen. Last year, some ol' trapper walked away with five grand!"

"Speakin' o' payoffs, do you realize the civvie pilots who ferry us back from Ladd are gettin' paid a whole lot more than the fifty clams a month they pay us?"

"So what. If one o' them had to fly solo, there'd be no one to pour their coffee or serve their sandwich and lady fingers," one replied, lifting his beer can with his little finger poised daintily. "The extra pay is to keep them from having tantrums!" The men burst into derisive snickers. Someone belched.

"I bite my nails every time I load into one of those transports flown by a guy in a clean white shirt. They get their wings by readin' books.

They sit in their heated cockpits – it's just an office job to them. What if one had an engine out? Would he know what to do?"

"You know who earns their civvie pay around here . . ." another began. "Really! The Norseman drivers – those bush pilots who come to get us after a forced landing in the toolie patch. Those guys not only land, they load up what's left of a busted up pilot and take off again."

———————

The following day Hopie and Caspari boarded the transport headed for Gore. Caspari's next flight was as leader in a pair of B-25s. Hopie was assigned to another P-39 flight group. The two friends passed once in a while along the route and always had plenty to talk about – their latest flights, their sweethearts back home, and how much they missed them.

On his next trip to Ladd, Hopie approached a few of the more outgoing Russians, one at a time, offering to trade patches, coins, lighters and card decks, mostly with sign language and lots of pointing and nodding. He wanted to bring some Russian mementoes home for Beverly. One of the men gave him a Russian magazine with a snazzy painting of P-39s on the cover. Hopie tried to give the man an American magazine, but he refused it. "Not allowed," he'd said, holding his big palm out and shaking his head back and forth.

The tough, rustic-looking men fussed over small luxuries like shrewd old maids. Hopie watched as they jealously showed each other the little trinkets they'd found in the local stores. When Ladd's kitchen turned out their newest delicacy – chocolate chip cookies – they disappeared quickly as the Russians sneaked handfuls into their tunics.

CHAPTER 19

Aishihik

Out of oblivion the gold has been smelted: there
it gleams in the lights of the airport.
– ANTOINE ST. EXUPÉRY, *WIND, SAND AND STARS*

Hopie was promoted to first lieutenant. Along with it came the position of flight leader and the sole navigating radio of his group. As he pinned the single silver bar on his collar, he imagined Beverly watching, a glow of pride on her pretty face. With her beside him, he was going to go far in the Army. His promotion had come quickly, thanks to this ferry duty. There would be better opportunity, once he proved himself, but there was no time to imagine all that now. He grabbed his flight manual and took a deep breath at the thought of leading other Airacobra pilots safely from Great Falls to Fairbanks.

Hopie and the pilots of his squad met before daylight for his briefing. Cigarettes glowed as the men shifted nervously on the wet pavement. They approached their airplanes. One of the men dropped his strip map and ran after it, lunging comically, trying to step on it before it flopped hopelessly away.

Flying to Edmonton, Hopie reflected on his first flight and how much he'd relied on Caspari. While they fueled, Hopie got a weather briefing and tried to appear cheerful in spite of the sour news about rain forecast along their route. He dialed the winds into his Dalton Wheel. Once they checked over their aircraft, they headed right out under high, yam-shaped clouds. With a strong voice, Hopie radioed their position at Grande Prairie. He told his crew they'd land for fuel at Fort St. John. The rain began. It peened them, their hollow aluminum airframes amplifying each impact over the sound of the engine. Hopie feared it was hail and would shatter their windshields any second.

"Flight leader to 'cobra squad. Any trouble with that little wash job we just got?" He asked, pushing cool confidence into his voice. No one reported any trouble, and they landed at Fort St. John and fueled.

They took off again, planning their next fuel stop at Watson Lake. From there, Hopie wanted to make Northway by dark. It would be their longest leg, nearly five hundred miles, leaving minimum fuel reserve. Whitehorse would be their alternate if weather or headwinds got worse. He navigated through the ninety-mile radio-silence section. Ground fog was forming in patches. He hoped the valley along Kluane Lake and the Alcan would stay open for them.

The longer he flew, the lower the clouds got and the more gas and daylight he was burning up. At the south end of Kluane Lake, the ceiling converged with fog, smearing his view of anything. The sun was no brighter than an old dime and fading fast. Once it dropped below the horizon, its usefulness as a herald of direction was lost. He decided to reverse heading and return to Whitehorse. It meant executing a tight turn within the narrow valley, which was risky in a fighter as fast as the 'cobra. Forcing himself to remain calm, he radioed the others. "We'll make a one-eighty and get outta here. Slow down and use half flaps," he ordered. "Watch your stall speed. She won't give you any warning."

He'd just handed each pilot their "desert rattler."

"Follow me close," he added.

"Roger, wilco!" came through his headset.

He reduced power, eased back on the yoke and pulled on flaps, slowing to a hundred. He rolled toward the left in a sixty-degree bank. His right wing clipped the clouds tattering above him. The two-g force pressed him against the seat. His arms felt heavy and his face sagged. He had to add power to maintain altitude. Through holes in the fog, the ground rotated below him. Individual treetops menaced, their lusting fingers reaching up from a frosted hell. It shocked him how close they were. His airspeed needle wavered around the ninety-five hatch mark. He kept his eye on his turn-and-bank indicator. A sloppy turn at this slow speed would stall a wing. The plane would spin, and he'd crash within the first rotation. He watched the others begin their turns, and they all rolled out on faith that the sky behind them had stayed a little lighter than the ominous gray wall they'd just faced.

By the time they got to where the valley widened, expecting to follow the highway over lower terrain back to Whitehorse, the ceiling had lowered there as well. Now, the only passable direction was north. They'd have to leave the security of flying over the highway and customary route. Hopie would have to navigate to the emergency field at Aishihik.

"At Kloo Lake, we'll fly a heading of zero-two-zero. From there it's about fifty more miles to Aishihik," Hopie announced. "We can't miss the field. It's at the end of a forty-mile long lake," he added, to firm up his own confidence. It would be dark soon. He hoped the field would be visible by the time they arrived, since he'd only seen it on maps. They flew on, surrounded in darkening grays. Now his hopes had turned to prayers that the route would stay open long enough for them to reach the runway and get their damned airplanes on the ground. Any worse and it would force them down into the trees.

He looked at his watch again and again, trying to remember the exact time they'd taken off from Watson. Would they have enough fuel? He recalculated their fuel burn and each time came up with "probably." It didn't keep his bowels from threatening an angry release. Fifty more miles of this. And three other men hurtling among obscured mountains at a couple hundred miles an hour, trusting him for safe passage. He calculated it should take twelve minutes, but running out of gas even an eighth mile from the airfield could be lethal over these dark woods. Will I ever see Beverly again? He imagined Caspari in this situation – he wouldn't let his feet go to clay. The outcome was going to be the same anyway, so why cave in? In his wishful imaginings he saw illusions – a rift of light, the highway below, the other aircraft glinting in the sun – just tricks of his strained eyes and hopes.

Peering through the gloom, he spotted a thin plume of white smoke rising from the forest. He aimed for it and the field came into view. It was just a wide swath in the scrub, but Hopie was mighty glad the Canadians had put it there. It would save them from becoming four more gruesome landmarks stuck in the muskeg. Hopie pushed that grim thought from his mind and tried to raise someone on the facilities radio for an altimeter report. The steamy green-spruce smoke was his only windsock in the fading light. He angled in parallel to the clearing. "I'm on downwind," he radioed, "so follow me in, fellas." By the time he heard the cheerful reply from the ground, he had turned onto final.

His main gear hit with a sickening clamor. He'd mistaken the gravel along the side for the runway, but he was committed to roll out in a straight line. He tried to hold the nose gear up, but it dropped and dug into the soft grit. Hopie was pressed violently against his shoulder harness as the nose gear collapsed. A series of metallic thuds sounded as the three five-foot-long prop blades blasted a corona of gravel like giant buckshot. It was over in an instant. He shut off the gas and grabbed his microphone but it was dead. He released his harness and bolted onto the canted wing of the craft to watch his flight mates. There goes my career, he thought. His men were on their final approaches, their landing lights sinking eerily toward him in the dusk. His heart was in his throat. And I'm gonna kill these guys! But they had seen his rooster tail and abrupt stop, and had the presence of mind to land alongside him on the hard turf. Hopie was enormously relieved for their heads-up landings. But his self-respect was as badly damaged as the twisted prop on his kneeling aircraft.

Hopie helped the men tie down their planes. He looked up as stars were swallowed in the closing crevasses of cloud and a cold drizzle began to fall. He felt a flood of warmth rise from the soles of his feet. He wanted to hug his men and cry.

They entered the friendly log building and the Canadian weather observer greeted them warmly. "I'm Bob, 'Radio Bob' some call me."

The men introduced themselves and stood near the stove. One of the pilots pulled out a flask.

"Aw, Lieutenant Stanhope, you musta hit a crosswind right on final," he said, handing it to Hopie. "Blew you right off the runway."

Radio Bob cocked his head to the men.

"Or one of them williwaws," another added.

Hopie grasped the flask with a shaking hand. Now he felt chilled, in spite of the warmth of the stove. He appreciated their theories. "That williwaw was a long way from where it started," he said with a sheepish smile, taking a long pull at the flask. He carelessly wiped his mouth with his sleeve. "Thank God you fellas didn't copy my bone-head landing."

The liquor was good medicine, but the men's attitude was even better salve for his shattered ego. "Goddamn! Now I'm gonna get my chops busted."

"No need to snap your cap over it, Lieutenant. We'll vouch for you." The men nodded and agreed.

Bob was pleased to have company. He chattered on while he rustled in cupboards and drawers. Even though they were unexpected, there was food and a bunk for each of the pilots. "Lucky the lake is still open," he said. "The barge just brought plenty o' fresh whitefish. Last trip o' the season. From now till it opens up again, me and the others here will eat an awful lotta chili con-con," Bob tossed each of them a can of beer. "Even brought more hen eggs and two kinds of apples! Tree apples and dirt apples, you know, what the French call 'pommes de terre.' " He started peeling potatoes.

Hopie took another swig and passed the flask on. His hands had steadied and his gut was radiating heat from the whiskey. They passed the can opener around and punched their beers open.

"So, now that I've radioed in my damage report, what do you suppose happens to my plane, Bob?" Hopie asked.

Bob rasped a stick match and lit the gas burners. "A Norseman will drop a coupla mechanics in with parts and fly you back to civilization for another ferry job." He cranked opened another tin can. "You aren't the first one who came in here needing a little fixing up."

A warm buzz let down his tangle of nerves. Hopie asked the way to the latrine and Bob gestured.

"Bob, how do you cope with the cold and long winter up here?" another asked.

"Well, it's a lot better than duty in the Aleutians. Now *that's* the place where you start seeing blue rabbits all around you." He turned back toward the stove and began gently shaking a splattering fry pan. The smell of hot lard covered up the wet-dog smell of scorched eggs.

"Blue rabbits?"

"You know, bushwackiness. Conditions where you're ready to start cuttin' out paper dolls." The men chuckled and slurped their beers.

Hopie returned and they found chairs at the table as Bob laid out fried fish, real boiled potatoes and canned peas and carrots. He entertained the pilots throughout the meal with stories about the Yukon.

"My father started out at sixteen as a wood monkey on the river," he began.

"Wood monkey?"

"The riverboats burned wood. All along the Yukon between Whitehorse and Dawson City, timber was cut, hauled and stacked, and when the boat pulled in, the wood monkeys lugged the cordwood down to the boiler room. Worked for rations. 'Nuther beer, anyone?" He got up and fetched more cans from the stoop and continued. "Got promoted to stoker, then porter, and after the wreck of the Sophia, became pilot. During the short season the route was free of ice, he hauled everything from priests to prostitutes."

Hopie smiled for the first time since his mishap.

They thanked him for the great meal and beverages, and moved back around the stove.

"That was some good navigating, Lieutenant. Glad you got us here," one said, hoisting his beer can. The others did the same. They finished the flask before turning in.

Hopie reflected on the junior pilot's comment. Sure, he'd gotten them this far in spite of demonic weather. But his decisions had also led them into a situation where he had to depend on luck – that there would be a passable way out and that an airport would appear before it got dark or they ran out of fuel.

Is it a good pilot who leads his men into danger then manages to get them down safely? Or would a good pilot have made different choices?

The question nagged him like a toothache.

CHAPTER 20

Judas Peak

When I was a boy with never a crack in my heart.
— WILLIAM BUTLER YEATS

"**S**o that was *you* who clipped the nose gear up at Aishihik," Caspari said, laying an empathetic arm on Hopie's shoulder. They had run into each other back at Gore.

"Fraid so."

"You saved our Army Air Forces a valuable asset, my friend."

"You mean the crankshaft wasn't bent and the engine was okay?"

"No. By the time you're a trained pilot, *you* are the most valuable asset. Parts are easily replaced. Not thinking, decision-making pilots."

"Even pilots who make *bad* decisions?" Hopie asked.

"Hey! Cheer up. They're so hard up for pilots, you'll get a chance to redeem yourself very soon, Lieutenant," Caspari said cheerfully. "C'mon. I'll buy you a beer. I just made captain and I don't fly out till Tuesday."

"Yes, sir!" Hopie snapped to attention and saluted with a huge smile.

———◆———

Hopie was ordered out the next morning to lead a squad of P-39s. After returning to Gore, he was in the mess hall sitting down with the pilots when two officers entered.

"You're not much good to the mission if you go hypothermic and fly into a mountain," the major was saying to his companion. The comment piqued the men's interest. "You heard that Caspari crashed a 'cobra between Teslin and Whitehorse on Tuesday."

Caspari? Crashed? The thought knocked Hopie's breath out.

"It was a flight of two 'cobras. Salinas was in the other one. He noticed Caspari go off course after making the turn between Atlin and Marsh Lake. Salinas tried to raise him on the radio, then Caspari hit Judas Peak. Salinas circled over the site. He says no way Caspari could have survived, going in like that at cruise speed."

The shock jammed Hopie's thoughts like a bad radio signal. Captain Caspari, his good friend, gone. Their paths had crossed often. Their conversations had turned from flying technicalities to personal talk. Hopie told him about Beverly, and Tony was always eager to talk about his fiancée Angela who he'd also met in college. She was living with her parents until Tony returned from duty. They were planning to marry and settle around Aurora, Illinois. He and Hopie promised to meet after the war for beers. They would get their new wives together and make a foursome. Caspari had never been stingy with his knowledge or lorded his seniority.

Hopie recalled Colonel Horner saying you could freeze in your own sweat. It was starting to make sense to him. Even in the cold, exertion inside a bundle of clothing causes a body to sweat which can freeze and bring on hypothermia. An insidious killer, it anesthetizes the brain while shutting down the body. Hopie felt a void in his chest as the major went on speaking.

"They think the pilot just passed out. Could have been exhaust fumes, but more likely he was hypothermic. They couldn't get to it for a couple of days and when the salvage crew got there . . . well . . . carnivores had strewn and picked over the . . . evidence." Hopie was facing the speaker, but he wasn't hearing anymore or seeing anything but Caspari's face. His chest felt like everything had been sucked out of it, even his heart.

His friend had loved the P-39. In the cold air, it performed beauti-
fully, Caspari had said.

"That plane hit so hard the wreckage would fit on this table." The
major spread his arms wide over the eight-foot-long chow table.

Like a light switch, Hopie thought. You're on and alive; then you're
off. At nearly three hundred miles an hour, it was a merciful, quick end,
but still an end. He could not believe his friend was gone. Caspari never
knew what hit him. But that was small comfort to Hopie.

It wasn't the first time Hopie imagined wrecking. All pilots pre-
pare a small part of their mind for the possibility of something going
wrong. And flights had gone wrong for names he didn't know. Now a
wreck had a face. A dimpled smile. A lively body with a life outside the
cockpit – parents, a sweetheart at home and brown-eyed children never
to be. There would be no wedding night blunder and bliss. A future
was slammed shut by a wall of frozen rock. His lively friend would be
reduced to a line-item entry marked "fatality," shrouded in a manila
folder in some Army file cabinet. Hopie couldn't shake the captain's
dispassionate words or his open-armed gesture from his mind – the
crumpled scraps of a thirty-foot long, fully-armed airplane – and mangled pilot – lying on an eight-foot table.

I can put up with being a goddamned "test pilot," he thought. I can
put up with crummy food, cold tents and exhaustion. Hopie shoved his
tray away and slumped, grabbing his head with both hands. But I don't
know how to put up with losing my friend Tony Caspari. I feel so *alone*.
More than ever he wanted to hold Beverly. She'd keep the bitterness
from rotting his soul.

Maybe Salinas was right. It would have been a lot less painful if
they'd never been chums.

CHAPTER 21

Risks

You may take the most gallant sailor, the most intrepid airman,
or the most audacious soldier;
put them at table together – what do you get?
The sum of their fears.
— WINSTON CHURCHILL

Some of fellows invited Hopie to go hunting, but like most of the pilots, he stayed out of the weather except to fly. Hopie tried to pass a Friday night at Gore's weekly dance. As he approached the hall, young Victory Belles were pouring out of a steamy-windowed bus. He got stuck holding the building's door open for the giggling swarm. The base orchestra was doing a good job of Glenn Miller's "Tuxedo Junction" when he entered. The room was very warm. He'd never seen so many young women in one place. He timidly looked at a few nearby, thinking of Beverly. He partnered with one for a clumsy dance, but his heart was thousands of miles away.

Gore and Ladd had formed intramural basketball teams, but that didn't interest Hopie, either. They were rougher than he remembered from high school. There were plenty of fouls and the offender stayed in the game. At Ladd, the Special Service started matching up willing boxers for fights on Wednesday nights. But still the stress bubbled over and once in a while hotheads threw a few punches at each other away from the ring. Those were the scraps that did not get reported in *Tailwinds*, the Seventh Ferrying Group's newspaper.

"Be glad we're not huddled someplace in the Aleutians fighting the Japs," a captain was saying when Hopie entered Gore's officers' club for the evening. "Now that place is dismal! And windy? Hell! They'd use a five-hunnerd pound bomb for a windsock, except it would blow around too much!" Hopie found a chair and joined the group.

"I was bringing a B-24 outta Gore to deliver to Anchorage for the Eleventh Air Force," Lieutenant Greger began. "I laid over at Watson. It got down to forty below overnight. When I saw the plane in the morning, it looked like she'd bled to death! Red hydraulic fluid had leaked onto the snow from shrunken seals. The struts were flat, and she looked like she'd never fly again! It took us three days to get everything thawed out. The plumbers' heaters wouldn't start, so we built a fire to get them running, then started heating her four engines. We finally got her heart beating again, but once I got her flying, I lost an outboard engine, and the prop stuck in high rpm on another one, probably because of bad hydraulics."

"What did you do?" the others gasped.

"I turned around and headed for Watson. We cooled our heels for a week while it warmed up, and we got all the hydraulics working."

"Go on, Greger, tell these greenhorns about your landing," another said, passing beers around as Greger continued.

"Well, that plane musta been jinxed. She did get us all they way to Anchorage, but when I came over the threshold, I could see the runway was a sheet of ice. I slowed down as much as I dared, and set her down and tried not to use brakes on roll-out. If one had grabbed, I'da gone off the side."

"Who cares if you use the whole runway," Hopie interrupted. "I think Uncle Sam prefers a whole airplane."

Greger nodded and pointed at Hopie in agreement.

"That wasn't the end of it. I taxied off the active, but a C-47 came in right behind me too fast, and that gooney slid right into the tail of my boxcar!"

"No shit!" one said, piercing his can open.

"Criminy!"

"Holy Joe! Hey, pass that can opener over here."

After pausing for their reactions, Greger changed the subject. "You boys wanna check over your survival gear real good. When my pea-shooter went down last fall in the mountains near Swift River, I opened my survival gear. Know what was in there? Mosquito netting, bug repellant, canvas boots, cotton socks, chocolate bars and guess what else! A goddamned machete! Of course, the machete was in there to cut the chocolate bars!" The men burst out in mocking laughter.

"What did you do then?" Hopie asked.

"I wrapped myself in my parachute, and burned the shrouds all night to keep from freezing. If you go down in these god-forsaken mountains, build a fire and warm up your mess kit and fork – if you don't, your fork will freeze to your tongue!"

Another pilot brought over a magazine. Leafing through it he announced with fanfare, "Here's some real fresh news!"

"Whaddya mean, it was actually published *after* the last war?" another quipped.

"Listen to this by some guy named Price:

"The Russians' flying habits are combat style, taking all the airplane has to give, bending everything forward to the firewall and racking the P-39 around in screaming verticals. They had to fly to Nome and beyond and they were in hell's own hurry."

Hopie wondered how a guy with paper and pen got anywhere near one of the spooky Reds.

"Hell's own hurry," one of the pilots repeated, punching open a beer. "He got that part right! I was coming in on final in a 'cobra and just as I was on short final, you know, gear down, doin' about ninety-five, full flaps, fallin' like a rock . . . " he paused to belch. "Here come two idiots in 'T-6s from the side. They crossed right in front of me, knowing full well I was there! One was so close I saw him grinning at me out his left side window. I recognized him after we landed, with that silly gap-tooth smile. I haven't seen him since. I headed back south for another flight."

"He's probably dogfighting and grinning at the Germans right now," another added as he headed to the latrine.

"No shit! I guess we gotta cut 'em some slack," Hopie said, swept up by their frat house talk. "It must be tough flying." He got up. "Anybody else want another beer?"

"Those poor guys in the tower," another said, piercing his can with the opener and taking a gulp. "Watching the Reds come in full speed the wrong direction, and being helpless to do anything. I watched one guy land *across the taxiway*. He weaved between a half dozen 'cobras then he swung around, shut it off and jumped out. Major Crane was the Ops officer, and bee-lined out there to chew his ass."

"Crane's as tough as a two-bit steak. What did the sonovabitch say?"

"It's not what Crane said . . . the Ruskie says to Crane, he says, 'Yah, I joost land the vay I vant, okeh? But I got *eight Nazi planes*. How many *you* got?' "

"I bet that ended the conversation!" They all laughed.

"Hey, toss that opener back over here!"

"Even identical makes of aircraft fly differently," a captain with gray wisps at his temples said. "The last peashooter I picked up at Bell, I hardly had to move the control before I was at a seventy-degree bank, and with that damn aux fuel tank, I easily could have stalled. And I wasn't more than a thousand feet in the air. I'da had no time to bail out."

"And how would you feel trashing a thirty-five-thousand dollar piece of taxpayer hardware?" one chimed in, rhetorically.

"That's more than my folks paid for their whole ranch!" another said.

"Then if you survived, you'd feel guilty." Hopie asked, shaking his head.

"Hey! Ever break up with a girl? You break her heart. She cries and tells you she will never be the same again. You feel real bad for a minute. But a guy's gotta move on. No regrets, right? Hey! Grab me another brew while you're up, will ya?"

Hopie thought about Beverly. He could never do that to her.

"Hey! I heard Scary Harry got caught buzzin' caribou again. He really got a chewing, 'specially after Punkie hit those trees and burnt up in his wreck."

"Wonder why Punkie didn't pull up sooner?"

"Harry had told him he wouldn't believe he'd *really* buzzed anything till he brought back caribou turds on his leading edges."

"Well, in Punkie's case, there wasn't much need for search and rescue. He scattered his own ashes." The men nodded solemnly.

"We haven't got much S and R anyway," the captain added. "No one wants to risk more pilots and airplanes when the chances of a live recovery is zip."

" 'Specially since that spotter went down trying to find Mills."

"Yep. Goin' down like he did in the muskeg, his plane just stuck like a fly on flypaper. Helluva neck-breaker."

After opening his third beer in the amity of Gore's officers' club, Hopie wasn't motivated to get up and leave even though the conversation had turned to the macabre.

"If you hadta bail, *and* dodged gettin' whacked by the tail or a propeller blade on one of the multi's, *and* survived the drop," one pilot began, "what are your chances of landing someplace another airplane *could* pick you up?"

"Harding was one lucky sonovabitch when he bailed out and landed so close to the Alcan that he got picked up within a day."

"That wouldn't happen again in a hunnerd years," one added in a boozy voice.

"Well, first a Norseman would drop you some supplies – an over-under rifle, a sleeping bag and some food. If your hands and arms still worked, you could play boy scout and camp out till the dogs arrive."

"What's an 'over-under'?" Hopie had to ask.

"Never heard of the 'food-getter'? Your forty-five will just turn a rabbit into mincemeat with fur on it, so they came up with the 'over-under.' One barrel takes a four-ten shotgun shell and the other is a twenty-two caliber. Pretty handy."

"*If* they spotted you in this empty backcountry in time," another added, crushing his empty beer can and throwing it at the garbage can. "How would you feel, layin' there in the snow all busted up, waitin' for a goddamned dog team to trot out and get you?"

"Sometimes they'll drop in a sawbones."

"You've got to give *those* guys credit," the captain defended. "How many doctors like Harve Jourdan do you know willing to jump out of airplanes in the snow with a dog sled for an ambulance?"

"*If* the wolves don't get you first," one said sarcastically. "Mush Fido! Mush! Can't you trot any faster?" he mimicked, cracking an imaginary whip. "Extra kibble if we get to the pilot before the wolves do!"

"I wouldn't knock it," another said, throwing his empty beer can at the joker.

The room got quiet. Hopie's mind wandered. What if you broke an ankle, or worse, had a compound leg fracture? Or burned a hand or two beyond use? You couldn't even use your forty-five to signal for help . . . or end your misery quickly. "I'm turning in," he said, and got up unsteadily. No one said much as they all broke up and made their way toward their bunks.

———◆———

Hopie had made dozens of flights by now, all in the P-39. He thought of Caspari each time he dropped into the seat. Pilots didn't need combat to encounter risk. As an ALSIB pilot, Hopie had faced winds jetting between peaks of rock blown bare. Like water over boulders, the air keeping his wings aloft was churned, pitching and rolling him over rapids as flotsam. He'd whispered the airman's prayer that every bolt and spar would hold fast as he was wracked by invisible forces. And he'd added his thanks to the heavens after outrunning the violence. Back on the ground among his cohorts Hopie might admit the mountain pass was "a little choppy."

He wrote Beverly often. He wanted to brag but left out a lot of detail so as not to frighten her. He mailed her a clipping from a newspaper, and asked her to show it to his mother. He thought it would be less boastful, coming from the pen of best-selling writer and aircraft designer Major Alexander deSeversky:

> The ferry pilot is by all odds the hardest-working, most versatile airman in the Service. He must be able to – at a moment's notice – fly any plane in existence to any part of the world.

———◆———

Everyone was struggling against a winter that was throwing the full force of an Arctic record-breaker at them. Cold weather slowed flights down but didn't stop them. If the plane started, you flew. No single-engine aircraft were to fly into weather that required instrument flying, but weather doesn't follow tidy rules. Once aloft, rules were nothing more than good suggestions. Hopie had learned to carry lighter fluid to clear a hole big enough to see out an icy windshield. If what he saw outside the cockpit wasn't any better than a windshield caked with ice, he climbed or looked for the closest runway.

Pilots were expected to manage risks. And good pilots didn't waste mental effort on "what-ifs." They concentrated on getting their aircraft and themselves to the destination in one piece, even if some risks were beyond managing.

Record-breaker

Gore Field, Great Falls, Montana – January, 1943

"**E**ven a small amount of frost on a wing or tail surface can cause a wreck," Mel told Dugan. "It spoils the airflow, and raises the stall speed. So be thorough scraping the ice off. We don't want to make Hell any more crowded."

At the first hard freeze, there were still only two large heated hangars. Aircraft were lined up in the biting wind awaiting adjustments and modifications.

The ground crew had to get resourceful. Dugan learned how to turn surplus canvas into wing covers to keep ice from forming on the planes parked outdoors.

Choking cold settled over Great Falls. Ice crystals floated from invisible clouds and sparkled in the winter sun. The thermometer fell below zero but the work went on.

"Gapping plugs and setting timing is precise work," a mechanic complained. "How can I do all that wearing gloves, especially under orders to hurry? These ships can drop outta the sky if I cross-thread a drain plug, or mess up a safety-wire. Then it's on my head!"

Patrick,
We lost another airplane yesterday. The pilot said he hit freezing rain a few miles out of here and iced up too heavy

to keep flying. They let me go with them to the crash site. Everything looked fine. There wasn't no ice left. I felt bad for the pilot having to defend his choice to land in the field and tear up the airplane so.

Good news tho. One of the Russians brought us a furry little half-grown Samoyed pup. He can't be a sled dog cuz he's blind in one eye. We watch out for him. His name is Sammy. He stays in the hangars while we work. We made beds for him out of surplus blankets. He sure adds joy to our lonely life.

"I grabbed a torque wrench, and it felt like a hot poker on my hand!" Mel told Dugan. "When I set it down, it took my skin with it!" It was so cold, the mechanics had to work in relays. One would work for twenty minutes, then the second fellow took up the wrench while the first one went inside to warm up. When a mechanic got frostbitten standing behind a Mitchell that fired up, posters appeared near each tool area:

FROSTBITE WARNING:
Never get in propwash at sub-zero temps

The wind blew, driving the wind-chill well below zero, frosting noses, chins and ears. Dugan and others watched in awe as an eighty-five mile-per-hour gust blew a C-47 over the embankment.

When the wind blows here – and that's almost always – it sucks the breth right out of you. The inside of your nose freezes. It sends spooky ice vapor across your path just above the ground. It's like walking on clouds.

Engine oil gets thick as sludge. I seen rivets come out of their holes. I was careless and touched a radio antenna. It snapped off and blew away.

I'm supposed to pre-heat the airplane engines with porta-
ble heaters. Sometimes even the heaters freeze up and I have
to preheat the heater before I preheat the aircraft.
Your brother Dugan

At the other air bases along the route, it was worse. Winter temperatures usually reached minus thirty. The land was in the clutches of
a deep arctic freeze, worse than anyone could remember. Engines that
sat for several hours were too cold to turn over until the ground crew
used pre-heating tricks they'd learned from the bush pilots.

"At these temperatures, the pilot's gotta remember to pump av gas
into the engine oil reservoir before he shuts down," Mel explained to
Dugan. "It just burns off when the engine runs a few minutes," he continued. "The Allison V-10's are liquid cooled."

"Don't they freeze up?" Dugan asked.

"We knocked our brains out trying to come up with the right ratio
of glycol to water to keep 'em from freezing, but glycol lowers the boil-
ing point, and they were overheatin' and blowin' relief valves. Then we
realized that the tricycle gear allows for the aircraft to tilt slightly, and
we were not quite filling the radiator to capacity. Now it's up to the
pilot. And a pilot can still overheat an Allison by forgetting to open the
coolant shutter. We seen 'em start fires in the cockpit."

Dugan's new job was to gather and clean five-gallon buckets, and
before the engines cooled off he'd pull the oil drain plug, filling buckets
until the engine was drained. He'd shuttle the buckets inside by the
heat for the night. In the case of the Havocs, each engine held twenty-
two gallons of oil, so he needed five buckets ready for each side.

"Make goddamned sure you don't drop the plug in the snow," Mel
said. "It's a bear trying to find it again. You gotta take off your gloves so
you can feel it. There goes a half hour, while you run in and thaw out
your fingers."

In the mornings, Dugan had to help fasten the roughly-fabricated
tarp over the engine nacelle, and drag out one of the industrial heaters

to pump warm air in. The warm oil was refilled, and while the pilot primed the engine, someone pulled each prop through a rotation. The magnetos were switched on, the starter engaged and with luck, the bombers' big radials would fire, after protesting the cold with a series of explosions that sent smoke and fire out the exhaust pipes.

———•———

New fighters and bombers were arriving with sappy messages chalked on their noses. Some had provocative images elaborately drawn along with the messages.

"Get a load of these headlights!" Dugan and Mel leered and joked. Other fellows heard and gathered.

"Too bad we have to erase all this great cheesecake! Looky here at the gams on *this* babe: 'Able Grable!' " Dugan wolf-whistled at "Too Hot To Handle," a rear view of a voluptuous girl in tight shorts touching her rump with a pink-chalk fingertip. "These should be painted on for good."

Some had themes of destruction. "Special Delivery for Adolph," "Rain of Terror" and "Aiming for Helmut's Helmet" had images of nose-diving bombs. "This Bell Tolls for Jerry" was inspired by Hemingway's new book. The "Jolly Roger" had a skull and crossed bones chalked on it.

"Bouncing Betty's Revenge," one of the men read aloud. "Didja know the Krauts use land mines that explode ten feet above ground? It splatters shrapnel into everyone within fifty feet!"

"Those bastards!" another seethed. "The message *should* read *Castrator's Counter Strike!*"

"Uh oh. Here's a FUBAR," Mel observed. "Musta malfunctioned en route here. Let's get 'er in and find out what's wrong."

"FUBAR?" Dugan asked.

"Fu . . . fouled up beyond all recognition!" The others laughed at Dugan's ignorance.

———•———

Mel had just finished checking a hydraulic fitting on a P-39, cursing that anyone was expected to function in "a deep freeze like this." Dugan rolled the heater away, over snow so cold it squeaked. Mel waved the pilot off, the plane started and began to taxi toward the runway.

When the men returned through the hangar's man-door, Sammy bolted out and ran toward the departing aircraft.

"Sammy! Come Sammy!" Mel shouted, taking off after him in a desperate dash to grab the dog before he got near the spinning propeller. The pilot never saw the animal, and continued toward the runway, Sammy merrily barking and chasing him. Mel sprinted after the dog, having taken no precautions to cover his face. He ran until he finally caught up with Sammy very close to the tail of the plane, and right in the prop blast. He gathered the dog in his arms and headed back to the hangar, struggling to catch his breath. He staggered in the door, panic on his face, and managed to release the dog before collapsing in front of Dugan.

His friend and mentor lay writhing in front of him on the floor. Dugan grabbed a litter and yelled for help to carry Mel to the infirmary. But Mel never recovered. His lungs had frozen.

———◆———

Dugan found a clerk and asked for Mel's family's address so he could write them.

> *Dear Folks,*
> *I worked with Mel. I am very sorry for his death. He was a good man and a very good meckanic. He died trying to save our dog, but he would of done the same for any of us men.*
> *Sincerely,*
> *Frank Dugan, Gore Field – Great Falls, Montana*

He sealed and addressed his message. He sat next to Sammy's bed and with the dog's head on his lap, wistfully rubbed its ears. He remembered the bottle of bourbon Mel had swiped. Dugan knew where he'd stashed it in a corner of a workbench. He found it and removed the grease rag draped over it. It was over half full. He sat on a crate and took a huge swig. He slowly looked over the space they'd shared, the tools Mel had handled. His stained coffee mug. His cap with Mel's gray thumb print on its upturned bill. He stopped when he saw Mel's dark blue coveralls, one empty shoulder hiked up on a hook. He took another big gulp and as the 160-proof bourbon scorched its way down his throat, he stood, walked slowly to the door, and heaved the bottle into a snowbank, shattering it in sacrificial tribute to his dead friend.

CHAPTER 23

Weather Rules the Skies

ALSIB Route, Yukon Territory – January, 1943

Winter's cold seemed to freeze out the sounds of natural life. Deep quiet settled on the land. There was no birdsong, no leaves rustling in a breeze or creek water riffling between gravel banks. Even the mighty Yukon River slowed to a halt, its coursing water silenced. Those sounds would not be heard until spring breakup. Many of the pilots Hopie had met along the route were from southern states and like him, were coping with itchy woolens and moving around in layers of clothes stuffed inside their jackets.

Hopie and a couple of pilots were remaining overnight at Whitehorse.

"Hey, that's a nice coat. Where'd you get it?" Hopie asked an officer who'd just entered and was taking off his knee-length quilted coat with a fur-lined hood. Hopie only noticed his rank after his coat was off.

"Bush pilot told me where to buy it in town. With a serge pullover under it, It's a lot warmer than that leather GI bomber jacket you're wearing."

"I didn't notice your rank, sir. I guess it's hard to pin the oak leaves on such a heavy garment," Hopie said, concerned that he'd offended the major for not saluting.

"Lieutenant, up here, commanders let that detail go once they've flown the route." he replied. "Any sane person realizes how important it is to keep warm."

Pilots were on their own for rousting up warmer clothing. That part of the supply chain was still disconnected. Hopie had found extra wool socks at the post exchange, but they limited him to two pairs. He would have bought a dozen.

"This morning, our thermometer was pegged at forty below," a mechanic began. "We went out to warm up a Mitchell, and it looked like it had hibernated!" The pilots, always keen to hear mechanics' stories, paused from their cards and looked at him, so he went on.

"The hydraulic seals had all shrunk, the gear struts collapsed, and the tires were nearly flat from low air pressure in the cold. The darn thing was just begging to be left on the ground."

"When it gets cold, an airplane becomes a disintegrating collection of miscellaneous parts," remarked a senior mechanic during a lull in his cribbage game. "Steel, aluminum, glass, rubber . . . all shrink at different rates and the fluids try to turn to solid at different rates, too."

"Yeah, but the good thing about blowin' a hydraulic line en route," a pilot interrupted, "it lays down a nice red track in the snow for the next pilot to follow." Someone heaved a magazine at his head.

"And then there's Anson here," said another, placing a hand on the pilot's shoulder. "Lost his radio beam outta Northway. Flies back and forth trying to pick it up again. Now you're really lost, right, Anson?" Without waiting for the pilot's reaction, he went on. "Spots the Alcan. Flies all the way back to Snag before he realizes he's following it *south* by mistake!"

Anson interrupted the laughter. "Hell, I wasn't really lost," he protested, "I was just . . . temporarily disoriented." Another gave a sideways shove to the embarrassed pilot.

By now, most lakes had frozen over and blended into the snow-covered land. It was harder to locate them on their charts. The rivers and drainages were hard to interpret, even when you could see them.

"None of the rivers up here flow very far in the same direction, so first you need to know where you are before you spot one to find out where you *really* are," Anson half-joked. The others silently agreed. Each one had been "temporarily disoriented" at one time or another, and luckily got re-oriented before running out of gas – or worse – flying blind in the clouds and into terrain.

The rushed ALSIB route planners gave little thought to weather forecasting. They thought they understood cold, but knew little of blinding arctic conditions that swirled down from the polar ice cap. They were sending hundreds of men in airplanes over thousands of miles of mountains and frozen waters through skies obscured with ice fog or precipitation. Williwaws blustered out of the craggy slopes and tossed the planes around like dry leaves. Wings iced up and stopped lifting, and propellers threw chunks of ice at fuselages and canopies, enough to dent or shatter them. Native Inuits had dozens of words for the way snow fell from the sky, and how it laid on the ground. Pilots just knew it could ground them – hopefully with a runway beneath them. At a hundred times the speed of a native dog team, pilots had mere seconds to make life-and-death decisions.

"Did you expect the bad weather to just hold off until the Army got around to installing decent forecasting equipment?" Hopie heard an officer shout into a telephone. "Some of our weather stations are nothing more than a rusty anemometer spinning from the top of a shed and a faded windsock planted on a pole someplace near the field!" Before the man slammed the receiver down, he barked, "Around here, a windsock doesn't stand a chance, when a thousand-pound bull moose rubs his ass against it!"

———————

"Hopie, have you given blood yet for the Dawson Creek disaster?" a pilot asked. News of the explosion, death and injuries had flashed along the route. The Red Cross was desperate for blood.

"On my way," Hopie replied. "I heard we lost a bunch o' guys there, working on the Alcan."

"Jesus, who'd park a truck full o' dynamite in a place like that?" the man asked, incredulously. "Makes a grain elevator fire seem like a marshmallow roast."

The truck of dynamite had been parked inside an old livery stable full of construction materials and tools. Sixty cases of explosives blew at once, triggering other explosions and fires that consumed other buildings and leveled the main part of Dawson Creek, on British Columbia's eastern edge. It killed five and injured one hundred and fifty civilians, nearly one third of the little town's residents. People were sliced by flying glass. Half-melted crowbars flew through the air like rockets, some wedged into the sides of buildings. Burning tires landed on cars or started other fires. A keg of nails exploded, impaling people. Cabins were blown off their foundations a half mile away. Men scurried about with buckets of water trying to control the conflagration, dodging red-hot metal debris and wildly unfurling coils of copper cable. The little hospital was thrown into chaos. The waiting room was turned into a makeshift clinic where Hopie's Army cohorts were giving blood. Lying on a cot, Hopie bared his arm for the procedure. He could hear moaning as Red Cross women rushed about with glass vials on a floor spattered with blood.

"Seems like giving a pint of blood is the least we can do," he said.

"It's red gold to us," a nurse told him.

———

While waiting out the weather for his return out of Fairbanks, Hopie'd heard a rumor that two hundred and seventy-five planes were marking time on snow-drifted airfields all along the ALSIB route. Posters depicted the route as the "Air Bridge to Russia" but it had become a rickety bridge, failing often against the elements. It dropped promised aircraft and men to endure dead hours seeking refuge from blinding, blowing snow. The Soviets had no patience over the delays and heated up phone lines between Moscow and Washington. All Hopie knew was that a string of pilots lay shivering in their sleeping bags, getting up in the night to chuck wood into the little stoves in their "winterized" tents. He was happy for the warm latrine and plenty of hot food and showers for a day or two. No need for fir boughs under his sleeping bag here at Ladd.

He settled in the officers' club for the evening.

"There aren't enough hangars for all these planes sitting overnight," a mechanic said between poker hands. "We've learned not to haul 'em in and out of the warm hangar anyway. It's best to leave a cold plane cold. The alternating freeze-thaw causes condensation which corrodes cams and cylinders. It's really tough on hydraulics, seals and stuff. It cracks windshields and canopies, so we just leave 'em out in the cold, and roast the engines before start-up."

"I'm still waiting for some decent wool socks," a pilot said. "I got large enough boots so I can wear two or three pairs."

"Just make sure yer boots aren't too big to waggle out of a Havoc," another said, partly in jest. "Bailing outta one o' them is dicey enough, with them big fans on both sides of you. One little slip and you can lose a vital part."

"Yeah, but it's so cold, at least you won't bleed!"

"I wonder how any of them Ruskies could bail out in an emergency. They're all so stocky and broad. Have you noticed their taste in women runs along the same . . . uh . . . dimensions?"

"Whuddya mean, Lieutenant?" another asked, feigning ignorance.

"Next time you take in a movie, listen to 'em hoot and howl when a chubby, over-endowed female appears on the screen!" The ham stood up and ogled and made a gesture suggesting a very wide figure.

"Seriously fellows," a captain interrupted, "a couple of Russians in Havocs had a mid-air at Nome last week. No chance of bailing out."

The group fell silent. It was like a cold stab in the gut anytime a pilot was killed. There was mutual respect among the pilot brotherhood, even if the cultural divide was too broad to bridge.

After a pause, the conversation changed direction. "You still tryin' to keep warm in those DVGs?" the lieutenant asked Hopie. "The Reds use felt. Much warmer."

Hopie looked down at his sheepskin-lined Gaffney boots, nick-named with the three initials of the notorious Colonel. He'd bought them at the PX. They looked plenty warm.

"I was flyin' with Peters when he went down shy of Northway. All he had for boots were those idiotic fleece-lined things," he said, pointing to Hopie's feet. "When he walked in the snow, they just scooped it in and he froze off three of his toes." Hopie looked back up.

"See if you can trade one of the Russians for a pair of theirs. They like women's makeup and perfume."

"Better yet, show them some fancy underwear. You know, lon-ger-ray!" another added. "Be sure to get a large size!" The men snickered as he held his hands out, a yard apart.

"Wouldn't it be simpler to just give them some American cash?" Hopie asked. "Isn't that like gold back in Russia?"

"No way. If they get caught with U.S. dollars on them, it's considered treason," the captain explained. "One of them approached me with some old U.S. currency he needed to get rid of. I could tell it was old because it was oversize and printed in blue ink. He wanted to trade it with me for something safe."

"What did you do, Captain?"

"I went ahead and took it off the guy's hands and traded him some jewelry I'd bought for my mother. Then I sent the bills home instead, telling her they were a collector's item. They were a lot easier to mail, anyway. You better know this too," the captain added. "There's a good reason they keep to themselves. We've got flying in common, and some of them have incredible combat experience, but they are drilled to be one hundred percent loyal to the motherland. If they're seen being too chummy with us, they can get yanked back into combat. Or worse."

"Do you think any of them are tempted to defect?" Hopie wondered aloud.

"Sure. But their government keeps an iron grip on their valuable assets. Don't try to get any of them in a private conversation. I think they are being watched constantly."

CHAPTER 24

Deadliest Week

*. . . a fabulous world filled with snares and pitfalls, with cliffs
suddenly looming out of fog and whirling air-currents of a strength
to uproot cedars. Black dragons guarded the mouths of the valleys and
clusters of lightning crowned the crests . . . but from time to time
one or another of them, eternally to be
revered, would fail to come back.*
— ANTOINE ST. EXUPÉRY, *WIND, SAND AND STARS*

ALSIB Route, Yukon Territory – February 1943

"**N**othing but gibberish!" Colonel Mensing blurted. He was trying to get reliable weather information. He and his pilot needed to return their planeload of ferry pilots to Gore when a blizzard forced them to land their Skytrain at Watson Lake. Hopie's Airacobra squad was grounded there as well. Everyone bent over the radios trying to catch a readable forecast as indecipherable code crackled over the airwaves.

"The Navy broadcasts vital weather information but the fools are trying to keep their information from helping the Japanese, so they scramble their goddamn transmissions. It's worthless to us!" the colonel thundered to everyone in earshot. "Men are *dying* because it isn't *protocol* for the Navy to share code books with the Army!"

The longer they had to wait, the more irritated the colonel became.

"Even Napoleon knew that weather could mean losing a battle! He ordered his scientists to learn to predict it to improve his chances!"

The man was nearly unhinged, Hopie thought.

"I'm going to send a broadside of a report about this!" The colonel stormed into the little administration office, scattering the corporal and his sheets of typing and carbon paper from the manual Underwood. He banged out a visceral letter to his superior.

Colonel Mensing's flight was finally cleared to take off, even though they knew they would have to find their way around blinding storms. With his letter draft, he and ten others loaded back into the transport and fired up, raising clouds of snow on their takeoff run. Hopie watched as they disappeared into an opaque sky.

———————

Hopie was still grounded at Watson Lake when the news came in that Colonel Mensing's flight never reached its destination. Sickened at the news of the downed flight with so many souls aboard, Hopie and the others were stunned with more bad news. The weather had wrested the lives of eight more lend-lease pilots. Fretting out storm after storm from the hangar, he watched through the windows as a C-47 attempted to land during a snow flurry. He stepped outside to watch. "I thought he'd just make another approach," Hopie told another pilot. "I heard him add power for a go-around. Then the engines sounded like they were getting farther away, and got kinda muffled by the heavy snowfall. Then they just faded to silence. It was spooky."

That evening, news spread that bad weather near Fort Simpson had brought down another C-47, and three transports in Alaska. Meanwhile at Ladd, the winter's late dawn was dimmed by a blanket of low clouds and a B-24 crashed twelve miles south of the airport, killing seven more Americans. It was a deadly week that Hopie would never forget.

"This carnage has overwhelmed our search and rescue crews!" a major rasped into the hissing phone lines. "Get everyone with two eyes into the air to help our aerial search the instant the weather opens up! I don't have to tell you that every little skiff of new snow hurts our chances of spotting a wreck."

Hopie and the other two pilots surged out of their chairs now that they'd been ordered to help. With the two big transports down nearby and so many personnel suddenly lost in the cold, they were eager to begin searching. But first, they needed a break in the weather. Drinking burned coffee, Hopie watched through the iced-up windows as snow pelted their airplanes. Captives of its forced idleness, they paced back and forth between the varnished walls like billiard balls. It was less annoying than sitting, bouncing a leg and going nowhere. Only after dark could the men relax their vigilance. But each minute haunted them as they imagined the cold draining the life from the missing.

The moment the cloud ceiling lifted a few hundred feet, Hopie scraped the snow off his Airacobra and took off, straining his eyes at the whitened woods for anything resembling an airplane, airplane part, the flash of a signal mirror, smoke, human tracks . . . or telltale evidence that they'd become prey. As darkness ended the search each evening, Hopie pretended not to have lost hope. He knew the others probably felt the same way. No one wanted to admit to the futility of the effort and trample waning morale. They spoke little of the predicament, or of anything. After a week of searching, Hopie was ordered to fly on to Fairbanks with the others. The entire search was called off a week later.

The lethal week left a pall of melancholy. But deliveries continued.

———◆———

Hopie was grounded by yet another blizzard on his return. Waiting out the storm at Pine Lake, the small group of pilots chatted.

"On my last transport outta Ladd," a lieutenant said, "I found a blowtorch, lit it, and we took turns keeping our feet warm with it. The inside of that C-47 musta been fifty below."

"Can you believe there are men who hold nothing more than a private pilot license, writing letters to Ferry Command begging to fly this route for us?" a captain asked the group as he walked past, dunking a rolled up piece of jellied bread into a paper cup of coffee.

"Just imagine how many wrecks we'd have if we let those cowboys come up here and fly! Old coots with a few civvie hours in a Piper Cub only on severe clear days?"

"They call themselves pilots. If they could look out these windows now!"

A phone rang in an adjacent room. A buzz of talk shot through the building. The second C-47 out of Watson had been spotted, and a dog team was dispatched to the site. The only clue was a scar in the heavy timber where the aircraft had clipped treetops before crashing in the snow. When the rescue team reached the wreck, they reported that both the pilot and co-pilot were killed on impact. But they discovered that rations had been consumed so they tracked through the new snow. They found the two survivors, near death. After two weeks of not being spotted, they had crawled out in the direction of the airport.

"Can you imagine how pissed off they musta been, hearing all that aircraft flying right over them for two weeks!" Hopie groaned when he heard the news. "A helluva lotta good their signal mirrors and police whistles did them! It got down to thirty-five below every night!" He felt a weight sinking in his heart. He'd let fellow pilots down. "I flew over that site a dozen times. How could I have missed it?" he nearly wailed.

"Drop it," said the captain. "Stop beating yourself up over it. You weren't the only one who didn't see it. Even slowed down to a hundred, stuff goes by awful fast, and besides, the low-wing peashooter is no recon plane."

Of course the officer was right, but Hopie couldn't calm himself. "They stayed in the aircraft for two weeks with those two dead pilots sitting there, staring straight ahead. They knew that was their best chance of being spotted. *Two weeks!* They each had a broken leg, so they put rubber overshoes over their *hands* so they could crawl out on their *bellies*. They made it halfway to Watson before they were picked up *nineteen days after wrecking!*"

He went to get another cup of coffee. He reread the hand-written poem tacked to the wall. It began,

> While Weather Rules the Skies
> 'Tis a frigid winter evening
> In the north country at Ladd
> No workin' no flyin' no nothing,
> Cause the weather is too damn bad.

This time, the silly phrases had become a requiem for those lost. Hopie felt a new emptiness. He wondered why he didn't cry. He solemnly filled his cup and sat among the others' conversations, lost in his own thoughts.

CHAPTER 25

Mitrov's Offer

Gore Field, Great Falls, Montana –
Early March 1943

Dugan watched the flights depart while handing tools to the mechanics. They installed bigger heaters, readjusted valves and re-timed the magnetos but he yearned for more action. He could tell his dream would probably not materialize. Caulking windows and loading freight was a piker's way to fight a war, Dugan thought.

He was working alone one morning, pulling the masking from around the freshly painted red star on a Havoc, feeling envious of the pilots. He really wanted to fly to Alaska. He paused to watch another group of P-39s take off in a sequential roar. He wanted to smash the wad of masking into the trash can and kick it across the shop. Just then, a strange man approached with a pack of cigarettes outstretched in his large hand. He smelled of cologne and had a heavy accent.

"I watch you work. You do good. You dedicate to your work, yes?" the man said, his voice rising at the end.

Dugan dropped the wad into the trash and looked into the man's eyes.

"Sir, we have not met . . . and no thanks for the smokes."

"Colonel Mitrov, Mr. Dugan." He did not extend his hand. "I remain sorry for your passed comrade."

"Mel? He was a good man."

Mitrov stood for a moment then broke the silence. "Do you have family at home that you would like to send extra money to?"

"I don't understand."

He explained that he had a different kind of job for Dugan, managing special cargo.

"That's above my pay grade, sir," Dugan said, walking toward the opposite side of the fuselage. The man followed him.

"We have need of help flying special . . . materials to Ladd Field in Fairbanks."

Dugan turned back to face the stranger. "I'd fly in one of these bombers?" Ignoring his own advice, he added indiscreetly, "I'd do just about anything to get in one of these planes and actually fly somewhere."

"I can arrange that. You would fly to Ladd. Maybe more flying too. But it's important to talk nothing to others." As an afterthought, he added, "Maybe you get to meet Colonel Niki Vasin. He commands our ferry regiment in Fairbanks. A Russian taran hero who earned 'Hero of Soviet Union' medal for ramming a Messerschmitt BF-109 with his old Rata in mid-air!" The man puffed out his sizable chest. "He now has steel teeth to prove his love for Russian motherland!"

That intrigued Dugan.

The Russian spoke just enough English to get his request across. Dugan understood it was a way to send his sister and Patrick some money and show that he'd made something of himself, even if it wasn't in a pressed uniform with stripes on the sleeves.

"You would be doing something good for a friend of your country," the man went on in his heavy accent. "As you know, we Russians need to get rid of Chormans who are attacking our homeland. They kill, burn, steal and our women they rape. But you must understand I have selected you because I can trust you with this important chob."

Dugan looked down as feelings of inadequacy shaded his enthusiasm.

"You hate the Nazi, yes?" Mitrov asked.

"Of course."

"Then this is your way to help your country."

Dugan stopped thinking beyond that. He could fly on a mission that would help Russians kill Germans. It was more important to the war than re-puttying windows and splitting firewood.

"When? And how do I manage it with my superiors here?" Dugan asked impulsively.

"I make arrangements and you will oversee special cargo." It was then he extended his hand to shake. It felt like an oversize sausage but Dugan appreciated this man. He seemed kind and obviously trusted and valued Dugan.

He was eager to act. The seed of Dugan's bigotry had been sown in an alley in Butte and nourished in prison. He couldn't hate a face he knew, so he had turned his hatred toward a faceless enemy he labeled "Germans." He could help his country by helping a friend of his country. And he would fly. He would do his best so they would ask him again. It wasn't dogfighting with Zeros or Messerschmitts, but he could say he played an important part in the Ferrying Command.

It was the solution he needed.

———◆———

Dugan was sweeping the shop area after the mechanics had left. Mitrov appeared again, his small eyes darting side to side to be sure they were alone. He told Dugan that arrangements were made for him to get his flight.

"You come here tonight. Alone. Nine o'clock." There would be crates and locked briefcases for him to load into a Havoc. He would fly at ten in the morning. Someone in Fairbanks would greet him when they landed at Ladd. A man named Alexey Pavlovich would ask about the "Havoc Red" shipment. Only Mr. Pavlovich could accept the cargo and permit him to leave the aircraft. Now Dugan could demonstrate his trustworthiness. Duty was calling now, and he was going to do his best.

"Are you clear, Mr. Dugan?" The man interrupted his thoughts.

"Yes, sir. Only Mr. Pavlovich can remove the cargo."

"One more thing," Mitrov said, with an indulgent smile. "There will be closed letter for you attached inside bomber's place in nose of your airplane. It is for you only. Do not talk of it to anyone."

"I understand." A little thrill shot through him. What would he find inside this "closed letter?" He assumed the man meant "sealed envelope" and visualized it bulging with crisp, new greenbacks.

"And please, my friend, dress warm. It will be cold where you go."

The Russian had said that Dugan needed no tools, but he wasn't specific on how long Dugan would work in Fairbanks. He packed his warmest clothes, mechanic's overalls and all the cash he'd saved. He started looking forward to working in the big Cold Weather Ops shop there. Mel had called it "legendary." He was eager to find out what that meant.

He returned to the hangar that night and met Mitrov. The two dozen pairs of white hickory skis looked legitimate. There were also crates and a half dozen black fake-leather suitcases sealed with red wax with "DIPLOMATIC IMMUNITY" stenciled on them. He noticed tags on the handles with "HAVOC RED" in crabbly-backslanted handwriting. There were also some Cyrillic letters. He puzzled over the colonel's unusual choice of the Havoc. A Skytrain would hold so much more. The Havoc could handle one thousand pounds of bombs, but bombs fit snugly inside the fore and aft bays, not like the crates and briefcases he had to struggle with under Mitrov's fragrant scrutiny. But Mitrov had specifically wanted this Havoc to haul his "special" stuff, because it was so much faster. It really made a difference on the three thousand-mile leg from Fairbanks to Moscow, he'd told Dugan in his broken English.

At ten in the morning, Dugan hauled his bag out to board the Havoc. One of the ground crew was rolling a bulky heater up to it and told Dugan he may as well go back indoors where it was warm. It had gotten down to twenty-eight below in the night. Dugan watched as another A-20 taxied out and took off, solo, northbound.

"We thought you two Havocs were flying out together, but Colonel Mitrov ordered us to warm the other one up fast and get him outta here," the man told Dugan. "These Wrights ain't eager to fire up in the cold, and I tried to explain that to him over and over. I tried to stand my ground." He was obviously shaken from the encounter with the overbearing man. "That pilot wanted to fly up together with you guys, too," he said, nodding toward the vanishing airplane, "and he told the colonel so, but the ol' man was irritated by that idea. Him and the pilot had words, and the ol' Russian really threw him some rhubarb. The pilot wasn't happy about it, but went on ahead and, well, you seen him take off just now." He adjusted the ductwork to blast heat into the first engine. "It's gonna be awhile while we warm up your bird. Your pilot was firm about a complete preheat, but the old crabpatch didn't give a darn over your flight."

Dugan waited in the hangar, busying himself wiping tools and putting them away. Colonel Mitrov was nowhere around. It was like a vacuum after all the hovering he'd done.

At about noon, the mechanic shouted at Dugan that his pilot was ready to start up. He hurried back to the plane. The long hatch was propped open, and a youthful pilot was seated in the cockpit. He looked small up there. Dugan hopped up on the left wing. The pilot was studying the gauges and levers. A neat arc of sandy-colored hair showed beneath his fleece-lined cap.

"Hello," he said absent-mindedly without looking at Dugan, as he glanced between a detailed chart and the compact array of indicators, switches and controls.

"Howdy," Dugan said. He could smell the plane's newness, and a hint of aviation fuel. He didn't want to interfere with the pilot's concentration.

"Bomb bay doors secured?"

"Yes. Affirmative."

"Do you have the 'Form F' on the load for me?"

"Right here, sir." Dugan produced the weight and balance paperwork. "And I'm your passenger."

"Oh! Well, looks like you won't put us over gross." The pilot stopped in the middle of his checklist, turned partway around, extending his hand. Dugan noticed the silver lieutenant bar on his collar through a gap in his heavy coat.

"I'm Stanhope. Lieutenant Daniel Stanhope. Call me 'Hopie.' Forgive me for not standing up."

"I'm Dugan." They shook hands.

"Once you get seated, you have to sort of wear this thing. There's no easy way to get in and out." Hopie gave him a half-way apologetic smile, but his eyes gleamed with anticipation. He didn't explain that this was his first time actually taking the controls of an A-20. His only flight in one had been while laying on his belly on the radio shelf, watching over the pilot's shoulder as he demonstrated a couple of touch-and-goes. Dugan noticed a softcover manual was spread open on Hopie's lap.

"We always use these. We fly so many different planes you know, that they make us use a dope chart."

"I'd like to ride in the bombardier's seat, if that's okay with you. For the view."

"Sure. Settle yourself in up there and strap in then. It'll give you the best sightseeing. It's not built for guest comfort as you can see, but there's a socket for your heated suit. Oh . . . it doesn't look like you're wearing one."

"This was a surprise assignment, and I don't have a heated flight suit," Dugan replied. This pilot was no older than himself. His face wasn't etched with creases of experience like the grizzled pilots of movies and magazines. Still, Dugan was in awe of his vaunted position as pilot in command.

Hopie mentioned that Dugan would find a headset that he could plug into the bomber's interphone jack box. "Be sure the switch is set on 'INT' so you and I can communicate." He crunched his headset over his cap and returned to studying the instruments. Stepping off the wing, Dugan stooped beneath the nose and squirmed into the bomber's seat. He snatched the envelope, just a corner of it visible from where it had been tucked in a cranny beside the switch panel. It had a satisfying bulk to it. He slipped it inside a pocket to open later, and put on his headset. Hopie switched on the radios, and they each tested for sound.

"Sorry about the delay," Hopie said. It took awhile to get her warmed up. Let's see if this bird is as eager to go help Uncle Joe as our CO is to get it to him."

A ground man approached, and waved up to Hopie. "Fuel on, switch off?!" he yelled.

"Fuel on, switch off!" the pilot replied with the canopy still open.

The man pressed his shoulder against a blade of the right-side propeller and rotated it, to the clacks of pushrods and valves.

Dugan heard the fuel pump and saw a cup or so of raw gas spill out of an overflow.

"Clear!" Hopie shouted.

The starter engaged on the engine. Dugan watched the prop turn slowly as puffs of smoke came out the exhaust. He heard a couple of backfires, then with a quick tremor the propeller spun into a transparent disk and the engine came alive with a muffled throbbing through his headset. They turned their attention to the left engine, and after a similar process, both engines were running smoothly.

"I'm gonna do some extra taxiing to round out the tires before we take off. They get flat spots in this cold," Hopie explained. The thump, thump, thump was amplified by the metal fuselage. "Before pilots paid it any mind, it was shaking the gauges loose." Hopie added, his intercom voice interrupted by the jarring.

Take all the time you need, Dugan thought.

The midday sun was bright and had warmed the day to just below zero as Hopie turned the plane onto the runway and pushed the throttles forward.

Dugan loved the feel of the two Wrights revving up, pulling them forward for the takeoff. The runway became a blur beneath him and the aircraft lifted from its shadow with effortless urgency. He felt like he was being shot from a cannon toward a place near heaven. He couldn't stop smiling as he watched all around him through the plexiglass. After a while he pulled the envelope out, slipped it open and counted out twenty-five well-worn ten-dollar bills. They smelled of tobacco and Chiclets gum. There was no note, nothing. Just the cash – plenty to buy a nice car. He slid it back in his pocket feeling the glow of good fortune.

Once the craft was in level flight, Hopie explained a few flying details. Dugan ignored the scratchy sounds that accompanied Hopie's intercom voice. He didn't want the flight to end, even though he was miserably cold. He kept asking questions and said nothing about himself. After all, what could interest this lieutenant about his civilian life, during which his biggest accomplishment was getting released from the state prison?

CHAPTER 26

New Bomber

Hopie was glad not to have to worry about weather as he got more familiar with his new bomber. The cockpit had heated up but his feet were cold. He kept wiggling his toes to be sure he could feel the sensitive rudder pedals. Lethbridge slipped by beneath them in clear skies. He wanted to try some maneuvers.

"Wanna see how much this bird loves to fly?" he asked Dugan.

"Sure!"

Hopie rolled into a tight left turn and revolved completely before leveling again. He was not pleased that he'd lost five hundred feet. He made another turn to the right, this time adding power and back pressure. After porpoising a little, he was able to maintain level fight. "Doin' okay up there?" Motion was more pronounced in the nose and he thought his passenger might be getting woozy.

"Great. The view up here is amazing."

"Roger. Now I'm going show you the stall characteristics." He wanted to sound experienced, although he'd never felt a stall with the control in his hands. He slowed, dropped the flaps and pulled up. It gave plenty of warning, shaking the control wheel before the nose dropped gently. He recovered easily with more power and airspeed. He could see why pilots loved the A-20. But this lovable machine was designed to destroy. Machine guns aimed forward and aft. It shed bombs as effortlessly as a bird molts feathers.

He wondered what it must feel like to release a load of bombs from thousands of feet above the target. Lofting among clouds, so remote from the grimy devastation below, sure is a sterile way to fight a war, he thought. You wouldn't even get your hands dirty while people below grasped their children and dove for safety from falling death and debris.

Since their departure had been delayed, Hopie decided to stay over in Edmonton. Tomorrow would offer plenty more flying, and the probability of weather delays in less desirable places. If ferry pilots were waiting on a repair or overnighting, Hopie knew where they'd go to grab dinner and a beer. They taxied in, Hopie pulled the mixture controls, and with a brief shudder the engines shut down.

Hopie hopped down and went forward to open the bombardier's door latch for Dugan.

"Thank you. My hands are a little cold," Dugan said, struggling to remove his headset.

"I know a good place to eat. We might run into some other pilots there. You must be frozen stiff!"

———

They took a cab to a Chinese restaurant. The hand-lettered sign over the door had faded but an electric sign flashed brightly. Ornate lanterns were visible through the steamy windows. It reminded Dugan of the noodle parlor on Main Street in Butte. He had nothing to run from, but he felt a new surge of freedom on this first venture away from Montana with all that cash in his pocket. They glanced at the grease-stained menus and Dugan eagerly ordered two entrées. He and Hopie pushed aside the fat pot of tea and chipped cups and tried the Canadian beer. Dugan asked Hopie about his flight training.

"I'm from Fresno. I started my training in California then went to San Antonio. They moved me over to Kelly. In an accelerated program. I got 'class-four' certified for twin bombers, gearing up for these lend-lease flights."

Two more pilots entered, waved, and joined them. More beers came, and the hangar talk started, relieving Dugan of the need to steer the conversation away from his own past. Through mouthfuls of noodles, chopped meats and blanched vegetables, the men shared light-hearted insults and anecdotes.

"This route is pretty half-assed," one said. "We almost stayed up at Fort Nelson. Glad we made it down here where there are facilities. Sure beats the tents!"

"And what passes for latrines!" Hopie added, and the others laughed.

"Didja hear that last night at Snag, their thermometer was pegged at eighty below? At that temperature, you can toss water in the air, and it freezes solid before it hits the ground."

"Water? When ya take a leak outside, it'll made a pee-icicle," the other said, making an arc with his arm to barks of laughter.

"Thank God for the new highway, cuz there ain't much other navigation up here."

"It isn't much of a highway," Hopie said, "but once you spot the cut through the woods, at least you've got a better chance if you need to land."

Hopie offered to pay for Dugan's meal and he accepted, figuring it wouldn't arouse any suspicion over the bribe he'd just taken. They all squeezed into one taxi to share the cost of the ride back to the airfield. They found bunks and turned in.

At first, Dugan just felt the pleasant buzz of the beer, the bliss of their beautiful flight and joyful anticipation of more flying the next morning. But in the quiet of the night, twinges of guilt seeped in and he began questioning his latest decision. As much as he'd wanted to fly, he was beginning to wonder if the money was worth it. Their hot cargo, the behavior of the Russian man, his own inexperience, the wad of bribe money – it all added up to goods of more importance than just the standard black market stuff.

———◆———

Laying in the silence, Hopie recalled the camaraderie but felt none of the joy of anticipation about the next day's flight. He lay awake in a pensive mood. The joke about the pee icicle didn't cheer him now. The heavy load of responsibility weighed on him, now that he had a passenger and no escort. Colonel Mitrov had told him that the other Havoc leaving that morning was ready hours before his, and the other pilot insisted on leaving immediately to take advantage of the daylight. It surprised Hopie. Pilots always preferred to go in groups wherever possible for safety. "What could I do but let him go?" Mitrov had said with a histrionic shrug.

He began thinking about the effect extreme cold has on an airplane. Gaskets shrink. Rubber shatters. He recalled the mechanic up at Whitehorse say that at these temperatures, a solid airplane is just a maze of loose parts, or something like it. He imagined Greger's cold B-24, bleeding red fluid in the snow. He thought of the cold weather preparations they'd completed on his new Havoc at Gore. He simply had to trust them. Then there were the navigation problems he'd had on previous flights. The variation between true and magnetic north up here. Your compass needle points to Canada's Prince of Wales Island, when your navigation charts are laid out on true north, thirteen hundred miles away. The flux fields cause quirky magnetic disturbances and the northern lights tease your compass into insanity. The best guides a pilot has are the strip maps, but outside those zones, there's nothing to keep you on course. The low-frequency radio stations are two hundred miles apart. They're hard to pick up in mountainous terrain, and cut out when the weather is poor – when you need them most. The Army hadn't yet retrieved a B-26 that had gone down before reaching Watson Lake, so the pilots used it for a ghoulish landmark. The risks up here don't come from enemy fire – but flying into a mountain is every bit as deadly. It was enough to twist your gut into knots.

———

In the morning the warm-up process was repeated for more promising engine starts. Hopie and Dugan prepared to load back into the cold-soaked airframe.

"The upper gunner's compartment might be warmer. You won't have cold ram air and the engines may throw a little heat at you up there."

"I won't argue, Hopie."

"In the event I become incapacitated," Hopie added, "you can take the gunner's controls and land us, 'without calamity' as the Brits say."

"I feel sorry for the ground guys, having to pull the props through this morning," Dugan said.

"Ditto," was all Hopie said. He helped secure the door behind Dugan, hopped onto the wing and climbed into the cockpit. A ground person approached, an unrecognizable form hunched in layers of clothing.

Dugan slipped up into the gunner's seat, and with a thrill noticed the M-2 fifty-caliber machine gun stowed neatly in its compartment. A thirty-caliber gun was stowed below, as well as a control stick. He placed his feet on the rudder pedals, and imagined himself flying.

Both engines reluctantly started, and the Havoc lifted off into the frigid air over Edmonton. Dugan looked back and watched as they kicked up a swirl of sparkling ice crystals. Riding in the upper waist canopy was like being drawn through the sky behind a team of power-ful horses.

Hopie wasn't as conversational as yesterday. He announced when they entered British Columbia and Dugan noticed the landscape turn from gentle to jagged, an empty and desolate splendor. As far as he could see, forests spread up the mountains. Distance paled them to an unearthly blue. Dugan imagined dozens of recumbent giants with gro-tesque silhouettes. A random nubile breast emerged among the profiles. The gargoyle horizons changed shape and darkened as they flew over them. Dugan had never seen so many shades of blue.

Hopie announced they'd entered Yukon Territory as they crossed the frozen Liard River again. They landed at Watson Lake because the weather was closing in to the northwest. As the plane turned on its approach to land, Dugan realized clouds had swallowed the view in their direction of flight.

He hopped out onto the snow, ignoring the pain of chilblains in his feet. He looked around and saw nothing but snow-covered terrain. "Hopie, where's the 'lake' part of Watson Lake?"

"Right alongside this runway," the pilot replied, gesturing toward the expanse streaked with tufts of snow fingering the prevailing surface winds. "At this temperature, a loaded bomber could probably land on the lake. This ice is probably stronger than some of the runways we've used."

A ground crewman approached and Hopie ordered him to top it off. The Havoc had a twelve-hundred-mile range, but he did not want to have to worry about fuel in case he had to divert around weather.

"So, where are we exactly?" Dugan asked.

"Well, here's one way to look at it," Hopie replied, pointing to the signpost that some homesick GI had erected.

Dugan read the hand-painted mileages aloud. "Chicago, two thousand, seven hundred. New York, three thousand, six hundred. Tokyo, four thousand. Man! Standing here, we are nearly as close to the Japs' capital as we are to New York City!"

"When you're midway from everywhere, you're farthest away from everywhere else," Hopie said in a wry tone. "Let's get the hell indoors and get some hot coffee and dinner."

Dinner was merely functional, with none of the beery camaraderie they'd enjoyed the night before.

"I'm gonna do some reading," Hopie told Dugan. "Can you find us a tent with a stove and get it warmed up? Then you'll probably want to come back in here where it's warm."

Hopie wanted time alone to review his A-20 manual. He reflected on the day's flight. When he'd looked out, he saw stark terrain, with thin assurance from the narrow slice of road through dense stands of spruce. He'd spotted a few deceptively open patches where drifted snow blanketed the knobbly ground underneath, rough enough to mangle a forced landing. You could try to land between spruce trees, letting them slow your forward motion as your wings broke through them, but the damn pecker poles were so dense you'd probably get skewered. There you'd be, between two ruptured tanks full of high octane gasoline. The frozen lakes were the only reliable clearings and you might find one large enough to land on safely . . . if the ice held. No wonder the Army made each man sign a will.

He was glad they'd made it all the way to Watson, considering how fast the weather changed on them. No doubt the earlier Havoc had made it through in good weather. He was annoyed all over again about losing his flying companion. At least Watson had a minimal crew to help fuel and warm his engines back up in the morning. There were a couple of mechanics here. One in particular was a withdrawn fellow who said little to anyone – probably just too serious about his job to be chummy, Hopie decided.

He kept wishing sleep would come once the clattering diesel generator finally silenced, but he lay awake. He envied the ground guys – entrenched under roofs and between walls of security while the pilots hurtled aloft into the changing moods of sub-arctic wind and ice. The rhythmic white-white-green light of the rotating beacon flashed steadily on the tent wall through the night, reminding him of the responsibility he faced in the morning. He envied its imperturbable heartbeat.

A record-breaking nighttime temperature was settling on Watson Lake. And it would be critical that Hopie's oil cooler flaps functioned properly for the men to continue their flight safely. As Hopie tossed and turned on his cot, the taciturn mechanic received an order to make a linkage adjustment to Havoc Red before he turned in for the night. An order that paid off in worn ten-dollar bills – plenty to buy a nice car.

CHAPTER 27

Final Leg

It's the cussedest land that I know,
From the big, dizzy mountains that screen it
To the deep, deathlike valleys below.
— ROBERT SERVICE, THE SPELL OF THE YUKON

Hopie saw no reason to rise early, since they wouldn't take off until the mechanic had preheated the aircraft. He and Dugan delayed emerging from their warmish sleeping bags into the frigid tent air as long as possible.

"This is colder than I've ever seen in Butte," Dugan muttered, "and it's a mile high."

They wiggled into their pants and coats while lying in their sleeping bags. Dugan muffled his laugh at Hopie's thrashing and cursing. The bitter air stung their noses and nearly choked them on their way to the mess shack, even though they'd covered their mouths. Hopie was astounded that anyone or anything could function in temperatures like this. They had breakfast and a couple of leisurely cups of sweetened coffee before heading to the plane.

Their takeoff was energetic in the dense air. Hopie had to watch his manifold pressure gauges to be sure he didn't over-boost the engines. Ice crystals swirled off the wings in the weak sunlight as they climbed to cruise altitude. Hopie closed the oil cooler covers. The levers seemed to move very easily in spite of the cold. He had no time to give it any thought. His side windows had already iced up and ice was building up

162

inside the windshield. He grabbed the can of lighter fluid he'd tucked in the map pouch, and squirted some right in front of his line of sight and scraped a hole large enough to see through.

There was a solid low overcast, so Hopie decided to climb higher, taking a chance that the cloud layer wasn't very deep and that he'd get above it quickly. He flew on instruments but kept scraping a hole to see through. He hoped there would be enough cabin heat soon to stop the accumulation of windshield ice and to keep his instruments from freezing.

At about six thousand feet, he broke out above the cloud layer. The outside air temperature showed fifty below zero. Through the open patch in his windshield he spotted higher mountaintops emerging above the blanket of cloud, revealing landmarks he'd used on previous flights. He decided to climb another thousand feet. They were about forty miles out of Watson Lake when he noticed the oil pressure on his right engine was nearing its redline mark of 90 psi. But the temperature was low, not yet reaching its green arc. That didn't make sense. He tapped the glass face of the temperature gauge, thinking it was at fault. Then he tapped the pressure gauge. Within a minute, the temperature needle rose steadily, and redlined at 185°. He scraped enough of a hole to look out at the engine. Slugs of oil lumped along the cowling. The engine began to miss and vibrate. Hopie snapped into emergency engine-out procedure. He turned the aux fuel pump on and tried carb heat. It made no difference. The engine shuddered violently and clunked to a stop. He feathered the windmilling prop to reduce drag.

The damned cold probably caused an oil line to rupture. He decided to turn back and land at Watson, ignoring that the cold was making identical demands on his remaining engine. He heard Dugan ask something in his headset, but stayed fixed on his engine instruments.

He felt a sharp thump in his chest as he saw the same bad news on the gauges of his left engine. Both engines had blown all their lubrication. His second engine was tearing itself apart. He feathered the second dead propeller. Now he faced a blind approach in mountainous terrain with a passenger in a ten-ton tin glider. They immediately began to sink through the clouds. He started wishing things were different but realized it was wasting valuable seconds. To keep his bad situation from becoming worse, he needed to concentrate on his instruments and hold a steady heading as his altimeter steadily unwound toward whatever lay below. They were full of fuel, but at least there were no bombs to worry about.

It seemed an eternity until they broke out beneath the clouds. There was rising terrain ahead. Holding this course meant certain impact with the face of a mountain. He scanned the area the best he could through the iced window for the least-deadly place to land. He didn't have time to ask Dugan to help look. Ahead and to his left, he spotted an open patch in the timber.

Hopie's intense concentration forced all sounds out of his head. It was as if he were flying in an airless pocket of suspense. He barely perceived the rumble of 150-mile-per-hour air rushing past him and his dead engines. In a bubble of silence he functioned like an automaton. He pulled on full flaps and slowed to one hundred and fifteen miles per hour, hovering just above the stall. He shut off the fuel supply and pumped the gear down – a sacrifice to absorb some of their forward energy. He knew his plane wouldn't need landing gear any more. He began a gentle turn to the left, aiming for the most open area. He needed to slow as much as possible yet maintain control. Trees, snow and rocks the size of trucks rushed beneath faster and faster as he got closer to the ground. He tried to steer between trees. The left wing dipped and the left main gear struck something. A tree caught the left wing and thrust the craft into an outcrop, abruptly stopping them. Even the sickening crunch of metal on rock didn't register in his mind before the young pilot was knocked unconscious.

PART III

CHAPTER 28

Confessions

It was quiet except for the ringing in his ears. Dugan sat, stunned, as clouds of loose snow settled around the wreck. The strong smell of gasoline brought him out of his stupor. They were sitting between nearly four hundred gallons of leaking high octane gas. He yanked his heavy mittens off and grabbed at the clasps on his safety harness.

"Hopie! Get out before she blows!" His voice banged within the plexiglass.

Dugan kicked the lower door open. His arms bumped through the sides of the opening as he dropped into snow up to his thighs. The plane rested at a cockeyed angle, its left gear collapsed, its tail in the air. He scrambled onto the contorted left wing and forced the canopy open from its jammed position.

Hopie was silent, his arms inert. His eyes opened slowly. He rolled his head from side to side and finally focused on Dugan.

The rock outcrop, scraped naked by the aircraft, protruded into Hopie's deformed cockpit.

Dugan struggled to release Hopie's harness with the pilot's slack body lying against it. He was seriously banged up. He vomited, barely managing to keep from choking. As moments passed, Dugan understood the risk of explosion or fire wasn't likely. He decided to leave Hopie where he was.

He was too concerned about the pilot to care about the crates and black briefcases that lay jumbled behind him. Dugan began to comprehend his predicament. He wanted Hopie rescued, but did not want to be discovered until he somehow got rid of the suitcases. A wave of panic overcame him. The Russians would punish him severely for his incomplete mission; the Americans would punish him for his attempted mission. He'd never had to take this kind of control. He was as unprepared as a child.

After several incoherent mumblings, Hopie began to comprehend the wreck.

Dugan wiggled out of his seat parachute. Thoughts of survival were now foremost in his mind. He ransacked some of the cargo for combustibles to make a fire. Planning a run from oncoming doom would have to wait. He cleared out a small area a safe distance from the damaged, leaking wing and cleared a place for a fire. He'd endured cold winds off the Rocky Mountain front while working outdoors in Great Falls, but this challenged his body and his state of mind. Everything was an effort in the stinging cold. He could only remove his mittens for a few seconds at a time. Even his teeth ached. He wrangled some skis from the cargo and one of the canvas wing covers stowed in the aircraft. He rigged it over the propped canopy to form a shelter. Hydraulic fluid leaked from a severed line in the wing. With his knife, he cut some aluminum skin, bending it into a vessel to capture some. It would help keep the fire going in the snow. Cutting a chunk of aircraft skin was very risky, as his fingers were so numb he couldn't trust the accuracy of his knife blade. It was like watching someone else's hands trying to work. Clumsily he finished. The fire was ready to light.

He stood back and struck a match and with a soft whoosh, the flame triggered a vivid memory. There was no time to ruminate on the past. He hurried to line up more skis for fire fuel and added them judiciously, not knowing how long they would last. He dug around and found loose stones and placed them in the fire. When the stones were hot he placed them inside the cockpit to keep Hopie warm. He spotted the canister of lighter fluid that had wedged against the windscreen. It would come in handy later. He sliced more aluminum skin and bent it into a shape for melting snow to drink. He recovered Hopie's thermos where it had wedged beside the pilot's seat. He knew liquid was important for survival, and warm liquid would help Hopie. He wanted to cry. For the first time in his life, he was driven to sacrifice for another.

Over the next hours, Hopie was lucid and talked. Dugan realized he was hurt badly. Moving him would surely cause worse injury. Dugan situated his parachute pack on the rock so he could sit close enough to reach inside the cockpit.

Hopie told Dugan how to work the radio, and how SOS messages were to be transmitted at fifteen and forty-five minutes past the hour. Their watches were broken and useless. Dugan got the coffee grinder radio tuned to the emergency frequency and sent a few SOS's into the empty air. He feared his signals just ricocheted between the boulders. It would take at least a day for anyone to find them – if they were lucky enough to get spotted. In that time, he could tend to Hopie, and disappear. The powdery snow would cover his tracks. Losing his trail would reinforce the story beginning to take shape in his mind.

Sympathy overwhelmed him and Dugan talked too much. He admitted to his friend that he'd been chosen to carry serious contraband. It all added up: the Russian, the need for secrecy, the dirty cash. He spilled the entire secret to Hopie.

Hopie panicked. "My father was a decorated war hero! My widowed mother expects no less of me!"

Dugan wished to hell he hadn't said anything.

"As if this route wasn't risky enough, you had to add treason, too?"

"Please calm yourself," Dugan pleaded.

"Discovery means dishonor to my family name!" He ranted, nearly hysterical. "You son of a bitch! You've ruined my reputation!"

He quieted, and Dugan made him eat a candy bar from his emergency rations. Hopie calmed down, and seemed to rest.

Dugan periodically left Hopie to tend the fire, refill the thermos and exchange cold rocks for hot ones. Darkness overcame them. In spite of the lung-stunning cold, Dugan found peace in the dark. Drinking warm water kept the cold from penetrating their bodies, although their breath had frozen inside their noses.

Hopie began to talk again. "My little brother . . . Luke . . . "

"Rest, man," Dugan begged him. "Store up your strength for when they come to get us. You'll be hiking outta here tomorrow."

Hopie spoke again, determined to continue his story. "I let him die. The river was high. Too high. Luke wanted to fish. It was a stupid idea, and I should have said 'no.' It was May. The water was cold and high, and he slipped on some pine needles and fell in." Hopie paused.

"It's okay man, just rest now. It's okay."

"I started to go in after him, but the water was cold . . . dirty . . . brown. I closed my eyes against the cold water . . . I . . ."

Dugan remained silent.

"I lost sight of him. I saved myself but I lost him. I could have saved him if I'd kept my eyes open in the water. But I was scared and closed my eyes and saved myself . . . Luke was gone . . . so cold . . ." He drifted back into silence, his breath forming ice crystals around his mouth.

In the weak light of the fire, Dugan saw that his lips were a sickly blue color. Dugan held Hopie's mittened hand in his, wishing he could embrace Hopie's head and shoulder.

Hopie rallied again. "You don't understand. Luke wasn't normal. He embarrassed me cuz he was . . . *retarded*. People stared at him and I hated taking him places. I hated being out together."

"It's okay," Dugan repeated.

"But when he fell in that water, I *wanted* to save him. I *really* wanted to. I know my parents doubted me . . . at least my father."

He was silent for a few moments. Dugan could hear him breathing hard.

"Now I'm going to die a traitor! *A killer and a traitor!*"

Hopie's self-condemnation shocked Dugan. He was helpless to console him.

"I'm caught flying bad stuff out of my country. I can't let my mother know this! I can't let Beverly know this. She – they – will hate me! Father! Luke! Forgive me!"

"Please calm yourself," Dugan pleaded again.

Hopie's head slumped to his chest. He was quiet long enough to catch his breath.

"And we were going to get married when I went on leave." His words were barely audible. The hysteria was out of his voice, but the pilot was inconsolable until exhaustion overtook him again.

As Dugan lay wakeful in the eerie quiet, his thoughts returned to his dilemma. How do I erase Hopie's identity without destroying his worth?

Hopie passed urine. Dugan knew it would freeze and suck more heat from his helpless body. He rallied just long enough to croak out, "now I'll die a killer and a traitor. Worse than Cain and Herbert Haupt."

CHAPTER 29

Redemption Plan

"**D**aniel, you're not going to die!"
They both knew it was a lie.

"You're not going to die a *traitor*," Dugan added, forcing more conviction into his voice. He was grateful for the dark. It was easier for him to talk, not seeing Hopie's blank but living face. He was the one censoring communication now. He imagined black lines through a script. There are things I won't tell Hopie for his own good, he thought. Call it lying, he didn't care, if it gave Hopie some comfort. It was no use trying to bolster Hopie's ideas about surviving. He was losing that battle. "Listen to me, Hopie. You'll die a hero."

"Bullshit!" Hopie rasped. "I'm a traitor!"

"Listen, Lieutenant Stanhope! You had your orders. You carried them out. You are not a traitor. You will walk out of here in hopes of rescue. You will be the hero."

"I'm a goddamned doomed traitor!" Hopie could only force a hollow whisper. "I'm trapped in this tin coffin and there's nothing you can do about it." After a pause, he forced a few more words out. "Start a goddamned fire. They'll think the crash caused it. Soak everything with fuel and light it."

"Listen to me. This is what's gonna happen. I'm gonna help you into civvie clothes."

Dugan could hardly stop the sob rising from his chest, but he went on. "When your body is discovered, they will think it's the traitor's. Mine. Me, Dugan, I'm a nobody. Nobody will miss Dugan.

Lieutenant Daniel Stanhope is the one who's gonna walk outta here." He held Hopie's useless hand while talking calmly now, but with all the authority he could muster. He'd made so many wrong decisions, that he was sure this one was right. He promised Hopie that he would find his mother and tell her that Daniel was the hero. He'd tell Beverly, too, all the time wishing it were he, Dugan in the hopeless spot.

Hopie rasped out something unintelligible.

Still holding Hopie's hand, choking back the catch in his voice, Dugan continued talking. He sensed that it soothed Hopie.

"My life changed that night in Butte . . ." He'd said nothing about it to anyone since the trial, but his feelings blew the top off his bottled-up story and he went on. "I was only tryin' to make a little ruckus near the back of the building so nobody would notice the guys jimmying the front door and swiping a little beer. We didn't mean no serious harm. Well, I started a little trash fire. But the old building caught fire, fast. The other boys scattered. When I heard the old man inside that building, I busted inside to get him out. But the fire was too hot. We thought the store was empty. The old fellah did books at night. He was in a wheelchair. Got his legs hurt in the last war. He never made it out. He couldn't cuz the Germans blew his legs off. Germans! Blast them all to hell!" He took a drink of water and made Hopie drink some.

"I thought my eyeballs would explode in the heat. I couldn't breathe, so I panicked and ran back out without him. Right into the law standin' there. Lucky for me, a witness came to gawk. Saw me go in. The little cowards ran. I wouldn't squeal on 'em, even though the law woulda gone easier on me. Some folks saw the bastards running away, but all they needed was one scapegoat. I was it.

"They gave me a charity lawyer. Even though he hated what happened, he done his best. I got ten years for arson and negligent homicide. Got a little credit for tryin' to go in and save him. That man in there burning to death haunts me more than I can say – every day of my life. Here Hopie, have more water before it gets cold."

Dugan checked the fire and came back. "Maybe get out in five years for 'good behavior.' Now isn't that funny? Good behavior when the big inmates are ganging up on you, and will kill you or cut your balls off if you tattle on 'em. Good behavior means different things to different folks. But survival means the same to us all.

"Arson. So in the pen I got nick-named 'Arse.' " He slammed his fist against a panel of the aircraft, making a hollow metallic bang. Hopie gave a little start.

"Hopie, please try to swallow some more water. Got put in Deer Lodge. Three years go by, then the war come. We wrote that letter. We offered to enlist if they'd let us out. I was hoping it would be a way to pay back. Better'n rotting in prison."

Hopie's breathing was labored. He gave Dugan's hand a weak squeeze. "Tell my mother Laura . . . and Beverly. I didn't know. You gotta tell them I didn't know about the stuff . . . Laura Stanhope . . . Fresno." There was a rattling sound in his throat, and then all sound stopped.

Dugan sat, absorbing the bizarre peace. He felt a soft gust of wind pass through the broken canopy. It was a signal. He must begin to act on his plan.

———◆———

With a dead body sitting there, a body that was broken and had messed itself, he was repulsed by his insane idea. Did he really have to follow through with his idiotic plan, now that Hopie was dead?

Dugan had a choice.

He could just find his way out at first light. He probably could make his way to a trapper's sled trail in a day or two. If he didn't make it, at least this ordeal would be over. He'd heard pilots speculate that freezing to death, you just sort of go to sleep and the cold didn't bother you any more. That wouldn't be so bad, and at least this nightmare would end. No one would miss him, except maybe Patrick. Probably not Margaret. She knew he'd made it to Great Falls and was working with the military there. She wasn't interested in war news, and probably wouldn't understand even if there was talk of what he'd done.

But he had promised that the innocent pilot would not be dishonored.

He brought more fire-warmed stones in to keep the body and clothes from freezing stiff. The next thirty minutes would be the most challenging of his life. He had to carry out the plan completely. There was no half way.

It was difficult in the dark, but he found his small satchel of travel clothing and tossed it near the fire. He began the ghastly task of extricating the inert body from the jumble of confounding metal and the rigid control wheel. He hauled it out and laid it beneath the shelter near the fire. He removed Hopie's outer clothing, somehow suppressing his revulsion. He clumsily managed to get his own spare coat on it. He started to put Hopie's outerwear on himself for extra warmth, then decided against it. He wanted no identifying clues. He groped inside Daniel's shirt for his dog tag, recoiling at the touch of his cold flesh. He removed it and praised himself for thinking of it now, not later. He started to rip the name patch off Daniel's jacket to take to Laura, but thought of a better use for it, intact. He removed Daniel's prized silver wings pin and slipped it into his own pocket.

Done. Now, if anyone came upon this horrid mess, they'd discover a civilian spy, of no consequence to the Stanhope name.

What if they recognized his face? His teeth? My plan has a problem, and Hopie's family honor hangs in the balance, Dugan realized. A new panic hit him. He had to conquer it to survive. He paused, placed both mittened hands over his face, trying to erase the last hours. "Oh God, what new horrors and lies are in store for me?" he shouted into the black silence. "I want to go back to the beginning and shed this burden!" A hunk of snow fell onto the fuselage, sounding like the condemning rap of a gavel.

What about the cargo? Burning it would just create more suspicion. If the Russians reached the wreck first wouldn't he be in worse trouble for knowing what they were shipping and attempting to destroy it? If the Army reached it first, it would be better if they discovered the Russian's treachery, intact. It would be best to be ignorant of the contents. Leaving the evidence alone seemed to be the lesser of the evils. The decision relieved him of another arsonous act. He just wanted to grab some survival gear and get away as fast and as far as possible. He fought off a suicidal urge to flee right then, in the dark.

When searchers discovered that provisions were taken, it would support his ruse that the good pilot attempted to walk out and was swallowed by the cold. For Hopie's reputation to remain intact, the Lieutenant must simply disappear in the wilds. His mangled body would go the route of an unknown civilian casualty of war. It was not what the upstanding, earnest pilot deserved. Dugan had again ruined an innocent man in a devious plot. And he could not reveal the truth to anyone else without exposing his own treachery.

Before he struck out in the morning, something more had to be done.

CHAPTER 30

Desperate Act

The winter! The brightness that blinds you,
The white land locked tight as a drum,
The cold fear that follows and finds you,
The silence that bludgeons you dumb.
— ROBERT SERVICE, *THE SPELL OF THE YUKON*

He didn't sleep in the nightmarish hours before light. The cold was small discomfort compared to the pounding guilt and regret that roiled his conscience all night. He kept imagining Colonel Mitrov facing him, his expression halfway between a smile and scorn. Dugan was nauseous with shame and fear. He prayed for strength and forgiveness. In his disturbed rest he had decided to commit the last act in the waning shroud of benevolent darkness just before setting out. An act that revolted him through like he was being skinned like a live rabbit.

The sound of the .45 shot going off next to the fuselage was deafening. Dugan had steeled himself for this, his most depraved act. He felt blessed that he couldn't see the result. In the gathering light he picked up Hopie's musette and coat, and from atop the wing he heaved them as hard as he could. He grabbed what he thought would be of use – a sleeping bag, candy bars, the remaining skis for firewood and the .45. He climbed out of the fuselage for the last time, shouldered his pack and staggered in the opposite direction, taking the germ of many nightmares to come.

He punched through crusted snow to uneven ground beneath. From a distance, he looked back at the wreck. He thought of his decision, the bad luck of the engine failures, and his friend's effort to land the dead airplane safely. There it lay, ruined with a good man lying frozen and nearly decapitated alongside. Now Dugan had to forge ahead, yoked to a series of deceits.

The farther he got from the wreck, the saner he felt. His fate relied on his determination and luck. He would either die of the cold, or stumble on a trail leading to help. He'd heard of it happening to downed pilots. The fate of Hopie's body was split into two possibilities as well. It might never be found; or would be discovered beyond recognition. Because of the clothing, it would be documented as the civilian passenger with no known kin. Either way, Lieutenant Stanhope would be assumed missing and the damning mark of conspiracy would not darken his record.

Dugan convinced himself that he didn't care anymore. He was going to disappear. This wild place was going to swallow Frank Dugan, dead or alive. If he survived, it would spit him out with a changed identity. He headed downhill. He had to make the most of the short daylight hours. A light snow had begun to fall, his only good fortune. It would cover his tracks out of there.

He weltered on, wondering if his civilian status would create an entry on a form somewhere. He had no record of kin because of his name change. No doubt his Russian connection would want to know exactly what happened. And no doubt the Army Air Forces would come in earnest to rescue their pilot. Even the State of Montana would hunt him down, for busting the conditions of his parole.

His face burned with the cold. Wearing the skis would be useless in this palsa terrain. He cursed the sedan-size humps ringed with moats of drifted snow.

He heard a plane. The cold air amplified the sound so it was hard to tell how far off it was. It seemed low enough to be reconnaissance for the wreck but it flew on without circling for a position fix.

Hopie should have lived out a stellar career with the Seventh Ferrying Group. He was conscientious and loved flying. Now his misidentified body was doomed to a dishonored grave in some god-forsaken graveyard; his Army service record would hover forever in the shadow of "missing in action." An official car would pull up in front of a star-crossed Fresno home. A mother and an unfulfilled young woman would hear the tragic news, unleashing tears and hand-wringing with no end.

He decided not to speculate any more. He fixed his mind on the need to find Mrs. Stanhope in Fresno. And young Beverly, alone now.

He'd lost all sensation in his feet. They were only responding to a primal order to maintain a slow cadence. He lifted one leaden foot and levered it in front of the other with a swing of his upper leg. Beneath plates of ice, water sluggishly secreted downgrade. He stayed in thickets of dense willows, choosing their snapping brittleness, over the chance of punching through a glazed pool of water. A dunking would end his life within the time of a gasp or two. In the spruce and aspen groves the timber was so dense, he had to sidle shoulder-first. He fought his way over shin-tangling downfall. Black spruces had the telling white stripe of the north wind, but it didn't tell the way to the nearest help. He spotted frantic hare tracks. He was hungry.

His mind wandered. He tried to hold an image of Beverly in front of him, to replace the hopeless face of the dying man. The old iron-barred door of his prison cell appeared. It rolled open silently. The arched portal in the outer prison wall was so far in the distance, it was just a slit of yellow light in the gray stone. The only way to gain his freedom was to keep walking toward it, one labored step at a time. It was crucial to get as far from the wreck as possible before summoning help, even if the cold took a costly toll on his body for the passage. He'd already sacrificed his extremities in order to keep enough blood in his brain and vital organs to stay alive. His cognition would be the next to drain to uselessness. He'd drift into everlasting sleep.

He made way until dusk. Once, a fire condemned him. Now it was the only thing that could save him.

———

The cold needled his body where it contacted the ground. He had to turn often, creating a bed of ice. He forced each cold-cramped limb out of his fetal position to add firewood during the night. As if the spirits were taunting him, the northern lights shimmered above the horizon with a surreal glow. Green and pink shafts wavered upward like satin in a slow breeze. In his torpor, shivering between sky and ice, he was sure he'd piqued the ire of departed souls and they were foretelling cosmic punishment. He heard discordant tones, changing keys as the light intensified. Make them stop! Would a catharsis make it stop so he could get some rest? He began babbling confessions to the sky. How far back in his past must he go to purge his bad acts?

He woke to the sound of a wolf howl. He waited in the silence – but it had been his own voice, his soul wailing for peace. Where heroism should have been, all Dugan could feel was shame. He was nothing but a worthless stiff now. Why go on? Then his sluggish mind recalled the promise. He allowed himself to sweeten it with hopes that he'd gain Beverly's approval. That the pretty girl would restore his dignity.

He arose in frigid light and continued through the ice crystals that hung in the wan air. The clouds thinned and sun broke out but there was no warmth in it. He was glad it had held off until today. He regretted not packing the snow goggles he'd seen among Hopie's things. He couldn't keep his eyes open for more than a second or all he could see was a starburst of white light even when he closed his eyes. He pulled his knit cap down to shade the low sunlight, but the snow reflected blinding light upward into his face. Cramping his eyes nearly shut, he stumbled among hidden deadfall searching for some hint of a trail. He wanted badly to lie down and drift into mindless sleep, from which he knew he would never wake. He cursed out loud that he didn't care anymore, but his legs kept mechanically driving him on. He'd had no sensation in his feet or fingers since . . . he couldn't recall. Now he was a prisoner of gravity, his every step weighted with invisible leg irons. Each step drained a little more strength, reason and life out of him. His body hauled itself onward like a dead carcass.

He spotted a tree that had been blazed by an axe. A shard of hope pierced his sense of doom – the first positive thought since before Hopie's engine trouble. God a'mighty! That was long ago! He staggered to the crude cipher marking a trail. Now which way? Reason was freezing inside his skull like a jug of water left out overnight. He started down the narrow trail. The packed snow made walking easier but ice tricked him at random by sending one foot or the other akimbo, nearly flipping him. The Natives had a name for this kind of snow, too. Dugan called it obscenities every time he lost footing. But was he heading *toward* salvation? Dugan was certain there was now a roof over him – he felt warmth as the roof lowered and enclosed him. The crisp sound of his footsteps faded out, the wind hushed in the trees, and the ice crystals sparkled, suspended in place. The darkness and warmth soothed . . . he realized he was lying down. He resisted the urge to take off his boots. He tried to open his eyes against the overbright snow. The light pierced him blind. He squeezed his eyes shut but his brain was branded with the image of the spruce-peaked horizon. In the distance he thought he heard voices. He recognized the hymn they were singing. He was too weak to join in so he just listened to the chorus he imagined radiating from old St. Mary's:

> *God be merciful to me,*
> *On Thy grace I rest my plea;*
> *Plenteous in compassion Thou,*
> *Blot out my transgressions now . . .*

The voices faded to silence. Snowblind and stupefied with the cold, he knew he had to muster one last effort. He struggled through his outerwear for the .45 and using both cramped, quaking hands, managed to fire it three times. If this didn't raise someone, he'd yield his corpse to the beyond, a frozen monument to failure.

There was no way he could go on alone.

A trapper heard the shots and headed up the trail with a dog sled. He whoa'd the dogs to a jerky stop and hushed their maniacal barking at the inert body. Dugan heard the racket, but was blind to the man's shock at seeing his desperate condition. The man helped Dugan onto the sled. Dugan tried to form words but once in the air, all meaning was lost – it was hypothermia talking.

"Save yer labors, sonny," the man said. Between "gee" and "haw" commands to his dogs, he told Dugan they weren't far from his cabin, but the frozen rider lapsed back into semi-consciousness.

The joyous yawping of dogs and the heavenly smell of wood smoke stirred him awake again as they arrived at the trapper's place. The man helped Dugan inside, lit a coal oil lamp, stoked the cast iron stove and heated a cup of brandy for him along with thinned caribou stew. While he helped Dugan out of his frozen outerwear, he located the pistol sagging in Dugan's coat pocket and quietly set it out of sight. He gently dipped Dugan's frostbitten fingers and toes in a basin of warm water. The men exchanged only necessary words as Dugan endured the pain. The trapper laid out wool blankets and a fur cover, loaded up the stove again and returned to his trapline. Dugan lay back and looked around the place in the dim lamplight. It was barely a cabin – more of a cache squatting on the ground. The windowless walls were unplaned planks lined with gobs of oakum, but to Dugan they were as fine as the pearly walls of Heaven. It smelled of an unwashed man, wet wools and the rank of skinned fur-bearers. A fleshing knife, honing stone and a block of wax shared the bench where canned foods were opened. Skinning gambrels, traps and dog harness hung on nails. There was a wash boiler, probably as useful for bathing as for cleaning traps.

Dugan dozed, too spent to even conjure dreams. As he recovered his cognition, the balm of safety and warmth between the wools and furs gave way to a sense of exposure. The nightmare awoke with him. Heaven knew what he'd done; that he'd cracked the vault of spectral revenge. So far, it was taking the carnal form of excruciating chilblains and an endless loop of horrible images in his mind. He'd have sold whatever was left of his soul to be rid of the pain and memories.

He rose and rekindled the fire which had almost burned out. He felt pursued. Carrion beneath gathering vultures. He needed to get out without explanation. A stranger lying along a trail would be puzzling, but he hoped the code of the territory meant that folks didn't ask questions or do a lot of blabbing. He'd never have the dexterity to run a trapline and intrude on the trapper. And this was no place for an idler.

Dugan needed medical attention first. With only the possessions he had on him, he'd need to be clever. Then he'd find some way to strike out for someplace he could begin a new life and finish his obligation to Hopie. A person could get lost and find themself again in this big Canada country. He'd head toward the states without getting too close for the time being. While he waited for the trapper to return, he took five ten-dollar bills out of his envelope and slipped them under a can of corn where the man would find them after Dugan left. But then he decided against leaving the tainted bills. They could be a clue if someone came looking for him.

He was awakened by the shrill of dogs. The trapper entered, his drooping red mustache caked with beads of frost. He displayed a glass bottle of White's Cough Syrup that had frozen solid. "This here means it's under forty below! Good to see yer in color ag'in," he said cheerfully, hanging his beaver hat on a nail. "You weren't makin' much sense so I stoked the fire and let you sleep it off."

Dugan wondered what he may have said to condemn himself.

"I'm Morgan. Robbie Morgan. What's yer name, son?"

Dugan noticed a tobacco can on a high shelf. "Albert D-Doyle. I don't know how I can thank you for all you've done. I'd like to get help as soon as I can, sir. You can see I'm in a bad way. I'll find work as soon as I get healed up. Maybe in the farm country." He added that at present, he had no way to repay the trapper for his kindness.

Morgan waved off the comment. "Up here, a person has friends he don't know until he's in need. I've no want o' knowin' why a Cheechako wandered across m' path. Just return the kindness to someone else in strife." He retrieved the gun and handed it to Dugan. He refused it.

"Please keep that for yourself, sir. You have more use for it than I will. Where I'm going the only critters I expect to see will be cows."

CHAPTER 31

A Wreck of Special Interest

"Sounds like our flight detachment is in line to receive the dodo bird trophy this month," the colonel vented, his shoulders stooped in defeat toward the phone. He rang up the Arctic Air Rescue Group.

The Alaska Wing was getting too familiar with the hazards of the ALSIB route. They were overworked, spreading their thin search and rescue crew even thinner. But when Hopie's Havoc failed to land in Fairbanks, it was more than just another downed pilot to worry about. There was special motivation to get to this wreck as soon as possible.

"Get a crew out there at the first crack in the weather and find that plane!" he barked through the line. "Save our pilot if you can, and bring in anyone else involved in the flight."

"Anything special?" the major in charge of the search asked.

"Not yet . . . but make arrangements to retrieve all the cargo for close inspection."

"Yes sir."

"Could be a big fish on the line. Russian Bear bait. But keep it quiet for now."

"Yes sir."

Hopkins was sweating some of the promises he'd made. His brazen Russian collaborators were ratcheting up their demands notch by notch. He'd heard that personnel with authority had begun to suspect the shipments. That's all I need now, he thought. A bunch of Army meddlers slowing things down. Or worse, they discover some of the documents I promised Moscow, after I worked so hard with my Oak Ridge connection. Could make Teapot Dome look like a trifle. He felt a stress headache coming on.

The general barged into Hopkins's little office without notice. His brass buttons bulged toward the cadaverous man. Hopkins could have bitten his campaign ribbons. He could smell dry cleaning solvent.

"Russian guards are stuck like glue to these shipments. What the hell are they stuffing into the bellies of these aircraft?" Without waiting for Hopkins to answer, he snapped, "Why does a crate of ladies' intimate wear or bootlegged booze need armed guards?"

"We are handling this diplomatically," Hopkins insisted, taking a step back. "I am merely carrying out *our president's* wishes to *appease* our Russian *ally*."

"Now we get to see for ourselves what's in those shipments."

"How so, sir?" Hopkins asked, keeping his voice from revealing his alarm.

"Just got word that one went down out of Watson, and we've got intel on this Havoc. Someone who knew what they were about could stow an awful lot of sensitive material on an expedited flight to Moscow."

A Havoc? Hopkins was sure they were loading larger planes with his special cargo. But once he managed to get it to Great Falls, it was up to the Russian pipeline to get it to Moscow. What if they did use that Havoc? Sounded like the general was determined to find it, too. Hopkins peeled open another package of antacids. He hated being in the middle of this.

———

As soon as the weather cleared enough, the colonel sent a recon plane and spotters. They retraced the route out of Watson, and sure enough, found the wrecked Havoc and noted its position. No tracks were detected. Another snow flurry blew in right on their heels, and the colonel was forced to delay the rescue another day. He didn't want to risk any more personnel. "That plane isn't going anywhere," he mumbled.

The rescuers landed on a frozen lake and hiked to the site.

"We discovered the body of a civilian next to the fuselage," they reported. "It appears to have been shot in the head. The word 'SPY' was marked with charcoal on the front of the coat. Survival provisions were taken. We found no tracks, but did recover a few personal items of the pilot's. They were some distance from the crash site, so it is evident he attempted to hike out." They'd fallen into Dugan's bizarre plot, and presumed the pilot had shot the interloper and made his way out before the snowfall covered his tracks.

With no further sign of life, the colonel made a decision. "We're not going to use up more resources for a further search. Bring in the cargo and get the body to Fairbanks for . . . appropriate disposal. We're getting urgent orders to deliver a couple hundred planes this month and I want search and rescue available for the next . . . incident!"

The recovery crew bagged the frozen body and prepared to haul the cargo to the recovery plane. When they discovered what was in the jumbles of luggage, they decided to leave the cargo and instead document their discovery:

> An assortment of freight had been stowed throughout the bomb bays. Examination of the crates revealed nothing more than bottles of common inexpensive colognes, packaged borax-type soap, and bolts of fabric. The satchels marked 'Diplomatic Immunity' contained nothing but mimeographed documents pertaining to the operation of the subject aircraft.

The report had differing impacts on the men swiveling in their office chairs near the top of the chain of command. While it frustrated the colonel, Roosevelt was vindicated in his complete trust of the lend-lease operation. The president went on, presuming it was running exactly as he had visualized. Hopkins felt like he'd been shot at and missed. It was not one of the sensitive loads he'd covertly arranged. He was enormously glad to have been ignorant. It was easier to look Franklin in they eye that way.

But the colonel's order to classify the report was clear. "Until we figure this out, keep a tight lid on it, Major."

"Yes sir," he replied, slamming the file drawer shut on the scanty report.

But others watched, powerless, as volumes of "diplomatic mail" continued to Moscow. They didn't recognize the terms plutonium, deuteron, U-92, heavy-water or "energy produced by fission," – the kernels of nuclear war power. How could they know that the harvest would belong to a nation that would turn into America's enemy?

———◆———

Colonel Mitrov with his "special cargo" act was tying a colorful lure to his line to attract suspicious Army brass. The twin flight that Hopie had expected to accompany him to Fairbanks had been sent off by Mitrov, its single pilot knowing nothing of the plot. It was always best to keep the drawstring tight on an operation, Mitrov had learned. He alone, under the wavering beam of his flashlight, had struggled to load one large crate containing a set of engraving plates into what he called "Havoc Blue." Once mounted on Soviet printing presses, they would spew limitless stacks of U.S. military base scrip. Military certificates could be converted to American cash, ensuring plenty of grease to keep the gears of espionage turning. It was the perfect way to counterfeit. Hopkins came through with the plates only after Mitrov got his superiors to approve strict limits on the quantities the Russians could print. But that was a detail Mitrov could easily bury in the bureaucracy. The more scrip the Russians printed, the sooner they could construct their own nuclear arsenal. In the end game, they could print a flood of it, gutting the American economy.

Exhausted from his night's work, Colonel Mitrov wiped his reddened face, satisfied that his efforts were of supreme value to the motherland. And he hadn't had to risk a dogfight or ramming a nimble Messerschmitt to get what he knew was coming – his very own "Hero of the Soviet Union" medal. Soon Premier Stalin himself might recognize and favor him.

He reflected on his smokescreen to foil suspicions. "Havoc Red" was sabotaged at Watson Lake by a Russian collaborator paid with a pittance of U.S. cash. A forced landing would trigger a search which would reveal that the cargo was nothing of importance.

Mr. Dugan and his pilot were pawns in his game of Russian chess.

Pawns were disposable.

CHAPTER 32

The Russian Report

It is our good fortune . . . that the British and the
Americans in their attitude towards us
have still not emerged from their calf-love . . .
all their slobber plays into our hands
and we shall thank them for this in the
next world with coals of fire . . .
the whole of the free western world will burst
apart like a fat squashed toad.
— JOSEPH STALIN, QUOTED BY NIKOLAI
TOLSTOY, *STALIN'S SECRET WAR*

Mitrov could see that his simple report pleased the NKVD bureau
chief. The man's wolfish eyes keened over the summary paragraph:

Status of Havoc Red: US Army Search & Rescue en route to
crash site. Discovery of inert cargo assured. Condition of pilot
and accomplice of no concern to us.

US suspicions of inappropriate CCCP-bound freight success-
fully nullified.

Status of Havoc Blue: Landed Ladd 16:32; met by designated
personnel. Sensitive materials en route to HQ thus completing
our objective.

He closed the report and looked up at Mitrov. The bureau chief had revealed his scheme with no one but his trusted colonel in a tiny Nome office under a single glaring light. Now, Mitrov swelled with pride that he had done his assignment so well.

Once Germany was no longer a competitor, Russia would need muscle to flex as the balance of power shifted. They had reinforced the pipeline through which they would receive what they needed. Hopkins had proven he could come through as well. With just a phone call to him, pesky obstacles were derailed. Russia would gain economic and nuclear strength, girding for their fight for world preeminence.

The chief swiveled around to his credenza, reached in and with a smile cracking his stony face, offered the colonel a vodka.

"To Mr. Harry Hopkins," the chief said, raising his glass.

Mitrov followed. Too bad about the pilot of Havoc Red, they agreed. He'd acted exactly according to plan.

"To the dead pilot," they toasted.

Mitrov had brilliantly found a naïve accomplice with a prison record. If the man survived the crash, he'd sing to the U.S. authorities to avoid prison, reinforcing their ruse.

The men lifted their glasses in another toast.

"To Mr. Dugan."

"This is what the Americans call a 'red herring' " the chief said to the colonel. The two men lifted their glasses again.

"To our red herring!"

CHAPTER 33

Becoming Albert Doyle

Yukon Territory – March 1943

The trapper did his best to clean and wrap Dugan's raw hands and feet, and arranged for him to ride out on the next mail and supply flight. As Albert Doyle, he boarded a bush plane for Whitehorse. There, his frostbitten fingers and toes were tended as well as could be expected with such severe, two-day-old damage.

It cost Dugan all his earnings from Gore. He'd have to start using the cursed bribe cash. He had to concentrate to walk steadily on what was left of his toes. No matter how hard he practiced, he walked with a rolling limp. The slightest pressure triggered painful spasms. He'd have to cope with that.

He needed to find a place that would accept him as-is. He would find work where it was more important to grow wheat or raise cattle than ask a lot of questions. He jumped civilian bush flights back to Edmonton and rode the bus south.

At Lethbridge he found the post office just before closing time. He asked the clerk if he knew of anyone hiring. There was a farm family whose hired hand had recently moved on, the clerk replied, kindly giving him the name of the place and directions.

Dugan asked him to repeat the name. "Lotta Germans in these parts," the clerk added. "They spell it H-E-I-N-Z."

He hitched a ride to the place. Folks probably thought he was a war veteran, because he didn't have to wait long for a ride. He lolloped up the long gravel driveway and approached the farmhouse. Dugan was concerned that it was past sundown by the time he knocked on their door, but he decided to risk it.

"You ever done farm work, Mr. Doyle?" the farmer asked. He looked him over very closely, the light from behind him shining on Dugan's face.

"No sir, but I'm willing. I learned a lot of useful building skills during my time with the military." Dugan carefully phrased his reply. He wanted to be truthful, but if the man jumped to the conclusion that Dugan was *in* the military, he'd let it ride for now. He almost offered to show the farmer his base pass, but realized it was in the name of Frank Dugan.

"There's little farming this time of year, but there's plenty other work. I'll accept you on a trial basis."

"Thank you, sir. I can begin whenever you need me."

"No need to wait. We lost our hired hand, and if the little house is ready, we'll put you up say, for two weeks unless either one of us decides it's not working out." He left Dugan on the porch and stepped back in. Dugan heard him call to his wife, but couldn't hear his exact words. It was something about the milk house. After a short while the man reappeared with folded linens and a kerosene lantern and told Dugan to follow him. They walked two hundred feet or so to a neat gable-roofed cottage.

"Take these, Albert, and settle in here. This used to be a milk house, but we got rid of the dairy cows and turned it into a place for our hired man. 'Lectrification isn't here yet, so we put in an icebox. You can cook on the wood stove. The last man nearly burned the place down with it, so be careful. We don't allow smoking or drinking on the property. First sign of trouble of any kind, you're out." Handing Dugan a neatly folded wax paper package, he added, "the wife made a roast beef sandwich for you, and the water's real good here." He set the lantern down on the table. "You can return this in the morning."

"Why, thank you very much, Mr. Heinz. Please thank your wife for the sandwich."

Dugan found a box of matches and floundered to light another lantern with what was left of his fingers. The place had a single bed, table, two straight-backed chairs, sink and a two-burner cookstove. The ice box sat between some shelves. In the corner was an enclosure with toilet, claw foot tub and sink with a shaving mirror tacked to the freshly-painted wall. He could hardly believe his good fortune. There were even a few boxes of breakfast cereal, Kraft macaroni and cheese and cans of peas left on a shelf. Chunks of firewood lay between the stove legs.

At first, the quiet and solitude left him feeling empty and anxious. When he slept he felt vulnerable, laid out to all the haunts he'd provoked up north under the spooky Yukon sky.

The farm work was difficult, but Dugan was determined to make up for his injured hands and feet by being thorough. Working outdoors, he felt washed by pure air, wind and cold sunlight. The two weeks went by, and nothing was said about ending his situation. It was a big place with outbuildings, fences, ditches and equipment to keep him busy. When he finished one job, he'd find Mr. Heinz for another or split and stack firewood for them. Dugan appreciated that the man was clear in his directions, and not wordy.

He ate the main noon meal with the couple. The meals were wonderful. It was the only time he interacted with Mrs. Heinz. He learned that their son had graduated from college and was working in the east. The war seemed very distant to these folks and their undisturbed lives. Dugan never started conversation. He let them draw their own conclusions. When they asked him to drive the farm pickup into town for supplies and parts, he didn't let on that he feared being around strangers in town. They said he could use the farm account for his own groceries.

Dear Patrick,
I am working on a big farm outfit near Lethbridge now. I'm
all done with Great Falls. I have my own place, the hired hand

house. But I don't spend a lot of time in it cuz there's lots of work.

I eat the noon meal with Mr. and Mrs. H. Their boy is away back east so that's why they need me. They are fighting the war by growing wheat to make food.

When they asked me to drive the farm truck to town, I didn't let on I never drove one before. I seen men driving so I knew how to shift. I just got in and drove to town. By the time I got there I was pretty good on all the gears. Good thing I didn't need to back up. I will try that when no one is around to watch.

Please tell Margaret where I am and I am fine. I even got my own bathroom now.

I love you both.

Your brother Dugan

It always cheered Dugan to write to Patrick, but he wasn't done putting his thoughts on paper for the night. Since there was no one he could talk to, writing in his journal helped let out some of the thoughts sparring in his head. He'd recovered from the battering of the wreck and the trial of escape, but mentally he was as raw and unhealed as his fingers and toes. Every stranger frightened Dugan, but he tried to act unconcerned. He frequently scanned the long gravel road leading into the place for strange cars.

The Russians will try to find me. I failed them, and they are harsh. These folks probably think I'm a deserter, or a conchie. They are kind to me and don't ask. I won't disturb their think-ing. I'll just have to live with that, as discussting as it is. It's better than the truth. I dread the trips to town, but can't let on or they might get to wondering. I'm scared around strangers. What if word of where I am gets back to the Reds?

Again I invented a new name, but it hasn't changed me. I'm trying to create a new man to go along with the new name, but it's going hard. I am so afraid someone will ask me something. What if I spew the whole G D story? I can't get the picture out of my head. Hopie rolling around in his own mess. He didn't deserve what happened, even if it was his choice to fly. A lot of guys fly and end up with ribbons and medals on their chests. And jobs – wives – kids – homes. At least he didn't end up turned into wolf food. I was glad to hear them fly in after I got to the trapper's place. I was glad they come for him. I wisht I could of been there to load him onto his final flight. Like a ghost, I'd of just slipped back into the woods, forgotten.

Even though it's a long ways away, I am going to make good on my promise. My Gore ID and base pass will get me through the border.

I don't know when, but soon as I can afford it, I will go to Fresno. Time is my friend now. The longer it goes, the more will be forgotten all about me. But poor Mrs. Stanhope. Time is not her friend. I guess she must be every day wondering about her nice boy. And with no one to keep her company. Just Beverly. Maybe that just doubles the pain, the two of them worrying and wondering together.

———

Dugan put in long, days during planting and harvest. When those demands were over, he felt underworked. He understood why the last man had left. But Mr. Heinz found jobs for him and he stayed on, appreciating the unhurried rhythms of farming. He passed the Alberta driver's license test. It gave his new alias validity. Some of his fears faded. He liked Lethbridge. It had a mining heritage that fit him like a worn-in shoe. The peace of farm life and outdoor work felt healthy, like his happiest days at Gore before that Russian colonel showed up.

A second year went by with no change. Dugan was able to anticipate some of the needs of the place. He began thinking of Beverly. When the winter wheat was planted, his promise to Hopie and the idea of meeting Beverly pushed him forward to a decision. He respected and liked Mr. and Mrs. Heinz very much, and didn't want to disrupt their farm operation, but knew the time had come for him to leave. "Family urgency" was the only explanation he gave, and the kind man did not act surprised. He thanked "Albert" and paid him a generous bonus. Mrs. Heinz handed him a large double-sacked lunch and Mr. Heinz gave him a ride to the bus station in Lethbridge.

Dugan hated to leave the routine of the wheat farm, the noon dinners and the hard work that kept his mind off the wreck. Staring out the bus window on the long journey to Fresno, his mind returned to the scene, and what he would tell Mrs. Stanhope. He should have had plenty of time to come up with a plausible story, but he preferred to think about Beverly. Funny, he thought. I don't even know her last name. Probably best or I'd want to write her a letter. Hopie had provided a blank frame within which Dugan was creating a complete picture of the young woman. As his own creation, he was falling in love with it.

CHAPTER 34

Laura's Kitchen

Fresno, California – March 1945

The cab dropped him in front of the Stanhope home. As he stood on the porch he fumbled his nickel comb from a pocket and ran it along the sides of his head.

"I knew Daniel. I was with him on his last flight." That was all he said when Mrs. Stanhope opened the door to his knock. He was so nervous, he'd forgotten to greet her by name.

She paused, blinked several times, her face fixed on the tall young man. She asked him into the house, a mix of doubt and intensity on her face. She then turned from him and walked a few steps to a stuffed chair and sat.

"You must come in," she insisted, motioning him in. "Please. You have surprised me. But I am very glad you are here."

He came in and closed the door behind him. He stood in the little arched stucco entry. A clock ticked off the uneasy seconds as he waited for the thumping in his chest to wane.

She stood.

"Come in, please," she repeated. She acted like she didn't know whether to sit or stand. "Let's sit in the kitchen. I'll make coffee for us." She disappeared through another arched doorway. Dugan followed. Although she must have been more comfortable there, Dugan found the room to be very close. He pulled out a chair and sat facing her with his back to the wall. She was silhouetted in the light from the window, cheerful curtains framing her face. His long legs sprawled out. He kicked a table leg and tried not to wince. He resisted the temptation to stroke his hair with his stubby fingers. Instead he gripped his knees beneath the tabletop. He regretted choosing the seat facing her. He'd have been more comfortable facing the door but it was too late to change.

She leaned with her back against the sink, her gaze fixed on him. She smiled faintly. While Dugan was extremely uncomfortable, she seemed to trust him and didn't rush to talk. Sitting in front of her was the last person to see her son alive. He had answers to the many questions that had bombarded her quiet moments the past two years.

She began fussing over the coffee preparations. Dugan bounced his right leg up and down beneath the table. He said nothing. It seemed the right thing to do.

"Tell me your name, again, young man,"

He'd not yet said it. "F . . . Albert Doyle." He had almost forgotten to use his new alias. Her sincerity triggered his desire to be truthful, and he almost corrected himself right then.

"And were you also a pilot in the Seventh Ferrying Group?"

"Not exactly, ma'am. I was a civilian working at Gore Field in Great Falls. That's where the planes came for us to outfit before pilots like your son flew them to Fairbanks."

"I see. So you met Daniel there. Before one of his flights."

"Yes, ma'am. I helped work on the planes that came from Bell in New York, you know, the P-39 Airacobras. And the Douglas A-20 Havocs and a few C-47s from California, Mitchells and stuff. The pilots like the Havoc better'n the P-39s."

She got a glazed-over look while he prattled, but she didn't interrupt him.

He was more comfortable talking about the details of his job. It was a way to put off the part of the story that he dreaded telling. He knew she'd probe him about Daniel.

"We installed special heaters, electric dipsticks, we painted the red stars on the planes and so forth. And ferry pilots fly them to Fairbanks and turn them over to the Russians there. The planes go across Siberia, for the Russians to fight the Germans. Daniel and I were in the Havoc together."

At the sound of her son's name, her eyes focused very clearly on Dugan.

"I couldn't fly, but Daniel – I mean Lieutenant Stanhope – was starting to sort of teach me over the intercom, since only the pilot sits in the cockpit. He was a real good teacher."

She smiled, but he could see heartbreak in her eyes.

"You know, it's making a difference. Daniel was fighting a good fight when . . . when we crashed."

"We'll get to that, Albert. Was Daniel liked? Did the men like him?" she asked eagerly.

When she used his assumed name, he almost stopped her to correct it. He hated deceiving her, but now it would ruin his credibility to back up and try to fix it. He had to go right on.

"Yes ma'am. He was very well liked. Personally, I only knew him for a short time. We pal'ed around Edmonton. Daniel only went to the nice places. He never went in to no joints. He was always true to his girl here at home. The Canadians are very good to American servicemen. We had a Chinese dinner – it reminded me of Butte." He regretted letting out more information about himself. But Mrs. Stanhope didn't pursue that fact. She seemed intent on finding out everything he knew about her own son. There was a long silence. Dugan was glad for the chuffing sound of the coffee as it perked. Mrs. Stanhope delayed until it became awkward.

"Was he courteous?" she finally asked.

"Oh yes. He wanted to buy my dinner." Now he felt expansive and wanted to shine the best light on his time with her son.

The smell of coffee filled the room, and she stood and leisurely removed two cups, saucers, and spoons, and set them on the little cloth-covered table. She opened the Frigidaire, took out a bottle of milk, and poured a bit into a small pitcher. She brought out a tiny sugar bowl, and elaborately set it all between them. Dugan feared that her dawdling would give her time to think of more touchy questions. She removed the percolator stem and basket, coffee dripping on her spotless counter on its way into the white porcelain sink. She eventually sat back down facing him. He felt very warm. She poured their coffee.

"Help yourself to milk and sugar, Albert." They each sipped for a moment.

"I should call Beverly," she said and stood up again. Dugan felt his pulse speed up. "She lives nearby and could be here in a few minutes." But it was obvious the mother had mixed feelings about including her in this special moment. She twirled her apron sash around her finger. "I'll call her in a bit." She sat back down. After taking another sip, she laid her cup down, extending both hands toward Dugan, her palms facing upward, like he'd seen women do at church.

"Albert, I'm very glad you found me. It's a relief from the torment of the past two years since those two men shocked me with news that my son was missing."

He looked at her upturned hands and felt like reaching for them, holding them, but held back, afraid he would spew a gusher of facts. Instead he swallowed some coffee to press the revolting parts of the story back down.

"How can the military lose a man on friendly soil even if the soil is covered in snow?" she blurted. "I understood that Daniel was a ferry pilot, nowhere near combat. Are they hiding something? Was he carrying out some kind of secret orders?" Dugan felt his heart pounding again but realized she was just voicing her frustration, so he remained silent.

Without waiting for his answer, the questions she'd silently asked herself a thousand times came tumbling out.

"Why didn't the military do more to find him? How can they give up on one of their pilots? All they said was that Daniel was lost somewhere in a place called the Yukon Territory. They called it an 'incident.' That's it! When they left they took my heart and left me with nothing but pain." He felt she was looking right through him. She stood, reached for the percolator and poured their cups full again. "Finally, here is my chance to get some answers," she said quietly. "I *really* should call Beverly," she added, and twirled her apron sash around her finger, unrolling it again.

He took several sips and delayed any kind of response.

"I only met Daniel just before our bad flight but he was well-liked. I really looked up to him. I think everyone did." He decided to say whatever he could remember to satisfy her curiosity. "He was a great pilot. That was obvious." He recalled his first sight of the young pilot, the new manual on his lap. He decided not to mention that the fateful trip was Daniel's first in that particular aircraft – it might put a shadow of blame on her son.

"I was called to Fairbanks to help the mechanics up there. I'd been wanting to see the ALSIB – that's what they call the Alaska-Siberia route – and I was happy to transfer there, and especially happy that I'd be flying with Daniel."

There was another long silence. She continued fussing with her apron.

"He told me about Luke." Dugan looked down at his cup, rotating it back and forth by pushing its dainty handle with his thumb, keeping his four truncated fingers closed into a fist. Laura's response did not surprise him. He'd noticed a picture of Jesus on his cross on her kitchen wall.

"I've tried to understand why God took my little boy like that. Daniel had no way to save him. If he'd tried any harder, God would have taken him, too. I guess God decided one angel was enough for my family to send to heaven. One angel at a time, that is."

He left her painful comment to float away on the air. Dugan had lost a lot of confidence in God by now. Of course she was entitled to her version of him.

CHAPTER 35

The Legend of Lieutenant Stanhope

"You'll stay for dinner. I have more questions to ask you, if you don't mind." It was misery, thinking this would extend his visit alone with Laura, but he really cared about her. He wondered if she was ever going to call Beverly.

She stood and started pulling things from a cupboard. She peeled potatoes and expertly sliced them into a baking dish, adding slices of ham. She heated milk and flour in a saucepan and poured it over the dish and set it near the stove while she lit the gas oven. The percussive sound of the gas igniting reminded Dugan of the fire he'd started beside the wreck. With a clatter, Laura slipped the dish into the oven and sat facing him again.

"Please tell me everything, Albert. Everything you can. Now I understand his plane went down. But you . . . you walked out?" She glanced at his feet.

Dugan took a deep breath and looked at her. "That's the reason I needed to find you, ma'am." The thumping was so strong in his chest he was sure she would notice it. He brought out the dog tag he'd removed from Hopie's body and set it on the table between them. Her hand clutched at her heart. As if steeling herself from a cruel joke, she did not move to touch it. He forced himself to look in her eyes. Everything was sticking in his throat, even his words, his breath. He wanted something to drink other than coffee. Maybe arsenic.

With her head lowered, she positioned her hands flat on the table as if holding herself against an earthquake.

"What happened to him?"

He felt the load of two years' worth of her trauma weighing him down. His pulse rang in his ears. He took another deep breath.

"Your son was buried in Alaska Territory, Mrs. Stanhope."

She just stared at him.

"Tell me the whole story," she finally whispered. She reached toward him again, this time he sensed it was a gesture to absolve him for his knowledge that had been kept from her. The time had come for the legend.

"The Havoc is an attack bomber. Our military suspected loads of contraband was going out in the bigger cargo planes. No one would suspect a Havoc of hauling hot stuff. I guess the Russians chose Daniel's flight to better their odds of staying unnoticed," he continued, "since he was so honorable."

Her eyes craved more detail, almost boring through his face to his core. Her intense interest in this part of the story surprised him. Why couldn't she just leave it alone, now that she knew Hopie's body had been found. Why must a mother care about the details, the details I'm trying to protect her from?

He soldiered on, doing his best to stay calm and believable, in spite of the deception. "There were actually three of us in that plane." He decided to give the troubled woman peace, instead of truth. What did it matter now? It would be a lie of no consequence. Was that really an unforgivable sin? He was surprised at his own inventiveness. He hadn't rehearsed any of this. But he had thought about his own future. Hopie's future was settled there in the aircraft, but Dugan's was not. If the truth got out, he would be wanted by both the United States and the Russians. Maybe even Joe Stalin would want to find him. Whoever got him first would be sure there wasn't much left over for anybody else. And certainly there would be prison – one that would make Montana's seem like a resort.

The room was silent now. He heard a vehicle upshift on a nearby street, and he wished he was in it right then, getting away from this scene.

"We took off outta Watson Lake over the mountains and engine trouble began. There were no runways anywheres near. Daniel tried his best to land safely. He really did, but with both engines out, he had no choice. After we crashed into the rocks and trees, he discovered the plane had been filled with stuff the Russians should not have gotten. The third guy was a spy, we realized after the crash. And then some awful stuff happened, Mrs. Stanhope."

She picked up the dog tag, its chain dangling between her fingers, and pressed it to her heart. "Did he pray?"

There was no need to tell her Daniel's rant. In those last hours, he'd said that God gave him a thinking brain to make his own decisions. God had no plan for him other than to start his heart beating and his lungs breathing, he'd said. God couldn't take credit for whatever success Daniel made of his life, nor could God be blamed for any disasters – and this is a big disaster. "Just tell my mother and Beverly that *I* decided to be a pilot. *I* decided to take that risk. God isn't taking anything away from my mother," he'd declared.

Dugan paused to frame his reply.

"Daniel wanted you to know how much he loved flying. He knew you hated the decision he'd made, but it was his way to serve his country, *to serve God's will*. To live up to his father. He told me about Mr. Stanhope."

She looked down at his mention of that painful memory, then looked at Dugan again.

"Then what happened?"

He paused to extrapolate more of the story.

"As soon as Daniel understood what was in the plane, he fought with the guy and knocked him out. I was hurt too bad to walk – you can see my feet never healed up right – so Daniel handled me out of the plane, and helped me out to a trail that we hoped might lead to a trapper's place or something. Daniel was so cool and in control, I let him make all the decisions. He built me a fire and I'll be darned if he didn't head back to destroy the cargo. Then I passed out. I don't know how long. There was a single gun shot."

Mrs. Stanhope's jaw dropped and she covered her face with her hand.

"I made my way back to the plane, and . . . well . . . Hopie was lying there dead, dressed in the guy's civilian clothes. The guy must've forced Daniel to change to take the blame . . ."

"Then shot him," she added, nodding her head slowly.

He didn't dare mention that her son had been shot in the face. Or that Dugan had taken a charred stick and blacked the damning brand on his coat.

Mrs. Stanhope looked saturated, like she couldn't absorb any more. After a moment she nodded and motioned for him to continue.

"Daniel hated that he'd gotten mixed up in the mess. He knew it could ruin his military career, and you know how serious he was about that." Dugan couldn't look at her any longer. Instead, he just stared at the table top. "I saw the spy's tracks heading out. I headed the opposite direction. I admit, I was dazed and not thinking very straight. All I wanted to do was get outta there."

"You had no choice either, Albert. Go on."

"It started snowing. Things were unclear to me. I must have stumbled around a long time. When the trapper came by with his dog sled, I wisht it had been Daniel, ma'am, I truly do. Daniel saved my life, but I wisht it was the other way around."

"Albert, you had no way of changing the outcome."

"I know this is terrible news. Your son deserved a better end, but you need to know he loved flying in the north country."

"So his body was found. Then what?"

"They thought it was Lieutenant Stanhope who'd walked out and was lost to the cold, so they reported he was 'missing in action.' They figured they'd bury the unknown civilian's body and be done with it. I figured the best way to save Daniel's reputation would be to keep quiet."

He felt the relief of a sick man after vomiting. He tried not to pant. "That's the truth of it, and I'm real sorry, ma'am."

CHAPTER 36

Deception Deepens

Oh! what a tangled web we weave
When first we practise to deceive!
— SIR WALTER SCOTT

"**I**'m really not hungry, and I should go." It was a bluff. He really wanted to stay and meet Beverly.

The meal smelled good, especially the baking ham, but Dugan had swallowed such a big hunk of truth that his belly was full of anxiety.

"No, please stay a bit longer Albert. I'm going to call Beverly now. She will want to meet the person who has the truth." Dugan hoped she couldn't tell that his face was getting warm again. She dialed. There was an answer, some excited talk, and Laura hung up. Moments later, the girl was at the back door, letting herself in.

Finally seeing Beverly filled in the gaps of the image he'd created of her. She didn't have pin-up looks, but she had shiny auburn hair and freckles that made her look not much older than high-school age. When she hugged Mrs. Stanhope he noticed that she was several inches taller than the woman. Laura introduced her as Beverly Ellis. Finally, a last name. The green wrap she wore set off the color of her eyes. He tried to imagine what she would look like if she smiled.

Laura heated a can of green beans, set the table, and the three of them sat. Laura began saying grace, and he and Beverly glanced bashfully at each other before they bowed their heads.

"Dear Lord in Heaven, thank you for this gift of truth and forth-rightness," the older woman prayed. "We thank you for the courage it has taken this man, Albert Doyle, to find us and tell us where our dear Daniel is at rest and now in your divine care. Give us courage to go on, and bless this food to your service. Amen."

Dugan held his hands still to keep from fidgeting. He pretended he hadn't lost his appetite during the grace, when something had twisted like an auger deep in his gut.

"I wish Daniel was the one sitting here eating potatoes and ham and beans with you right now, miss," he said to Beverly as he accepted the hot dish. It was one of the only truthful things he'd said since he'd arrived. He helped himself to a small serving.

"Dinner smells real tasty. I have to say, though, I haven't much of an appetite, recalling all this for you." Dugan set the hot dish down and looked at Beverly.

She and Laura pushed food around their plates.

"I completely understand, Albert," Laura said. "You have been through so much. We all have. Then you came so far to find us . . ."

She asked him to repeat the whole story for Beverly and he felt the auger twist again. He had to do his best to reconstruct the story, buncos and all.

Each time he paused, Laura eagerly jumped in to finish his sentence.

It was a relief to Dugan.

The young girl listened silently with a pained expression. She wiped tears from her eyes with her cloth napkin.

"I am afraid that if you report what I've said, they will pin the con-traband on Daniel, since he was pilot-in-command. I know this is ter-rible news. Now you know why I had to be careful about setting you straight." Mrs. Stanhope looked at him, her empty fork in her hand.

"When I got the chance, I looked up the accident report. Your son is buried at Birch Hill Cemetery in Fairbanks, Mrs. Stanhope." Beverly gave him a long look through red, swollen eyes.

Laura squinted toward Beverly. "The military will always list him as missing," she said. "But at least now we know. We're not going to raise trouble by trying to correct any records. So we must be content to leave the situation as it is."

Dugan felt like his brain had just gone ten rounds. The last time he was in a tight place and told the truth, he was rewarded with ten years in Montana State Prison. He'd been loyal to rogues he never should have trusted. This time, he desperately wanted to bring some peace to a distraught mother and release a young woman from her hopeless grasp on a missing lover. Closure was worth the price this last lie might cost.

He thanked Mrs. Stanhope for the coffee and meal. He rose and said he'd better be going to the bus station.

"Beverly, would you like to take Albert to the bus?" Laura asked. "You can use my car."

"Of course," the girl replied, jumping up. This would give him more time with Beverly. He desperately wanted relief from the atmosphere he'd created in the tiny kitchen with his lies. Dugan felt he'd fouled the air with an invisible toxin.

Beverly brought the Oldsmobile around to the front.

Mrs. Stanhope held both her hands out to him in a gesture of good will and good-bye. He was relieved that she didn't move to hug him. He was afraid he'd have really spilled his guts if she'd held him. He liked her, and hated himself for the mess he'd caused.

Dugan left the orderly home yearning for things he had lost – mother, warmth, feminine presence, stability and now honesty. He imagined smelling morning toast in the sunny little kitchen. He felt like he'd just run his heart through a table saw – half would be left here, and the other half wanted to be far away.

Shutting the heavy car door shielded him from the mother's agony, but now there'd be more questions from the girl. The way Beverly kept glancing at him during his convoluted tale made him wonder if she believed him. He felt as if the cloven hoof of a large monster was bearing down on his chest, splaying wide with ever more weight.

Blessedly, the girl remained silent for the first few blocks. He could tell she took a few extra turns on the way. As they approached the bus station, she began.

"Did Daniel mention me?" She yanked the park brake and shut the motor off.

"Oh yes, many times," Dugan replied. "He was really looking forward to your wedding." She must be in shock, he thought. She showed so little emotion. She was beautiful in a way, even in her sorrow. He could see why Hopie had fixed on her. "I am *really* sorry for that," Dugan added.

"By now, I've gotten used to losing him," she said. "In my heart I knew he was dead, but I didn't want to crush Laura's hopes. These past two years have really been hard on her."

"I'm sure."

"In a way, now I feel better. I hope you don't think me cold or uncaring. What troubles me is . . ."

The auger twisted again. Dugan swallowed.

" . . . it wasn't a hero's death. He knew it and no doubt it tormented him at the end. He was desperately trying to live up to his father's fame. And he blamed himself for Luke's drowning. I was always afraid it would lead him into danger."

He looked at her.

She smiled for the first time. God a'mighty, she was pretty, and so alone.

"I am *so glad* you knew him and came here for us."

She reached for his hand and held it in hers. "I'm sorry it affected your well-being," and she looked down at their hands. "I'd really like to keep in touch with you, Albert." She let go of his hand to find a pencil and a scrap of paper in her purse.

He should have liked to spend more time with Beverly, but his thicket of lies had created a barrier. It was difficult for him to look into her lovely eyes. He felt like he'd just thrown everything of value off a high bridge. He hadn't anticipated any of this. There was no breaking through now to any fragment of truth. His sweaty hand cupped his door handle. He desperately wanted to bolt for the anonymity of the bus station.

"Wouldn't it be too painful? I mean . . . a reminder of all the bad news I brought with me? It's such a bad piece of history, and you can't change history," he added, nearly gagging on the irony.

"Albert, I've known for two years that Daniel was never coming home. I was crying in there for Laura, watching her finally accept the truth. You don't know how much you've helped me. Now I can get past the fairy tale that he was alive, and that we were going to live happily ever after."

Fairy tale, he thought. If only he could dismiss all his deceits as simple fairy tales! But fairy tales didn't wreck the lives of real people.

"Sure," he mumbled, taking the tidy note from her. His other hand still clutched the door handle.

"You look poorly," she said. "All this must be terrible for you . . . after your airplane accident and that horrible spy murdering Daniel." But she was pitying him for the wrong reason, Dugan thought. His right foot was pressed against the base of the car door in spite of the stabbing pain.

"Where will you go? I'm sure there's work around here."

He was so eager to be away from this, he wanted to board the first bus no matter where it was headed.

"North. I have good prospects back up in . . . well, near the border." He didn't want to explain any more. "Oh, here! You should have this before I go." Dugan removed Hopie's silver wings from his breast pocket. As much as he cherished the beautiful pin, it was a small price to pay for his freedom.

He got out of the car and thanked her for the ride.

She stayed and watched him. "Be sure and write!" she called out the open car window. He forced a half-hearted smile back at her, waved, and went inside. He checked the northbound departure time, got his ticket and went in the men's room. He stayed until he was sure she had driven off. He tossed her note in the waste can. He had to turn his back on the tidy peace of Fresno, a place where the war had mangled lives in heartbreaking ways.

———————————————

When they had gone, Laura pulled the shades closed in her small bedroom, and collapsed on her bed, still holding Daniel's dog tag. Shouldn't today's news have been salve for her splintered heart? She believed the man, but everything seemed unreal. That Daniel was *dead*.

Lying there, she decided that she'd go to Fairbanks and see for herself where he lay. Her heart pounded as if she were looking down from a great height. She'd been climbing a crumbling path for two years, each step planted with a mother's hope. Now she needed to leap.

A weight seemed to lift from her, as if a heavy blanket had been fluffed and pulled away.

She got up. She opened her jewelry box and lowered Daniel's dog tag next to Dan Senior's, making a tinny ping. She splashed cold water on her face, returned to the kitchen and opened the drawer beneath the calendar. She picked up the red and black crayons and marked a black "X" on the day's square.

Holding the two crayons like spent cartridges, she threw them in the garbage. She was finished with them, just like the day's coffee grounds.

CHAPTER 37

Living Two Lies

There was plenty of time to think on the long bus ride back toward Alberta. Dugan felt he'd done the right thing in Fresno, but his conscience was still beasting him. Was the lie worth the closure it brought the two women? He would long remember the look on Laura's face, as she heard and accepted his version of Hopie's noble end. He hoped her son's dog tag would give her something tangible to mourn over and end her hopeless waiting. And young, fetching Beverly would no doubt go on to other hopes and loves. Dugan was left to dwell in a stoneless prison – the inescapable bondage of regret and lies.

His money held out until he reached Montana's Hi-line. He was relieved to get north of Great Falls. With only an Alberta driver's license, he thought he'd best cross the border at a lax outpost. He left the bus station in Shelby and hitchhiked to the tiny border crossing at Del Bonita. He'd heard of it in prison. They made allowances for the farm folks who crossed regularly for parts and equipment. Now he could talk farming, if they asked questions. He'd had good luck on the road so far, and was confident he'd get a ride on to his final destination in Calgary where he'd find work and could blend in again with little chance of being discovered.

In a way, changing your name is a lie. You are lying about your family. I managed to become Frank Dugan but I never thought that lie had sharp edges. If my own mother had known

I was headed for the pen she would of named me Mickey or Jiggs. Proinsias would of been a death sentence in prison. Mother would forgive me my first lie, changing that swishy name to Frank Dugan.

But now I am Albert Doyle trying to live two lies at once and its tearing me apart.

Approaching the city, he asked to be dropped off at the Catholic Church. Out of desperation, he'd turned to church charity throughout his journey to Fresno. He hadn't done a thing to help the church but here he was, taking advantage of their kindness again. His father had always told his children to pay their debts promptly. Dugan would find a way to pay them back. The people were usually helpful, and he let them reach their own conclusions. He went in and asked permission to use their washroom and cleaned up the best he could. They told him of a barber who accepted pay with church vouchers and offered him a sandwich and milk from their kitchen. It was the first he'd eaten since yesterday, when a kind bus passenger headed for Conrad had given him an apple. He asked if they could put him up until he got a paycheck. They gave him permission to stay as long as he needed in their mission rooms, a few blocks away.

He found the barber. Since he'd left Gore and its base barber, he'd been on his own for keeping his shock of dark hair presentable. He'd borrowed Mrs. Heinz's sewing scissors for the job. Luckily his thick wavy hair filled in the notches he'd cut in back where he couldn't see. It felt good to get a real haircut again, and his first professional shave. He felt rich. He tipped his last half-dollar and walked out feeling ready to go door-to-door in search of any kind of work.

He walked toward the busiest part of town. After disappointing exchanges in a filling station, corner grocery store, implement dealer and auto repair shop, he entered Gunnar's Bakery. The man behind the counter was waiting on a woman with a little girl.

"She has just been to the dentist, and her reward is a trip to the bakery," the mother said, smiling at the little girl. "I'll take two loaves of bread – sliced, please – while Betsy selects a treat for herself."

The child was peering over all the sweets – rum balls rolled in coconut, pretzel-like kringle, wienerbrod and crullers. When the baker returned with the sliced bread, the girl pointed at the rum balls, and the woman ordered a dozen.

The baker winked at the woman as he conspicuously dropped a thirteenth into the crisp white sack and handed it over the counter to the child.

"You may have one on the way home, Betsy, and we'll save the rest to share later," the mother said kindly.

Dugan stayed back, waiting for the man to finish the transaction. By the time the child left the bakery, the rich little confections had already stained her sack.

The owner turned to Dugan with a harried look.

He probably thinks I'm selling something or a missionary, Dugan thought.

"Good day, sir. You have a very nice place here."

The man softened a bit.

"I am looking for work. I'm a hard worker and willing to work any hours. My name is Frank Dugan." He extended his hand, looking in the man's blue eyes, clouding with age.

The baker wiped his right hand on his chocolate-smudged apron and shook Dugan's hand, returning Dugan's gaze. His grip was firm as a half-thawed chuck roast from having kneaded thousands of batches of dough. If he noticed Dugan's shortened fingers, he did not reveal it. He studied Dugan for a moment, then asked him to wait. He spoke with an accent Dugan couldn't place. Gunnar disappeared in the back. Dugan could hear his and a woman's voice. He returned. "We can use morning help, beginning at four in the mornings except Sundays." Dugan eagerly accepted.

"Wash up there and put on an apron. I'll show you around today, Frank." It was the first time he'd heard his preferred name for a very long time. A warmth came over him, mixed with the smells of fresh breads, baking sugars and a hint of glass cleaner.

———•———

Dugan began in the windowless back room, washing oversize pots and pans, cleaning the floor and unloading and stowing the bulk baking supplies the truck delivered in the alley. Before opening, he swept the sidewalk, washed the front windows inside and out, cleaned the display cases and started the big coffee maker. Once a week he washed Gunnar's delivery truck.

> Patrick,
>
> I work at the best bakery in Calgary, no dout about it. At first it was hard for me to be indoors all the time, but the owners Gunnar and Bergit are good people. Gunnar showed me how to make bread. We use big mixers for part of it but I love to nead the warm doe. It makes my fingers stop tingling. And I like to take the raw ingredients and turn them into good things to eat.
>
> At seven I wrap goods for Gunnar to deliver. Bergit comes in at eight to frost cakes and keep the books. Bergit showed me how to run the cash register, and now I wait on customers.
>
> Sometimes kids stare at my fingers and go outside and call me 'dog paws' and walk back and forth like I do and laff, but I got no hard feelings toward them.

Gunnar started leaving Dugan in charge of the place so he could spend more time in their flower garden. As spring turned to summer, he brought in beautiful bunches of fresh flowers for the several little tables in the front of the shop – first gladiolas, then daffodils, peonies, hydrangeas and roses. Their fragrances seemed to be competing with the heavenly baking aromas. He tried marigolds and chrysanthemums, but Bergit and Dugan agreed they didn't smell good.

One day as the two men were bent over the big sink washing pans and utensils together, the old Dane began telling Dugan how the Germans occupied his homeland in April of 1940. As if he were on the verge of telling a big secret, Gunnar leaned toward Dugan and described the terror the Germans brought to their peaceful and honorable life. His gray eyebrows twitched. Dugan's hatred for the Germans surfaced again like it had in prison. Gunnar interrupted his thoughts with his story about how he and his countrymen foiled the invaders.

"They yanked me out of my shop and asked me what *useful* skills I had. They weren't interested in fancy Danish pastries. I told them I knew how to drive a truck." With a big wire whisk in his hand, he pointed out at an imaginary person and cried, "*Achtung!* You there! *Schwein! Schaffen die strasse!* You vill haul dirt! It is a job fitting of a Danish pig like you!" Bowing back over the suds, he continued, "I had to report in every morning with maybe a dozen others. Bergit was left to run the bakery."

"I bet that was very difficult, to do all alone," Dugan said.

"Yes, but every day we thanked God they left her alone so we could make a meager living. Other women were . . . not so lucky." He shook his head solemnly. "*Utilgivelig!* Unforgivable! But we tricked the brutes. We drivers made a secret pact. We knew of a back road connecting two of their construction routes. The next morning we loaded up our trucks as usual." He chuckled, straightened up, his forearms dripping suds as he grasped an imaginary steering wheel. "We drove our route, without dumping our loads. Both directions we had to pass a German sentry." He laughed again. "They didn't recognize that it was the same dirt, riding around the circuit!" He wiped his eyes on his rolled-up sleeve. "An awful lot of German-bought fuel was wasted on their project!" Gunnar was nearly crying as he finished the story.

"Good for you," Dugan said enthusiastically. "You fight the enemy any way you can!"

"Of course if they'd discovered our trick, we'd all have been shot," he added ruefully. He looked out at Bergit who was waiting on a customer. "I know many people who are running from their past. Some have a great distance to cover."

How true, Dugan thought.

Over time, the old Dane told him how the couple had escaped, giving up all they had worked for in Denmark. They came to Canada to start over. The couple worked long hours, sleeping on cots in the back of their rented space until they could afford a home. Now that Dugan was helping, Bergit didn't have to work late nights on the books. "Every night now is like vacation," he told Dugan. "Much more smiling at home these days." He swished his hips back and forth. His eyes twinkled.

I like this job as much as I liked the work in Great Falls. I found a room I can afford, and bought a used bicycle. One day you and Margaret should come up here and visit.
Give Margaret a hug for me. I love you both,
Your brother Dugan

Dugan heard about the Soldiers' Children's Home for Orphans, on a hill overlooking Calgary. "Gunnar, I'm sure the orphan children's home would love fresh white bread from Gunnar's. Would you consider giving me part of my pay in bread at wholesale? I will take it to them on my own time."

The Dane said he'd never thought of that. Baking communion bread for his Lutheran church had been the extent of his charity. "If you are willing to deliver it, you can take any loaves that aren't sold on

Saturday afternoon to the home," he told Dugan. "It need not come out of your pay, son. And use the bakery truck. It will be good advertising!"

"That's very kind of you. I am happy to do that." Dugan noticed that from that day on, the Dane measured out a larger portion of flour and ingredients for Saturday's batch of white bread.

———◆———

As content as Dugan should have been, when he was not with Gunnar, Bergit and their customers, an overcast of guilt and shame spread over him. One evening a wave of emotion drove his pencil to keep writing, dislodging Dugan's soul and peppering it onto the paper.

> There is a huge truth staring me in the face. It is almost blinding me. Facing it is hard.
>
> It wasn't the German's fault the old man burned alive, it was me. My bad choice. I had to prove I was just as tuff as Joker, Mash, all of them.
>
> I did a stupid, selfish thing.
>
> I need to quit living a lie.
>
> I did it. But I paid the price. Then I did another stupid thing taking that Russian bribe. I can't take blame for Hopie's death, but I paid anyway with all those lies. Looking at those two women as they swallowed my story – surely it's my one-way ticket to hell.
>
> I just hope Hopie's soul is at rest. I am evermore paying for that with my own restless soul.

His letters to Patrick left out the shameful parts. This wasn't a letter to Patrick. Instead, he slipped it under his mattress with the rest of his musings – just an old habit.

———◆———

Walking uptown on an errand, he spotted a used accordion in the window of a second hand store. A wave of longing passed through him as he recalled happy times with Pop playing and singing. This was a deep marbled red with pearl buttons. The grille was trimmed with chrome. Next payday, Dugan thought, when I have the money . . . but instead he jammed his finger stubs back into his pocket, and ambled past.

THE END

Afterword

I know "gratitude" very well. It is a sickness suffered by dogs.
— Joseph Stalin

*The argument is now put forward that we
must never use the atomic bomb
until or unless, it has been used against us first.
In other words, you must never fire until you have been shot dead.*
— Winston Churchill

There was no need for Dugan to live in endless fear of Russians pursuing him. He never learned that his tragic flight actually fulfilled its mission. The treacherous plan continued; information passed from Great Falls to Fairbanks into the hands and beneath the slide rules of Russian engineers. A person skirting the Oval Office continued to invigorate a nation that would soon aim nuclear missiles at America's heart, from behind what Winston Churchill would call an "iron curtain."

Russian citizens paid a horrendous corporeal price fighting Germany. Historians estimate up to twenty-four million deaths, or about fourteen percent of the Soviet Union's population. Joseph Stalin is quoted as saying, "the death of one man is a tragedy. The death of millions is a statistic." Red Army soldiers were ordered to advance into likely German bullets; or hesitate and be certainly shot from behind by another man marching beneath the hammer and sickle.

The United States paid a huge price in joining the Allied Forces. According to Oxford University's *Companion to American Military History*, over 405,000 soldiers paid the ultimate sacrifice; 670,846 were wounded, and 30,314 went missing in action, totaling over one million Americans. But another huge Allied prize was forfeited to the Soviets near Prague at the Krupp and Skoda armaments super-factories where Panzers and V-2 rockets had emerged. Reams of documents – the "cream of the German Research and Development on nuclear power ballistics" – were handed to the Russians, according to Tom Agoston in *Blunder! How the U.S. Gave Away Nazi Supersecrets to Russia*.

When Japan brought war to the Aleutian island chain, Alaska's Natives lost their aboriginal homes during and after the attacks. Home was never to return to normalcy for these people.

Unlike the annihilation of Europe's civilians, homes, factories, hospitals, bridges, railroads, cathedrals, schools and art of incalculable value, America's civilian loss was not so tangible. It was a loss of innocence, a shattering of confidence that we were safe in our homes.

After World War II, air raid sirens wouldn't warn of German or Japanese bombs creating small craters of localized damage. This time, sirens would howl for the Russian "atom bomb" on its way to destroy an entire city. Survivors would suffer radiation burns like the blackened walking corpses in filmstrips we watched. Americans regularly walked past stark yellow and black signs directing us toward the closest public fallout shelter. At science fairs we watched bizarre displays of radiation poisoning. Men in white coats pointed at radiated carrots and potatoes the size of punching bags.

Instead of an American hand extended toward Russia in friendship, we lived in neighborhoods where Nike nuclear missiles pointed at the citizens of Moscow.

Those of us who practiced diving under our spindly desks in grade school may have been too young to understand at first. But watching our elders build fallout shelters deep below our lawns to avoid the black rain after a nuclear attack brought gloom into our hearts. Ads for survival supplies permeated our lives. We digested the impending doom and it became part of us. We anxiously watched television during the Cuban missile crisis, a knot in our guts telling us "this is it – the Russians will bomb us now."

How the Russians were able to build atomic weapons on the heels of our own Manhattan Project may remain a mystery to the general public. To discount the largess of aid provided by the United States and Britain, the Soviets sealed all references to the lend-lease operation. Details again were "like an iceberg, slipping from public view." But to those with deeper knowledge, it is plausible that the White House over-trusted an unrepentant mass murderer some endearingly called "Uncle Joe."

Our grandest loss was our freedom from fear.

You can't hug a bear without getting mauled.

Acknowledgements

First, I must thank Montana pilot Chuck Jarecki for the two leisurely flights exploring the ALSIB route, and his patience while I followed leads into museums, libraries, bookstores, file cabinets and reels of microfilm.

Heartfelt thanks go to my editor Maggie Plummer, author of two gripping books about the enslaved Irish, and my friend and mentor Mary Barmeyer O'Brien, who brings determined American pioneers to life in her wonderful books of western history.

Stan Cohen is well-known among American military history buffs. I began my research in his Pictorial Histories Publishing office and warehouse in Missoula, Montana. Mr. Cohen was generous with his time, and every place I went – from Great Falls to Fairbanks – the mention of his name was like a master key opening the doors to the history I needed.

I am very grateful for the interest, time and care that Mr. Cohen, Ben Donnelly of the University of Great Falls, and Blake W. Smith each invested to check my manuscript for historical accuracy.

Alex Mumley-Dupuis, whom I met at the Alaska Aviation Gathering in Anchorage, steered me to rich resources in Fairbanks: H. Lee Griffin, officially the Environmental Scientist at Fort Wainwright, but passionately a warbird pilot and Ladd Field historian; and Pete Haggland, curator of the Pioneer Air Museum in Fairbanks. There I touched the truncated wreckage of a P-39, and a massive eighteen-cylinder twin-row radial engine. I could hear the ghosts whispering throughout the silent relics. Thanks to Fairbanks pilot Tom George for flying me there from Anchorage, over terrain and through spring weather the ALSIB pilots experienced.

Along my path many other people provided important facts and leads. Jim Blodgett, former Deputy Warden of Montana State Prison, was a wealth of facts about MSP, as well as military history. Among his meticulously-kept artifacts were items with significance to the pilots in this story.

Powell County Museum and Arts Foundation maintains Old Montana State Prison very close to its condition when it was vacated in 1979. If you pause in the group shower area, you might still catch the scent of Palmolive soap. I'd toured the prison on a hot summer day and noticed it was twenty degrees cooler inside. So I returned to tour it in early winter. I believe it was still twenty degrees cooler inside.

I wish to thank the staff at Montana Historical Society in Helena for their help. Kristin Bokovoy, Archive Administrator and Megan Trent and their staff at the Historical Museum of Great Falls assisted my search through their extensive Seventh Ferrying Group archives, in large part assembled by Byrnes Ellender. I deeply regret not having the chance to meet him in person.

CMSgt (Ret.) Curt Shannon, Director of Malmstrom Air Museum provided authentic photos to enrich the book's promotion graphics. Thank you, Ben Donnelly, for making the introduction.

Ben Ryan of West Glacier, Montana, flew the P-39 patrolling for Japanese submarines in the Pacific. He modestly shared anecdotes with me but more than once his eyes teared up with recollections of lost colleagues.

I am grateful to Ruth Baxter for sharing her photo album and stories of living along the ALSIB route. In 1943, she and her new husband Lyle became radio operators at Tanacross, Alaska. "I spoke to many of those pilots," she told me.

Murray Biggins of Whitehorse, Yukon Territory, graciously spent time with me and did extra research on my behalf. The staff at Yukon

Archives in Whitehorse; Janna Swales, and Kathy Gates of the Yukon Transportation Museum and the staff at the North Peace Historical Society in Fort St. John, British Columbia and Steven Dammann, Chief pilot for Absolute Aviation in Wetaskawin, Alberta, all gave me access to their materials. Roger Gregoire of Fort St. John shared further details.

Trevor Palmer of Faro, Yukon Territory, needs to be thanked for his hospitality and encouragement.

Polson's North Lake County library staff, as always, cheerfully assisted me in obtaining obscure resources cached across the country. Thanks go to Sue and Don Williamson for sharing Butte history and anecdotes.

Thank you to my son who years ago, had placed his 1:48 scale model of a Douglas A-20 Havoc – complete with the Soviet red star – on my dusty piano; later adding a beautiful P-39 model. He became a factual resource as well as providing the tangible study items.

There was a wealth of research in Michelle Reid's *Red Stars on the Horizon: The Seventh Ferrying Group in World War II*, published by Eastern University Press, 2010. Thank you, Stan Cohen, for that lead.

Viewing the stunningly beautiful ALSIB Memorial in Fairbanks had much richer meaning for me, thanks to *Allies in Wartime*, edited by Alexander Dolitsky of the Alaska-Siberia Research Center.

I am ever grateful for my long-time association with historian Paul Fugleberg, who mentored me in the newspaper business; and encouraged me to contribute my own works of historical fiction to the genre.

To those I inconvenienced by choosing to dwell over my keyboard rather than turn out for road cleanup, chair a local committee or bring a hot dish to a potluck, I hope you will forgive me for making this project a priority. I research and write slowly and I am determined that my historical fiction be told accurately.

About The Author

C. Margo Mowbray writes from her home in northwestern Montana. Her newspaper career began at age twenty, proofreading obituaries and legal notices at one of Montana's oldest weeklies. For nearly three decades, she continued in a fulfilling career of publishing award-winning weekly newspapers. Her 2013 work of historical fiction, *An Answering Flame – From the Journal of a Horseback Nurse-Midwife* won the 2014 Media Award from the American College of Nurse-Midwives.

Mowbray is a private pilot and aircraft owner with over 1,200 left-seat hours and remains active in organizations that advocate for general aviation.

She has served in the Montana Senate. She is the mother of four grown children.

Her website is: *www.authormargomowbray.com*

Made in the USA
Charleston, SC
23 March 2015